Josiah Keep

West Coast Shells

A familiar description of the marine, fresh water, and land mollusks of United

States, found west of the Rocky Mountains

Josiah Keep

West Coast Shells

A familiar description of the marine, fresh water, and land mollusks of United States, found west of the Rocky Mountains

ISBN/EAN: 9783337391973

Printed in Europe, USA, Canada, Australia, Japan

Cover: Foto ©Andreas Hilbeck / pixelio.de

More available books at **www.hansebooks.com**

WEST COAST SHELLS.

A FAMILIAR DESCRIPTION OF THE

MARINE, FRESH WATER, AND LAND MOLLUSKS OF THE UNITED STATES, FOUND WEST OF THE ROCKY MOUNTAINS.

Adapted to the Use of Schools, Private Students, Tourists, and all Lovers of Nature.

BY

JOSIAH KEEP, A. M.,

PROFESSOR OF NATURAL SCIENCE, MILLS COLLEGE.

With Numerous Illustrations by LAURA M. MELLEN, Teacher of Art, Mills College.

SAN FRANCISCO:
SAMUEL CARSON & CO.,
208 POST STREET.
1888.

PREFACE.

THE kind reception given to my little book on the "Common Sea-shells of California," has induced me to prepare this larger work, embracing a wider territory, namely, that part of the United States lying west of the Rocky Mountains.

The present volume includes descriptions of all the species mentioned in the former one, together with many others of the more minute and uncommon marine shells which are found from Puget Sound or Alaska on the north, to San Diego on the south.

It also describes the land and fresh-water mollusks of California, Oregon, Washington, Idaho, Utah and Nevada, thus making it of use as a reference-book for the interior, as well as along the sea-coast.

While not claiming absolute completeness, I trust it will be found sufficient to enable students and collectors to identify all the specimens which they will be likely to gather within the limits already mentioned.

The nearly two hundred engravings have all been drawn from nature, expressly for this work, and while materially increasing its cost, they will, I trust, even more increase its value.

Some additional matter respecting the authors of the specific names, a Glossary, and a brief Key for the Analysis of Shells, will be found near the close of the book.

The work is written in a familiar style, but is believed to be scientifically accurate. Though containing many hard names and technical descriptions, I hope that the indicated pronounciation of the names, and the interest of the subject, may render it available, not only as a school-library reference-book, but as a book for supplemental reading in the more advanced classes of our schools.

It is most desirable that the children and youth of our Western Slope should become interested in, and intelligently acquainted with, the rich and varied forms of life which are resting or moving all around them.

If this book shall awaken or increase an interest in the humble but beautiful creatures of which it treats, my purpose will be accomplished.

It remains for me to thank the many kind friends who have assisted me ; particularly Mrs. C. T. Mills, whose generous additions to the college cabinet have been of the greatest assistance; and Miss Laura M. Mellen, whose skill in illustrating the work speaks for itself, but whose patience and painstaking are known to but few. I also wish to thank those who have kindly given me valuable specimens and information, and to commend our united labors to all lovers of nature. J. K.

MILLS COLLEGE, CALIFORNIA, July, 1887.

WEST COAST SHELLS.

CHAPTER I.

THE ocean is a great home. Its waters are full of life. The rocks along its shores are thickly set with living things ; the mud and sand of its bays are pierced with innumerable burrows, and even the abyss of the deep sea has its curious inhabitants.

Huge whales steam along near the surface of the ocean ; fishes of a thousand kinds are at home a little lower down ; crabs and lobsters, star-fishes and sea-urchins, creep along the rocks or make their way through the masses of seaweed which grow near the shores. Clams and oysters lie on the bottom ; sea-snails, with their curious shells, mussels, barnacles, and a host of inferior creatures, all find their proper places in this great ocean home.

We are not able to see all that is going on under the water; in fact, our field of observation is quite limited ; but by keeping a sharp lookout we may be able to discover a great many interesting facts, and to make very probable guesses as to things which we cannot clearly observe.

So come with me some fine summer morning down to the ocean beach. We will choose a day when low tide occurs about sunrise, and we will be promptly on hand at that hour. There is a light fog floating over the water, and as we come down to the shore we are surprised to see what a broad stretch of mossy rocks has been left bare by the retreating tide.

We walk quickly across the sandy beach, clamber over the slippery rocks as far as the water will allow us, and then we look and listen. Some distance out the big waves come rolling in, smooth and glassy, till they strike the shoaling bottom. There the lower part of the wave is stranded, but the top by no means loses its shoreward motion. Rushing forward, it curls and breaks into foam with a roaring splash, while the water at our feet, feeling the impulse, presses in be- tween the rocks with a soft murmur and then flows back again to meet the next incoming wave.

There are tones of music in all this never-ending motion of the sea which can hardly be described, but which bring to the ear of the sympathetic listener the sweetest of nature's harmonies. The deep bass of the breakers mingled with the lighter notes of the throbbing wavelets, the dripping of the mossy rocks, and the rustle of little crustaceans—all these sounds, united with the sweet breath of the sea, and joined with the lovely forms and beautiful colors which are all around us, all these make us believe that we are in fairyland, and we almost envy the mermaids in their homes among the coral groves, where the dra- peries are mosses and the pavements are of pearl.

But we see no mermaids here, though there is plenty of life. Here is a huge arching rock, and under it is a pool of the clearest sea-water.

We stretch ourselves upon the soft moss, and partly enter the charmed grotto. In the pool are a few bright fishes, which dart round their little ocean, evidently alarmed by our presence. As they swim through the shallow water, they brush against the slender mosses, which wave to and fro and display their graceful forms; or perhaps they touch the frond of an irridescent sea-weed, which, as it moves, reveals its beautiful colors.

On the bottom, or attached to the sides of the stones, are star-fishes of brilliant and varied hues—red, yellow, purple and brown—contrasting strongly with the green sea-grass, and making it seem as if the sky had last night sent a shower of stars into the ocean, and some of them had been left when the tide ebbed away.

Brilliant patches of living sponge—scarlet, orange, or drab—paint the dark rocks; colonies of lace-like polyzoans are scattered over the stones and old shells; pretty sea-snails are creeping slowly along the roof of our grotto, or quietly waiting, with all imaginable patience, for the return of the tide; strange tunicates and other low forms of animal life add to the beauty of form and color, and excite our curiosity to know what they are and how they live; sea-anemones—those living flowers—open their tube-like petals and glow in the morning light; and a host of other things, "creeping innumerable"—all welcome us to this beautiful home in the sea.

Our liveliest hosts are the little crabs, which scamper off sidewise, backwards, forwards, or in any other direction, as we approach, crowding into the narrowest of cracks, whence they peer out with their curious stalked eyes, while they stand ready to defend themselves with their jaw-like claws. If we manifest no hostile intent, they will quickly come creeping down again, and begin anew the business of the day. How their glossy shells shine!—white, green, red, or brown, or perhaps combining all these colors in harmonious patterns.

There is such a thing as getting into sympathy with all these humble animals; and, as you lie on the rocks and admire the wondrous combinations of form and color, equaling in beauty the finest gardens of the dry land, there is such a thing as feeling an intense sympathy with all these humble creatures, and losing all thoughts that you are here for study in the consciousness that you are among friends.

How you wish to become acquainted with them all; to learn their habits and enter into their instincts and feelings! But, as among our own kind, we cannot possibly become acquainted with one in a thousand of all the good people on the earth, so, here in the sea, we must necessarily choose our special friends, and wait for future opportunities to become better acquainted with the others.

For good reasons, to my mind, I have chosen the *Mollusks* as special objects of study, and now wish to introduce them to any one who is seeking to make pleasant acquaintances. I will vouch for it that there is not one of them that carries a bag of poison, or that will harm you in the least; and if you only approach them in a friendly spirit, they will stand ready to give you the best of their possessions, and make your life sweeter and happier for having known them.

One thing I beg of you: never be cruel to my friends. It may be necessary and right to deprive some of them of life, but it need never be done wantonly or cruelly. And while you admire their lovely shells, think even more of the quiet and pleasant lives which they spend in their ocean home.

CHAPTER II.

ONE fine June morning, some years ago, I found myself in the pretty little town of Bolinas. The village is nestled among the cliffs and along the shores of Bolinas Bay, which is the first inlet north of the great entrance to the Bay of San Francisco. Bolinas, or Baulines, as you will find it spelled on some maps, is only about ten miles north of the Golden Gate, but it is so shut in by a high mountain on the east, and by the great Pacific on the west, that you would hardly guess that you were so near to San Francisco, the metropolis of the Pacific States.

The bay was once quite commodious, but now it is so filled with mud and sand that only the smallest sea-going craft can cross the bar, while at low tide great patches of gray sand and brown mud lie exposed to the sun.

Most of the houses are near the low shore, but some of them are perched upon the cliffs and serve a good turn as lighthouses.

A friend of mine, an old sea captain, was once sailing down the coast in a fog. He reckoned that he

was some miles away from land when, all of a sudden
—it must have been on a Monday,—the fog lifted, and
right in front of them, high up on one of these Bolinas
bluffs, they saw a whole line of newly-washed clothes
hanging out to dry.

Although these signal flags were white and not red,
they had the effect of the most emphatic danger sig-
nals ; and with a prompt turn of the wheel the vessel
swung off without striking, and with a blessing on the
good washerwoman the captain was soon speeding
away from the mainland towards a place of safety.

Behind the town rises Mt. Tamalpais, from whose
top, on a clear day, one gets a magnificent view of the
ocean.

The road over this mountain leads through groves
of fine trees, and is full of surprises and delightful
little views. If you want to enjoy real luxury of
scenery, within a little distance from the great city,
take a stage ride across the mountain from San Rafael
to Bolinas.

Well, on that June morning, I was up early to take
advantage of the low tide. There was no fog, and
when the sun showed his face over the top of the
mountain, the beach and bay and ocean were all beautifully lighted up, and invited one to a morning of
the most cheerful study.

I went up the beach, past the hull of a wrecked
vessel over which the waves were breaking, and then
struck out across a long expanse of mossy rocks
which form the shoreward end of the dangerous Duxbury Reef.

From the little patches of gravel between the rocks
came jets of water as I passed along, revealing the
presence of the clams which I will speak of hereafter.

I dug out some of them, but gave most of my attention to the inhabitants of the rocks.

Turning back the masses of olive green *Fucus*,
that most ancient of sea-weeds, I found a considerable
number of mollusks with shells like the one shown in
Fig. 1.   It is not a very common species for California, but is more abundant to the north, about Van-
couver's Island and southern Alaska.

The shell of a full-grown specimen is an inch and
a half long.   It is spindle-shaped, that is, it is largest

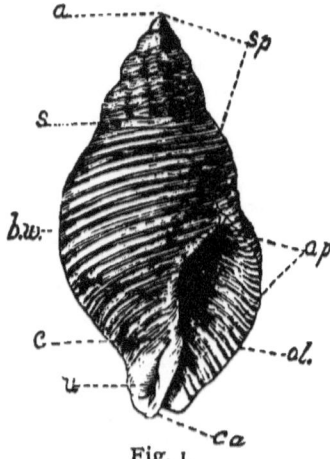

in the middle, and tapers towards each end.   There is an
opening on the right side of the
shell, extending about half way
to the apex or point.   This
opening is called the aperture,
and is marked *ap*.

This aperture is sometimes
called the mouth of the shell,
though it is in no sense the
mouth of the animal ; but since
it has been called the mouth,
the sides of the shell which

Fig. 1.

bound it are called lips.   The one towards your right
hand is the *outer lip*, and is marked *o.l.;* the inner
lip is usually so grown to the central axis of the shell
that it is not distinct from this part round which the
shell seems to revolve, and which is called the
columella.

At the lower end of the aperture is a little curved
canal, marked *ca.* in the figure.

Many shells do not have this canal, but have an
oval or nearly circular opening.   The animals which
have shells with canals are mostly carnivorous, while

those with circular apertures are usually vegetable eaters.

Just to the left of the canal is a little chink or hole called the *umbilicus*, marked *u.* In some shells the umbilicus is very large, and is the space left as the turns of the shell grow in a spiral form, curving around a central opening. Each turn of the shell is called a *whorl;* the last and largest one, *b.w.*, is the *body whorl.* The earlier and smaller whorls make up the *spire*, *sp.*, and the line of union between two whorls is called a *suture*, which is marked *s.* in our picture. Thus we come round again to the apex, *a.*, from which we started, and from which our little creature started also; for when it was hatched from an egg, it had a minute shell of two or three whorls, which remain, in part at least, as the whorls nearest the apex.

As time went on, the whorls increased in number, the outer lip being constantly built up, and the aperture thus going round and round the central axis of the shell, and all the time growing larger and larger. The outside of the shell is not perfectly smooth, but is marked by about twenty little grooves and an equal number of ridges, which follow the shell round and round, from the apex to the edge of the outer lip, where you see them very distinctly. We will call these markings *spiral lines*, to distinguish them from other markings on the shell.

The growth of the shell is frequently interrupted for a little time, and if you follow back from the edge of the outer lip, you can see numerous little lines, parallel with the present edge, and curved just as the edge is now. These marks, which run across the spiral lines, are called *lines of growth*, and show you just where the lip ended when the shell was younger.

Sometimes the animal pauses for a considerable time before it builds another whorl to its shell, and during this time it spends its strength in thickening the outer lip, or throwing out a ridge or frill; after this it goes on smoothly for awhile, and then builds another ridge. Each of these periodical elevations, which thus vary the surface of the whorl, is called a *varix*.

The number of varices to a whorl differs as much as their shape; some shells having but two, others three, while still others have many of these distinctive markings.

The varices on this shell are best seen in young specimens, and consist of nine rounded ridges to a whorl. In full-grown specimens the body whorl has no distinct varices, and those on the spire become somewhat worn off and obliterated. Quite often a piece of the outer lip gets broken off by an accident; then the patient animal builds on a new lip, often leaving a big scar to show where the break was repaired.

Inside, the shell is of a dark-liver color, with lighter spiral lines; without, it is about the same color, but is generally covered with an ash-colored powder, giving it a dingy appearance.

Now that we have examined the parts of the shell, let us study the living animal, which all this time has kept itself concealed in this spiral tube.

We will put a few of our specimens into a glass jar of sea-water, and watch their motions.

First, from out the aperture comes a little brown scale, which serves as a door, and which the tenant had closed after he had withdrawn himself into his house. This door is called the *operculum*. We shall notice how greatly the operculum varies in the different species that we are to study ; but for the shells now under consideration the operculum is a somewhat oval, horny plate, just fitting the aperture. If we examine it, we shall notice that it was once very small, and that there are additions around its edge, and fine marks which correspond to the lines of growth on the shell.

After the operculum, the body of this curious sea-snail begins to appear : first a flat, crawling disk or *foot*, by which he clings to the rock, and is able to slowly move along its surface. And now, in the front of this creeping disk, we see the animal's head, with its pair of tentacles or feelers. The eyes are set upon stalks, often at the base of the tentacles ; they are small organs probably of quite limited vision.

A considerable portion of the animal, however, never leaves the shell—in fact, the shell is grown to the skin or mantle by which it is secreted. We may often pick up the empty cases of little crabs, and may be pretty sure that they are but the cast-off, hardened outer skins of those crustaceans ; for the crabs shed their shells periodically, somewhat as a snake casts its old skin.

But if we find the empty shell of any snail, we may be sure that its former occupant is no longer alive. There are land-slugs and sea-slugs which look like snails without shells, and some people believe that they once had such protections ; but the fact is, they belong to species which never had and never will have any shells, except, perhaps, very small and rudimentary ones.

There are many other things which we might notice about our little animal ; such as his teeth, his gills, and his curious foot, with its transverse muscles; but the tide has turned, and we had better be getting ashore, since we belong to a class of air-breathing animals, and are wholly unprovided with gills. We will only stop to observe that this animal has no bones, but is soft in all its parts, except its teeth and shell; hence, it is called a *mollusk*, which name is derived from the Latin *mollis*, meaning soft.

Because it crawls upon its stomach, or *ventral sur-face*, as we would say, it is called a *Gasteropod*, from the Greek words meaning stomach-footed.

Nearly all the names of shells are derived from the Latin or the Greek. These names may sound rather barbarous to us, but no more so than if they were written in German or Russian. Why not write them in English, then?

A fair question, surely, and if English was univer-sally spoken, it might be hard to find a satisfactory answer. But an English name, to a Russian, would be as bad as a Russian name to you, and since the Latin language is studied by scholars of all nations, and since scientific names should all be written in one language, there is no doubt that the Latin tongue is best adapted for this purpose.

There are different methods of pronouncing Latin, but as some of my readers may not be acquainted with that language, and may like to know at least one way to pronounce the names, I shall indicate the pronunciation according to the English system, by which you pronounce a Latin word as you naturally would if it were an English one spelled in the same way. If you are a Latin scholar, and prefer to pro-nounce by the Roman or the Continental method, you may be sure that very many will agree with you, and certainly I shall find no fault.

Each mollusk has two names—that of the *species* or kind, which is written last, and that of the *genus* or group, which is written first, and which always begins with a capital letter. This generic name, as it is called, is a noun; while the specific name, or name of the species, is an adjective, and agrees with its noun in gender, according to the Latin standard. It may begin with either a capital or a small letter; with a capital, if it is derived from a proper name, otherwise, with a small letter. Some writers allow no capitals in specific names. Sometimes, instead of a proper adjective, the genitive form of the proper noun is used, signifying possession. The whole name strictly applies to the entire, living mollusk; but it is also used in reference to the empty shell.

To the specific name is added the name or initials of the naturalist who first applied that name to the species. These initials are added so that it may be easy to refer to the original specimen or description, if it is necessary to identify the shell beyond all doubt.

The name of the species shown in Fig. 1 is *Chryso-domus dirus*, Rve., Kri-so-do'-mus di'-rus. Near the close of the book you will find a brief sketch of Mr. Reeve, as well as of other naturalists who have given names to our species. It is an honorable list. Many of these men struggled bravely to obtain their knowl-edge, and they present worthy models for our imita-tion. Even in the hard names of shells the human element is present, and the initials of such men as Gould and Carpenter are a constant inspiration to one who knows something of their worthy lives. I trust the brief accounts given of these men may incite you to learn more of their history, and to study their writings with renewed zeal.

(2)

CHAPTER III.

WHILE I was out on the reef, that fine June morning, gathering specimens of the shell already described and of other interesting kinds, the tide began to come in and my investigations were somewhat disturbed. As the shore was a good way off, I began to make my way across the rocks for the beach; but the water gained upon me, though at last my wet feet were safely planted on the warm, dry sands. I would beg my readers to never run serious risks in collecting shells; especially on the sea-coast keep a sharp lookout for the waves and the tide, for more than one person has been swept away from a lack of watchfulness.

Considerable space has been given to a consideration of the first species, not because it is the most interesting shell to be found on our coast, but that an explanation of its parts may serve as a guide in the study of many other species.

Authors differ very widely in the order they adopt for the classification of shells; but as this book is not designed to present disputed points of classification, but to enable you to see and recognize the features, determine the name, and learn the haunts and habits of

the mollusks which you may find, it has seemed best
to essentially follow the order adopted by Dr. P. P.
Carpenter, in his report on "The Mollusks of Western
North America."

Many very small shells will be but briefly described,
and where there are several varieties of the same
species, the principal ones only will be noticed. Still,
I trust that every shell which ordinary collectors will
be likely to gather upon this coast may be identified
by the engravings or the descriptions.

Sometimes the same species has received several
distinct names, given by men who were not aware
that it had been named before, or who have named
two or more varieties of the same species.

In such cases, I have endeavored to give the most
approved name, sometimes referring to the others as
synonyms. For the study of such perplexing points, I
would refer my readers to the larger books and to the
reports of learned societies.

Chrysodomus liratus, Mart., li-ra'-tus, is a species
from Alaska, having a fusiform shell three inches
long, brown in color, and marked by a few sharp spiral
ridges, especially prominent on the body whorl.

Anachis penicillata, Cpr., An'-a-kis pen-i-sil-la'-ta,
has a minute, slender, brownish shell, consisting of
six finely-ridged and sculptured whorls. Its length
is only one-fourth of an inch. This, and the next
species, *Anachis subturrita*, Cpr., sub-tur'-ri-ta, which
is smaller and has fainter ribs, are both found in
southern waters, that is, from the region of Santa
Barbara to the coast of Mexico.

By the term ribs, I would indicate little ridges
which run across the spiral lines. The word is used

in a different sense by some writers, so in the beginning I would clearly define what is meant by the terms to be used.

In Fig. 2 we have a picture of the shell of a little mollusk which lives on the above-mentioned southern

coast. Its name is *Macron lividus*, A. Ad., Mák-ron liv'-id-us. The shell is small, seldom more than an inch in length, without sculpture, and of a brownish color. When found living it is covered with a brown epidermis, which is laid on in little ridges, and resembles a coating of fine, soft cloth.

Fig. 2.

We shall often have occasion to speak of the epidermis or outside coating of the shell. In this species it is very persistent, that is, it clings to the shell and covers it from the apex to the canal. In many species, however, it is easily removed; and when specimens have been knocked about a little their epidermis is nearly lost. Still other shells, like the smooth Olives, show scarcely a trace of epidermis.

The shape of our Macron is well shown in the figure; the whorls are five in number, the outer lip sharp and curved, and the canal short and bent.

The position to hold a shell for study is shown in the figure. The apex should be uppermost, and the axis, or the line which may be supposed to run through the center of the whorls, should be vertical. In this way the spire becomes the upper part of the shell, and we know that it is the oldest part, while the canal is the lowest portion. The French usually draw their figures of shells with the apex downward, but they observe the same rule in regard to the vertical axis.

Notice the strong white fold on the inner wall near the top of the aperture; it is a characteristic mark of this species. These shells may be found on rocks, between tides, and may be easily recognized by the figure and the description.

Macron Kellettii, A. Ad., Kel-let'-ti-i, is a larger species, found on the coast of Lower California. The shell is of a dark color, nearly smooth, or marked with low ridges. The aperture is very large, the outer lip thin, and the canal a mere notch. Its length is more than an inch.

Trophon multicostatus, Esch., Tro'-fon mul-ti-cos-ta'-tus, is a northern species, having a small, pear-shaped, white shell, with several sharp, frill-like varices. The sutures are deep, and the few whorls of the spire are very distinct. Otherwise it is smooth. Length, less than an inch.

Trophon Orpheus, Gld., Or-fe'-us, is smaller than the last, but similar in shape. The sharp, white varices make a crown at the sutures. These varices are crossed by small spiral lines.

Fusus Kobelti, Dall, Fu'-sus Ko-bel'-ti, is found on Santa Catalina Island. It is spindle-shaped, and very graceful in form. There are five or six whorls, with nine elevations on each whorl, crossed by fine, dark, spiral lines. Color, whitish; length, from an inch to two inches.

Fusus ambustus, Gld., am-bus'-tus, has a small, spindle-shaped shell, with a rather long aperture. The dark-colored surface is roughened by numerous knobs and spiral lines. Length, less than an inch.

A beautiful shell found occasionally at San Diego, and further to the south, is known as *Murex trialatus*, Sowb., Mu'-rex tri-a-la'-tus. It is a representative of the great genus of rock-shells, which are so abundant

in the warmer oceans, particularly about Panama.
The rock-shells, or *Murices*, usually are highly ornamented with frills, spines, or knobby varices, and are
sometimes gorgeously colored, particularly within the
aperture. Almost every house has a Murex among
its treasures, and a countless number of little children
have learned to notice and admire the beautiful shape
and color of one or more of these shells.

Brilliant shells belong to warmer seas than this
part of the Pacific. The rare species which we are
now considering is of a dull-white color, marked with
brown stripes. It may easily be recognized by its
three sharp frills, its small oval aperture, and its
tubular canal. Its length is two or three inches.

Another rare shell, sometimes found in southern
waters, is named *Siphonalia Kellettii*, Fbs., Si-fo-
na'-li-a Kel-let'-ti-i. My specimen is from Santa
Barbara ; it measures five inches in length, and thus
ranks among the largest of all our shells. It has a
regular, conical spire, three inches long, marked with
numerous rounded knobs. The aperture is elliptical
in shape, not very large, and the canal turns back-
ward. The shell is strong, heavy, white within, and
somewhat brownish without.

Muricidea incisa, Brod., Mu-ri-sid'-e-a in-si'-sa,
belongs to southern waters, and is not common. The
shell is marked by strong, rounded, transverse ridges,
which give the spire an appearance of being chopped
full of holes. Color, white, with cross-stripes of
brown ; length, an inch and a quarter.

We have, in Fig. 3, the shell of another of the
southern species — one which loves warm water too
much to emigrate far to the north. Its name is
Pteronotus festivus, Hds., Ter-o-no'-tus fes-ti'-vus.

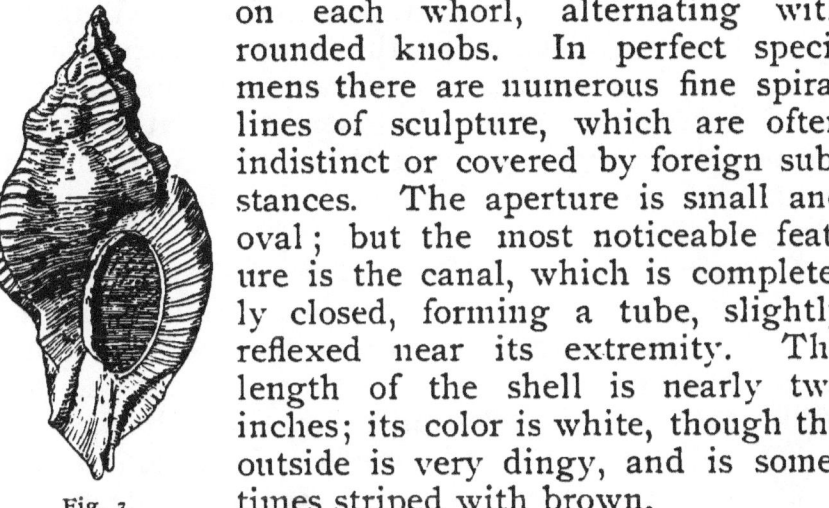

The shell is plainly marked by three reflexed frills on each whorl, alternating with rounded knobs. In perfect specimens there are numerous fine spiral lines of sculpture, which are often indistinct or covered by foreign substances. The aperture is small and oval; but the most noticeable feature is the canal, which is completely closed, forming a tube, slightly reflexed near its extremity. The length of the shell is nearly two inches; its color is white, though the outside is very dingy, and is sometimes striped with brown.

Fig. 3.

Ocinebra Poulsoni, Cpr., O-sin-e'-bra Poul'-son-i, has a strong, spindle-shaped shell, and is found about San Diego. Its surface is strongly marked with rounded varices, which are crossed by fine, dark, spiral lines. The walls of the aperture, in mature specimens, are pure white, and within the outer lip are five or six little round knobs or teeth. Let some one try to find out whether these teeth are merely for ornament, or whether they have some useful office.

The canal is open and somewhat curved, and the operculum is a thin, brown scale. The length of the shell is from an inch to two inches.

The other Ocinebras are much smaller than the last species, and some of them are rather difficult to determine. Fig. 4 represents the shell of *Ocinebra lurida*, Midd., lu'-ri-da. This pretty little shell is common at Monterey and other parts of the coast. It is spindle-shaped, and is marked

Fig. 4.

by fine spiral grooves. The aperture is oval; the canal sometimes open and sometimes tubiform. While the spiral lines are prominent, the transverse sculpturing is faint. The color, as is indicated by the name, is usually reddish yellow, but sometimes it is nearly white. The length is one-half or three-fourths of an inch. At low tide I have found living specimens clinging to stones.

Ocinebra interfossa, Cpr., in-ter-fos'-sa, Fig. 5, is of about the same shape as the last species, though it is usually rather larger. It, too, has spiral grooves, but it also has sharp varices and deep sutures. It varies in color through shades of yellow, gray and brown. It is found near the places which the preceding species in-

Fig. 5. habit.

And now comes another species of this genus, *Ocinebra circumtexta*, Stearns, cir-cum-tex'-ta. The shell is represented in Fig. 6. It is larger and heavier than the last, has a short spire, rather low varices, but very deep and distinct spiral grooves which give the outer lip a scolloped appearance. It is of a reddish color within, but externally it is

Fig. 6. whitish, with brown spots.

Ocinebra gracillima, Stearns, gra-sil'-li-ma, is a small, southern species, similar, in some respects, to Fig. 5, but smoother and darker colored than the shell of *O. interfossa*.

CHAPTER IV.

THE large mollusk whose shell is shown in Fig. 7 is such a lover of the warm waters which bathe the coast of Southern California, that it never migrates

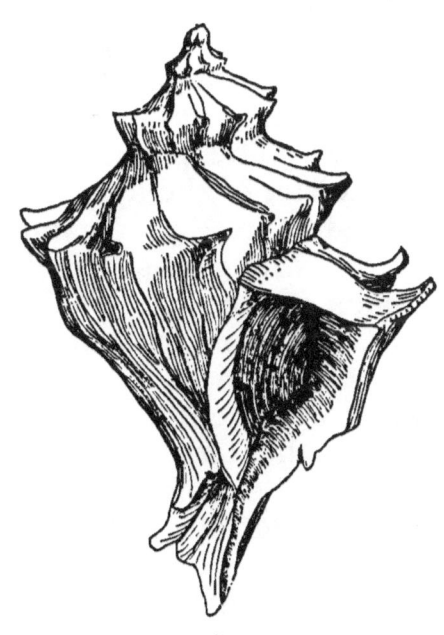

Fig. 7.

far to the north, but is found in the vicinity of San Diego. The engraving is of about half the length of a good sized specimen, though some of these shells are found which are fully six inches long. It may sometimes be picked up upon mud flats at the time of low tide. Its name is *Chorus Belcheri*, Hds., Ko'-rus Belch'-er-i, or Belcher's Chorus. The shell as a whole is somewhat pear-shaped, ending in a long canal, to the left of which is a deep, funnel-shaped umbilicus. The spire is

conical, quite rough and jagged, and the body whorl
is guarded by a crown of strong, sharp points. The
operculum, like that of all similar shells, is thin and
horny. The color of the shell is a dull white, somewhat tinged with brown.

Fig. 8 introduces us to another southern shell,
Cerostoma Nuttallii, Conr., Se-ros'-to-ma Nutt-all'-i-i,
which we may translate as Nuttall's Hornmouth. In
the latter part of the book you will find a brief notice
of Mr. Nuttall, for whom this species was named by
Mr. Conrad, about whom also you will find a few

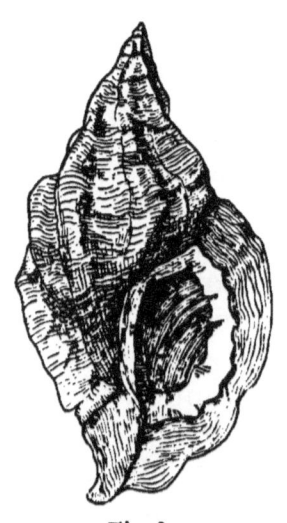

words. If you examine a full-grown
shell of this species you will find a
sharp tooth, or horn, near the base
of the outer lip. The presence of
this horn on the rim of the aperture
is so peculiar a feature that a name
was chosen for the genus which
should indicate its presence. We
shall find the Greek word for mouth,
stoma, combined in various ways to
form the names of different genera,
as *Chlorostoma*, the Green-mouth,
Calliostoma, the Beautiful-mouth,
and *Melanostoma*, the Black-mouth.

Fig. 8.

Our *Cerostoma*, or Horn-mouth,
as you see in the engraving, has a distinct spire
marked by ridgelike varices, a small aperture, and a
closed canal.

Some young specimens have no horn on the wall
of the aperture, and have an open instead of a closed
canal. Allowance must always be made for the age
and development of the specimen. Most of the draw-
ings in this book were made from adult specimens,

and may be supposed to be of the average natural size, unless something is stated to the contrary.

The shell of this species is about two inches long, of a dingy white color, somewhat marked with brown, and each whorl usually has three distinct varices with rounded knobs between them.

Cerostoma foliatum, Gmel., fo-li-a'-tum, which is thought by some to be but a variety of the last species, has a larger shell, which is very conspicuously marked by three broad, wing-like varices, which appear to be made up of overlapping plates, like shingles on the roof of a house. I have only one specimen in my collection, but that one is a beauty. It was found alive, under a stone, and was given to me a few minutes after its capture.

Whether we shall consider *C. foliatum* as distinct from the species shown in Fig. 8, or whether it is but a mere variety of the same species, is a matter of very little consequence in itself; but it is an inquiry which opens the door to very intricate questions concerning the definition of the term species.

By some it is believed that a species includes all the descendants from an original pair of ancestors. Dr. Isaac Lea, that patriarchal naturalist, said : ''A species must be considered a primary established law, stamped with a persistent form—a type, pertaining solely to itself, with the power of successively reproducing the same form and none other.''

Others, who have studied and observed extensively, believe that species and genera do not exist in nature, but are merely convenient terms to designate groups of similar forms and characteristics; and that, like other provisional terms, they will pass away when a better system of naming is devised.

It seems to me that varieties of living beings are like shades of color—indefinite in number, and blending into one another like the tints of the rainbow. Though there are shades in the middle of the spectrum which one might call green, and another might call blue, still, blue is blue, and green is green, and ever remain so. We may give names to the intermediate colors, like light blue or greenish blue, but no one doubts that each of these shades is distinct, though not easily defined. So, though we doubtless must reduce many of our present species to the rank of varieties, and though there may be many varieties concerning which there will be differing opinions, and which will be variously classed, even by thoughtful observers—still, I believe the great forms of life, the true species, exist unchanged, and can vary only within fixed and narrow limits, unless it be by the express act of creative power.

Next on our list comes a small genus of mollusks, which are almost exclusively confined to the west coast of America. A good representation of one of these shells is shown in Fig. 9, which illustrates the common Unicorn shell, *Monoceros lapilloides*, Conr., Mo-nos'-e-ros lap-il-loi'-des. The Greek name, *Mo-noceros*, is exactly translated by our word "Unicorn," which is derived from the Latin, and both of them mean single-horn. The specific name, *lapilloides*, means, resembling a pebble. The little horn near the base of the outer lip is the key to the generic name, and the rounded, granite-like appearance of the shell explains the second, or specific name.

Fig. 9.

It is a pretty little shell, about an inch in length,

with a spire of four whorls, a rather small aperture, within which are several knobs or teeth.

The outside is marked by fine spiral grooves, crossed by lines of growth ; and the colors, white and brown, are broken up into little checks, giving it a grayish appearance. I have found many of these mollusks on the rocks, near the upper tide-mark. In such an exposed position they are liable to receive severe knocks, as the the waves come dashing in, and if their shells were light and thin, like some of those which we shall soon have occasion to examine, they would quickly be broken to pieces. Shore shells are usually strong and solid ones. Whenever you examine a shell, please notice such points, and try to find out how it is adapted to its surroundings. In this way, shell gathering becomes something more than a mere pastime, for it brings us face to face with the great questions of life, of design, and of final causes.

Along with specimens of *Chrysodomus dirus*, shown in Fig. 1, I found on Duxbury Reef a great number of shells quite similar to those of the last species. They were on the moist rocks, under the heavy growth of sea-weed, and were of almost the same color as the stones to which they were clinging. A view of one

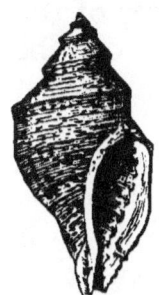

of these shells is shown in Fig. 10. The name, derived from the angular appearance of the whorls, is *Monoceros engonatum*, Conr., en-go-na'-tum. While the former species resembled a rolled pebble, this one has sharper corners and looks as if it had been less worn. In other respects it is very similar to *M. lapilloides*, and some observers think they are but varieties

Fig. 10.

of the same species. The remarks on a preceding

page, concerning the different kinds of *Cerostoma*, apply equally well to this genus, and a careful study of the variations seen in specimens which are found in different localities and under different conditions is highly interesting.

Accurate observations by any one may prove valuable, both to the observer and to the cause of science in general. There are many things yet to be learned about even our most common animals, and no one need despair of discovering some new truth.

It is a good thing to know the names of the objects which we are studying, for that enables us to speak of them intelligently and definitely ; but to this knowledge of the name we will try to attach all available facts which relate in any way to the nature and habits of the creature that we are studying.

Monoceros lugubre, Sowb., lu-gu'-bre, found on the coast of Lower California, and perhaps a little farther north, has a thick, heavy shell about an inch long. The wall of the aperture is of a brown color, and is marked with several rows of white tubercles. The little horn near the canal is very distinct.

In olden times, the inhabitants of ancient Tyre used to get a purple dye from the bodies of several kinds of mollusks which lived along the shores of the Mediterranean Sea. It is said that this dye can be obtained by pressing upon the operculum, and that it is of a light color at first, but turns darker by exposure to the air. Large quantities of shells are found near Tyre, which seem to have been broken in stone mortars, doubtless for the purpose of obtaining this precious purple dye. How successfully the coloring fluid may be obtained from our own species remains to be determined, but the ancient custom of extracting a

purple dye from similar mollusks has given a name
to a great genus, several species of which live upon
this coast. That name is *Purpura*, or the Purple
shell. The Latin name for our most common species
of Purples is *Purpura saxicola*, Val., Pur′-pu-ra sax-
ik′-o-la. We may call it the Rock Purple, as its name

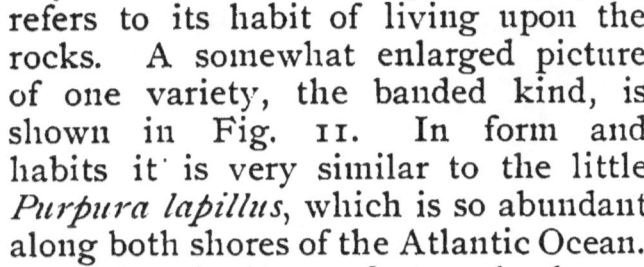

refers to its habit of living upon the
rocks. A somewhat enlarged picture
of one variety, the banded kind, is
shown in Fig. 11. In form and
habits it is very similar to the little
Purpura lapillus, which is so abundant
along both shores of the Atlantic Ocean.
Our Purples love to frequently change
their element, for they select for a home
those rocks which are alternately left

Fig. 11. bare and covered again by the tides.
The books state that the Purples are carnivorous,
boring into mussel shells and eating the unfortunate
inhabitant; also that they are quite destructive to
oyster beds. I have never seen them engaged in these
alleged atrocities, but would be very glad to hear
from witnesses who had caught them in the act.

The shell is rather less than an inch in length, and
has a short spire, a flattened columella, a sharp-edged
outer lip, a short canal and a small umbilicus. The
inside is reddish brown, but the outside varies greatly,
both in form and in color. Sometimes it is smooth
and almost black, sometimes white and coronated;
but often it is of a dingy white, decorated with double
spiral bands of dark brown, accompanied with spiral
grooves.

Various names, as *fuscata*, *emarginata* and *ostrina*,
have been given to the different forms, but probably

they all belong to one species. The Atlantic Purple exhibits similar varieties of form and color.

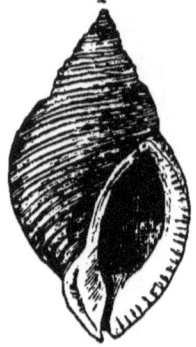

Purpura lima, Mart., li'-ma, which is the same as *Purpura canaliculata*, Duclos, is shown in Fig. 12. It is more rarely met with than the last species, probably on account of its living in deeper water. In size it is rather larger than *P. saxicola*, while in appearance its shell is more smooth and symmetrical. The spire consists of four whorls, separated by distinct sutures. The distinguishing feature, however, and the one which gives the name to the shell, is the presence of about fifteen spiral grooves on the whorls, giving its surface somewhat the appearance of a coarse file. The operculum, as in all the Purples, is thin, horny, and somewhat oval in shape. The color of the shell is light brown. It is a very pretty species, and may easily be recognized by its rounded and channelled whorls.

Fig. 12.

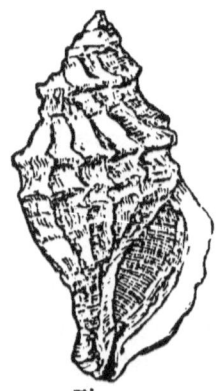

There is another member of the same genus which lives in San Francisco Bay, but which is more common and more finely developed, a few hundred miles farther northward. The shell varies very much in respect to its surface, a specimen being represented in Fig. 13, which is only moderately rough. You notice that the shell is widest in the middle, that it has an elliptical aperture, a short canal, a distinct spire, and numerous sharp varices. Its color varies from white to brown; some specimens are pure white and are quite smooth, others are almost wholly brown

Fig. 13.

and somewhat rough, while others are marked with bands of color and are richly ornamented with numerous wrinkled frills. This last characteristic has determined the name for the species, *Purpura crispata*, Chem., cris-pa'-ta, the Wrinkled Purple. One of the synonyms by which it is known is *P. lactuca*, Esch., which name was probably given to white specimens.

The shells are always strong and heavy, and have an average length of an inch and a half. Many specimens are longer and wider than the engraving, while some are even smaller.

Though the smooth white varieties are very plain in their appearance, some of the northern beauties, all frilled and banded as if to attract attention, are worthy of a place in any choice collection of handsome shells.

(3)

CHAPTER V.

WHEN the tide is high, the waves often wash up great numbers of little shells into sheltered coves, and leave them there to be gathered when the tide has ebbed away. It is very pleasant to lie down upon the warm sand, on a summer afternoon, and while the waves are rushing to and fro at your feet, to look for these beautiful bits of organic structure. Whenever you find a pretty one you put it in a little bag, or, what is more likely, you lay it away in some large shell which you have picked up for that purpose.

Among the most abundant of the shells to be thus found on our coast is the little Wrinkled Amphissa,

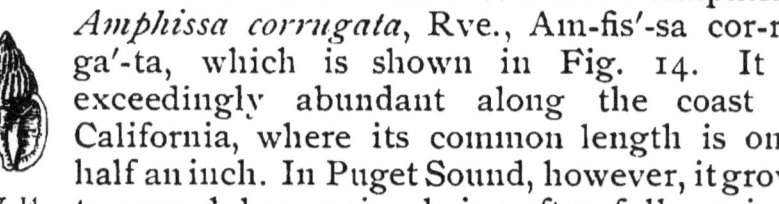

Amphissa corrugata, Rve., Am-fis′-sa cor-ru-ga′-ta, which is shown in Fig. 14. It is exceedingly abundant along the coast of California, where its common length is only half an inch. In Puget Sound, however, it grows Fig. 14. to a much larger size, being often fully an inch in length, and of corresponding proportions.

The spire consists of four whorls, separated by a plainly marked suture. Spiral striæ, or fine lines, may be found at the base of the shell, above which the whole surface is ornamented with numerous ribs or varices, giving it the corrugated appearance from which it takes its name. The color of the shell may be either red, orange, gray, light brown, or almost black ; and a collection of them, in a glass, furnishes a very pretty assortment of tints.

It is pleasant for you to find these pretty shells all clean and dry on the warm sand, but such collecting is not enough to give you the keenest relish for the work. You want to find the little animal at home, and see how he keeps house, before you can form a correct notion of his peculiarities. If you search among the stones at low tide, turning them over with a stove poker or some similar hook, you will probably be able to find some living specimens of our little Amphissa. Such a triumph is not soon forgotten. Don't be deceived, however, by the little hermit-crabs which get part way into dead and empty shells and then draw them around as a piece of armor, but search until you find the true living mollusk.

In your search along the beach you will surely find great numbers of a similar species, the little Eel-grass shell, *Astyris gausapata*, Gld., As'-ty-ris gau-sa-pa'-ta,

Fig. 15.

which is shown in Fig. 15. This shell, formerly called *Amycla carinata*, is about the size of a grain of wheat. The spire is conical, rather long, and marked by faint sutures. The aperture is small, and in adult specimens the lip is somewhat thickened. The color of the shell is either light or dark brown, and its surface is polished and glistening, and often mottled by dots or stripes. The figure is considerably magnified.

This little mollusk lives in great numbers at the roots of the eel-grass, and dead shells are washed up abundantly upon the beach. In the variety *carinata*

the l..'y whorl has a stout spiral keel, just below the last s...ure.

A...ris tuberosa, Cpr., tu-ber-o'-sa, has a very small, slender, brownish shell, the lower whorl of which is marked with two rows of minute, whitish tubercles. It is found on the southern coast of California, as are two other species of the same genus, *A. chrysalloidea*, Cpr., and *A. aurantiæa*, Dall, both of which are of small size.

The next genus which we will consider is named *Nassa*. The word literally means a basket for taking fish. Most of the members of this genus have a reticulated or checked surface, somewhat like network or the sides of a basket.

Our largest Basket shell is named *Nassa fossata*, Gld., Nas'-sa fos-sa'-ta. An excellent picture of it is

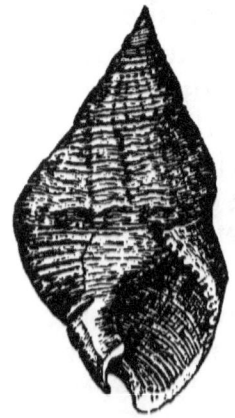

Fig. 16.

given in Fig. 16. The spire is conical, consisting of five or six whorls, and ends in a pointed apex. The surface of the whole shell is marked by spiral and transverse ridges, the former of which appear also within the outer lip. The thickness of this lip varies much with the age of the animal, as does the callus of enamel which is spread over the columella. This enamel, in mature specimens, is of a bright orange color, and contrasts finely with the light ash color of the general surface of the shell.

The canal is short and abruptly reflexed, while just above it is a deep ditch or *fossa*, showing at once from what the name is derived. The use of the canal seems to be to afford space and protection for a breathing tube which projects above the surface of the mud which the animal is exploring for its prey.

The Nassas are active mollusks, and are cordially hated by the oystermen, because they are so fond of boring a hole through the shells of young oysters and eating the contents with as much relish as any other judge of good living. They bore into various clams, too, and it is even hinted that they sometimes attack their own kind. But they are scavengers also, and consume the flesh of dead crabs and like animals which are so liable to be found near the shores. I have some beautiful specimens of this species which were taken from the stomach of a large fish, showing that the biter of other animals is liable to be swallowed whole when the avenging and hungry fish comes round. The length of an adult shell is about an inch and a half, and is seldom as much as two inches.

Nassa tegula, Rve., teg'-u-la, shown in Fig. 17, is a southern species. Shell, strong ; spire, conical, half the length of the whole shell, and marked with little knobs; aperture, small ; canal, reflexed ; inner lip covered with a large callus of smooth, white enamel. Color, dark gray ; length, three-fourths of an inch.

Fig. 17.

Nassa mendica, Gld., men'-di-ca, Fig. 18, is a variable species, having a shell about the length of the last one, but more slender. The surface is marked by numerous fine spiral lines, crossed by ridgy varices. It is light brown in color, with a white peristome, or margin of the aperture. It occurs all along the coast from Puget Sound to San Diego.

Fig. 18.

Nassa Cooperi, Fbs., Coop'-er-i, which has seven

ribs to a whorl, and fine spiral sculpture, is now considered as a variety of the species *mendica*.

Nassa perpinguis, Hinds, per-pin'-guis, Fig. 19, is

our last species of the interesting group of
Basket Shells.   It resembles the first one,
whose shell is shown in Fig. 16, but it is
much smaller, being less than an inch
long.   Its whorls are beautifully rounded
and cut into little squares.   The shell is
thin, light brown in color, with a trace of
orange inside.   It is chiefly found on the
southern coasts.   The name, *perpinguis*, simply
means fat, while *mendica*, the name of another species,
means lean.   Can you not see from the cuts why these
names were applied ?

Fig. 19.

CHAPTER VI.

ONE fine summer morning I rose very early, took
my long rubber boots, an old hoe, and a basket, put
a few crackers in my pocket, and silently stole away
from the little tent among the pines where the rest
of my family were continuing their slumbers. I followed the long path which led along the cliffs, here
coming down close to the shore, and there cutting off
a sharp headland of rocks, till I reached my destina-
tion. This was a little strip of sandy beach from
which the water had all receded, for it was at the very
lowest ebb of the early tide. I sat down on a rock,
took a cracker from my pocket, and began to investi-
gate both it and the prospect. In front of me was
the strip of sand sloping down to the light waves ;
behind me was the high bank of earth, and the rocks
were on either side ; but no shells were to be found
except a few well-worn specimens which had been
tossed up by some departing wave.

But I was not expecting to find shells in plain sight,
so I cheerfully pulled off my shoes and drew on those
very convenient appendages, the long rubber boots.

Now I was ready for work and taking up my hoe I began to dig in the sand. There was plenty of sand to dig in, in fact, too much of it, for it apparently took up all the room and left no place for shells.

At length I struck upon a spot where a little stream of water was oozing out from the bank of sand. As I scraped away the surface, I saw something which would have made me dance for joy had I not been weighed down by the long boots. For there, in very truth, was a live Olive, with its graceful shell shaped like Fig. 20, and a beautiful, pearl-colored body. It quickly withdrew this into the shell and closed the aperture with a very insignificant scale, which seemed to be an apology for an operculum.

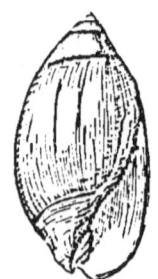

Fig. 20.

I picked up the pretty little creature, and scientifically mused somewhat as follows:

The Latin name for this mollusk is *Olivella biplicata*, Sby., Ol-i-vel'-la bi-pli-ca'-ta. The shell is about an inch long, apparently smooth and polished, yet showing under the microscope very fine and beautiful reticulations. The spire is short, the aperture long and narrow, the canal a mere notch, and the outer lip thin edged. Upon the inner wall of the aperture is a lump of white enamel, and at the base of the columella are two little folds, which are referred to in the name *biplicata*, twice folded. The color of the shell varies much in different specimens; some are almost pure white, others are very dark, but most of them are dove-colored, with purple trimmings. They are about the size and shape of the olives of our orchards, and their name has no mystery connected with it, but doubtless refers to their appearance.

Well, as I proceeded with my hoeing, my joy increased, for I found them by the hundred, and I had gathered about a thousand before the tide came in so far as to render further work impracticable. They seemed to lie in groups just under the surface of the sand, yet wholly concealed from sight. You must go at the very lowest morning tides, if you wish to gather them, and search till you find the bed ; for they seem to be active burrowers, and to travel rapidly from place to place.

I took some of them home and put them in a jar of beach-sand and sea-water. You will be pleased to do the same if you ever have the opportunity, for their movements are very interesting. You will then see the plow-shaped foot which quickly digs a hole in the sand, and the long breathing-siphon which curls up through the canal, and reaches through the sand up to the clear water, like the trunk of a swimming elephant reaching up for air.

To clean the shells it is simply necessary to spread them in the sunshine for a few hours, when the animal will be found to be dead and loosened from the shell. The soft parts can then be removed with a pin.

To clean most shells, however, it is necessary to throw them into boiling water. In a few minutes they can be taken out and the animal withdrawn by a little hook or bent wire.

If only a part of the body can be obtained, the shell may be securely plugged with cotton. It is well to fill even perfectly cleaned shells, and attach the operculum to the cotton by a drop of glue. They will then appear as if they were living specimens. Much will depend upon one's time and taste for this

part of the preparation, but the thorough cleaning of
the shell is indispensable, and should be attended to
as soon as possible after specimens are gathered.

Olivella bœtica, Cpr., be'-ti-ca, Fig. 21, has a more
slender shell than the last species, and is smaller in
all respects.   Some specimens are larger than the
engraving, but the spire is always quite tapering,
and the shell is usually thin and delicate.   The
color varies, but it is generally brown or bluish,
sometimes diversified with yellow stripes.

Fig. 21.   A short, yellowish variety is sometimes called
Olivella intorta, but it seems to me that it does not
deserve that name, which is applied to a species found
in the Gulf of California.   I think all our specimens
may be classed under one or the other of the two
main species.

Most of the Olives live in warmer waters than those
which bathe the west coast of the United States, and
some of them from tropical seas are very beautiful
and richly colored.

Mitra maura, Swains., Mi'-tra mau'-ra, is a dusky
relative of the beautiful Miter Shells which are found
in the vicinity of Australia.   Some of those southern
shells, like the Pope's Cap, and the Bishop's Cap,

look exceedingly gay with their yellow,
white, and scarlet markings and their crown
of graceful points.

Our species, however, as shown in Fig.
22, has a plain, smooth shell, while its color
is almost black, and it is wholly devoid of
the gay trimmings of its relatives.   The
shell is strong and firm, spindle-shaped,
obscurely marked by lines of growth and
spiral threads.   The columella is ridged by

Fig 22.

three strong, oblique folds which are very conspicuous. The length of the shell is from an inch to two inches or more. It is seldom found living, but dead and broken shells are not unfrequently thrown up by the waves. The folds on the columella, the dark brown shell, and the black epidermis are decisive markings.

The pretty little shell of *Volvarina varia*, Sby., Vol-va-ri'-na va'ri-a, is about the size and shape of a grain of wheat. It has a very short, rounded spire, a long aperture and a plaited columella. Its surface is very smooth and glossy, and varies in color from white to brown, the shades being often laid on in bands and stripes. It is a southern species and is found on rocks between tides.

There are several little pure white shells about the size of a grain of rice, all of which are popularly known as Rice Shells. Most of them live in the warmer oceans, but one which here commonly passes by that name is rather sparingly found on our coast.

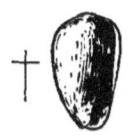

Fig. 23.

Its true name is *Marginella Jewettii*, Cpr., Mar-gin-el'-la Jew-ett'-i-i, a rather large name for so small a shell. Fig. 23 gives an enlarged view of the shell, with a little cross beside it to show the true length and breadth. You will notice these little crosses beside several other figures in the book.

The shell is pure white, pear-shaped, and has no visible spire. The columella is plaited, and the aperture extends the whole length of the shell, which is rather less than one-fourth of an inch in length.

Marginella subtrigona, M. regularis and *M. pyriformis* are three species similar in form to the last, but so very minute that they would hardly be noticed, except by one with very sharp eyes. They occur on the southern coasts.

From these very small shells we pass abruptly to a very large one, *Ranella Californica*, Hds., Ra-nel'-la Cal-i-for'-ni-ca, commonly known as the Frog Shell. The picture of a small specimen is shown in Fig. 24.

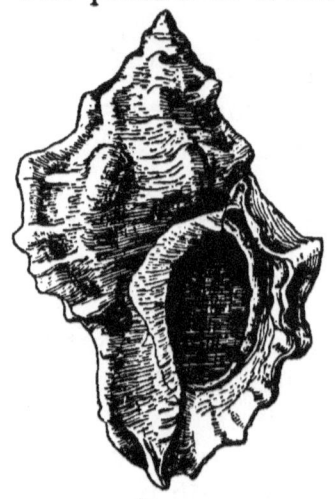

This shell is very strong and solid, and its surface is marked with many knobs and ridges. It appears to grow forward half a whorl, and then the creature pauses and builds up a thick lip. Leaving this ridge at length, it completes the whorl, and then forms another varix. The result of this singular method of shell-building is, that the shell has two ridges extending from the apex to the canal, on opposite sides of the whorl. This feature is characteristic of the whole *Ranella* genus.

Fig. 24.

Our species is essentially a southern mollusk, though I have seen a few good specimens which were collected in Monterey Bay.

The external color is yellowish brown ; but within it is of the purest white. The common length of one of these shells is three inches, though some of them grow to twice that length, and thus rank as one of our largest shells.

At this point, mention should be made of the rare *Priene Oregonensis*, Redf., which has a large, elongated, thin shell, with distinct, rounded whorls and a short canal. It is of a light color, and is covered with a hairy epidermis. Its home, as the name indicates, is on the northern coast.

CHAPTER VII.

Bad Habits of the Natica Family—Lunatia and Neverita—The Southern Sigaretus — Lamellaria and
the Velvet Shell—Triforis—Dextral and Sinistral Shells—Cerithiopsis—The White Opalia and
Scalaria—The Shining Eulima.

FIGURE 25 represents the big Moon-shell, *Lunatia
Lewisii*, Gld., Lu-na'-shi-a Lew-is'-i-i. It is a representative of the *Natica*
family, all the members of
which are distinguished by
their ferocious nature, and
might well be called Snails
of Prey.

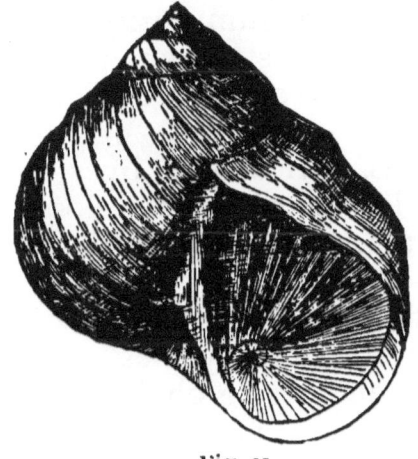

Plowing along through
the wet sand by means of its
enormous foot, it no sooner
reaches an unfortunate
clam, than the flint drill
which it carries in its mouth
is stretched out and begins
to accomplish its work of destruction. The helpless
clam has no means of flight from such an enemy; and
if its hard shell is not a sufficient protection, it is in
a sad case indeed. And in truth, the case is sad, for
the shell is no match for the drill, and when once it
has reached the savory meat inside, the robber makes

Fig. 25.

short work of his victim. A high-handed proceeding, no doubt; but then, it contrasts rather favorably with our way of opening clams and oysters.

The size of this shell varies greatly with its age and conditions. Specimens have been found as large as six-inch globes, but such giants are not common. They are ordinarily the size of average apples. The color is yellowish white and the form spheroidal; the surface is nearly smooth, the operculum horny, and the umbilicus large. This figure was drawn from a specimen collected at Olympia, Washington Territory.

A somewhat similiar species, which also lives in northern waters, may be distinguished by its closed umbilicus and shelly operculum. Its name is *Natica clausa*, Brod. and Sby., Nat'-i-ca clau'-sa.

Neverita Recluziana, Petit., Ne-ver'-i-ta Re-cluz-i-an'-a, shown in Fig. 26, is a southern species, more

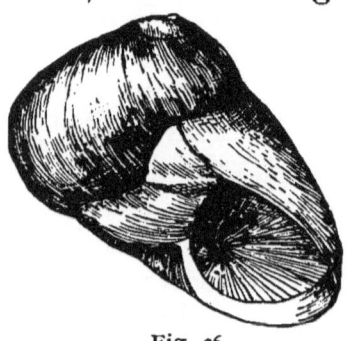

Fig. 26.

smooth and less globular than the last, and is easily determined by the thick, heavy patch of enamel which extends down the columella, and nearly or quite fills the umbilicus. The shell is very solid and strong. In color it varies between brown and white. Its average length is perhaps two inches, though many specimens are smaller.

The last three species, all of which belong to the Natica family, have strong, heavy shells, and grow to a large size. A very pretty shell belonging to the same family is probably found occasionally on our southern coast, though its real home is still farther to the south. Its name is *Sigaretus debilis*, Sig-a-re'-tus deb'-i-lis. It is pure white, very flat, and has a small spire but a very large aperture. Its breadth is about an inch.

Somewhat resembling this last shell, but smaller, is the one shown in Fig. 27, named *Lamellaria Stearnsii*, Dall, Lam-el-la'-ri-a Sterns'-i-i. It is pure white, very thin, and has so large an aperture that the interior of the shell is plainly visible. Its breadth is about half an inch. In this species, as well as in the next one to be described, the thin shell is wholly concealed by the large development of the mantle.

Fig. 27.

The little Velvet Shell is represented in Fig. 28. It belongs to the same species that lives on the coast of Great Britain, and its name is *Velutina lævigata*, Linn., Vel-u-ti'-na lev-i-ga'-ta. You will notice that it is one of the few of our species which received its name from the great Swedish naturalist, Linné, and the reason for this fact is obvious. As shown in the figure, the spire is short, the outer lip thin, and the aperture large and nearly circular. The color is light brown, and the size is about that of a pea. It derives its name from the velvet-like epidermis which, in fresh specimens, covers the shell. It is a northern species, and is found along the shores of Puget Sound and the adjacent regions.

Fig. 28.

Triforis adversa, Mont., 'Trif'-o-ris ad-ver'-sa, is a little mollusk, having a minute, spire-shaped, many-whorled shell, the surface of which is reticulated or netted, and the aperture of which is small.

There is one peculiarity about this shell which makes it differ from any of those which we have thus far studied. You notice in nearly all the cuts that when the apex is uppermost, as it should be, the aperture is on the side next to your right hand. All such shells are said to be right-handed or dextral shells. Our little *Triforis*, however, has the aperture upon the left side and is said to be left-handed or sinistral. As this little brown shell is less than one-fourth of an inch long, a picture would have to be magnified a good deal to show its form plainly, but you will see examples of sinistral shells in Fig. 107 and Fig. 108. There are some whole genera of mollusks which have sinistral shells, particularly the Physas, which are the fresh water snails so common in all little brooks. In some few species part of the specimens are dextral and part are sinistral, but, as a rule, left-handed shells are rare and quickly excite remark.

Cerithiopsis tuberculata, Mont., Se-rith-i-op'-sis tu-ber-cu-la'-ta, is much like the last species in its general appearance, though it is larger and its shell

is dextral, as shown in Fig. 29. The spire consists of six or seven whorls, the spire is tuberculated or covered with little projections, and the sutures are conspicuous. The color is

Fig. 29. dark brown, and the length is from one-fourth to one-half of an inch.

Cerithiopsis columna, Cpr., col-um'-na, has a shell of ten whorls; in form it is slender, its sutures are inconspicuous, and "the nodules are close, like strung figs" (Cpr.). Its color is light brown, and its size is the same as that of the last species.

A southern species should also be mentioned, *Cerithiopsis assimilata*, C. B. Adams, as-sim-i-la'-ta. In size and color it is like the last species, but it is marked by strong spiral ridges, winding from the apex to the aperture.

It is now our pleasant task to consider a few species of pure white shells regularly marked with frequent varices. All of them are quite rare, but if you search along the shore you will probably have the good fortune to find one or more of them.

The first one of the group is shown in Fig. 30, and is known as *Opalia borealis*, Gld., O-pa'-li-a bo-re-a'-lis, or the Northern Opalia.

The shell consists almost wholly of the spire, which is composed of about eight whorls, and each of these is crossed by eight blunt ridges. The aperture is entire, and the rounded lips are sometimes stained by the rich purple juices of the animal.

Fig. 30. The operculum is a brown scale, nearly circular, and showing lines of growth. The color of the shell is white, and its length is about an inch.

Opalia crenatoides, Cpr., cren-a-toi'-des, is smaller and blunter than *borealis*. The ridges are less conspicuous except at the sutures. According to Mr. Carpenter, there are "sutural holes behind the basal rib."

In Fig. 31 is shown the beautiful shell of *Scalaria Hindsii*, Cpr., Ska-la'-ri-a Hinds'-i-i. It is pure white, very delicate, and is generally less than one inch in length. The whorls are very distinct, finely rounded, and each one is crossed by about twelve thin, sharp ridges.

Fig. 31.

These shells are so highly prized that they are sometimes worn as the drops of ear-rings, while a foreign specimen, the great Chinese Scalaria or Wentle-trap,

(4)

used to be so rare and so highly prized that most extravagant prices were paid for a specimen. So greatly were they desired, and so seldom were they found, that the Chinese, it is said, made very perfect imitations of these precious shells from a preparation of rice. Beware of counterfeits!

Scalaria Indianorum, Cpr., In-di-an-o'-rum, is a northern species, very similar to *Hindsii*, which is found more at the south. Its shell is rather less tapering, and it is sometimes tinted.

Eulima micans, Cpr., Eu-li'-ma mi'-kans, Fig. 32, comes next on our list. This species has a beautifully polished, slender, spiral shell, with a very sharp apex and an elongated aperture. Its surface is bluish white and glistening, as its name indicates. Its length is commonly less than half an inch.

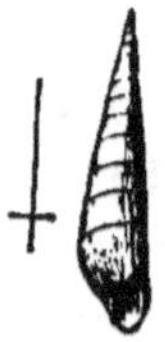

Fig. 32. *Eulima rutila*, Cpr., ru'-ti-la, is like the last species, but very small and slender. Its color is rosy, and the base of the shell is lengthened.

Every one of this group of shells possesses a peculiar beauty; and whether we examine the white Opalia, the sculptured Stair-case shell, or the polished Eulima, we shall be struck with the evident regularity of its parts, and the beautiful plan upon which it is constructed.

CHAPTER VIII.

A Group of Minute Shells — Why Mentioned — The Chemnitzias, or Minute Spire-Shells — The Best Way to Determine Such Specimens — The Odostomias and the Obelisk-Shell — The California Cone — Mitromorpha and Mangelia — Shells Marked by a Notch in the Outer Lip — Our Rarest Shell.

WE are now to consider a group of shells, several of which are so very small that they would scarcely be noticed by any one who was not looking sharply for just such specimens.

But though they are so very minute, still there are two reasons why I wish to mention most of them ; first, that the shells may be recognized from the descriptions, so far as possible; and secondly, that names which are already known may be compared with what is here said of the species, that thus they may be verified.

The first species of these little mollusks is named *Chemnitzia torquata*, Gld., Chem-nitz'-i-a tor-qua'-ta, showing clearly that names and dimensions do not necessarily agree.

The shell is so small that it would scarcely be noticed, yet when examined under the microscope it is very beautiful.

It consists of a very slender, many-whorled spire, with deep sutures and numerous and delicate cross-ribs. Its color is white, and the whole length of the shell is less than a quarter of an inch.

Chemnitzia castanea, Cpr., cas-tan'-e-a, is represented in Fig. 33. The shell is somewhat larger than that of the last, and is of a chestnut color, as the name indicates. Its eight or ten whorls are marked with numerous fine ribs, and though so small, it is a beautiful shell.

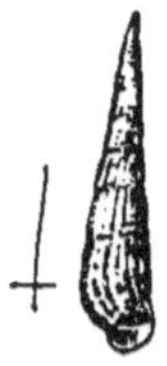

Fig. 33. *Chemnitzia tenuicula*, Gld., ten-u-ic'-u-la, is another representative of the genus which was named for the scholarly Chemnitz. It is a southern species, has flattened whorls, and is marked with fine and crowded ribs. Color, brownish; length, one-fourth of an inch.

Dunkeria laminata, Cpr., Dun-ker'-i-a lam-in-a'-ta, is the name of another similar mollusk belonging to a sub-genus of *Chemnitzia*.

Its shell is similar in size and color to that of the last species, but its eight whorls are more rounded and more finely cancellated.

Oscilla insculpta, Cpr., Os-sil'-la in-skulp'-ta, is very minute and has a spire-shaped shell, the five whorls of which are marked by a few strong spiral ridges. Whitish; length, one-eighth of an inch.

Miralda quinquecincta, Cpr., Mi-ral'-da quin-que-sink'-ta, Five-banded Miralda. The little shell is of the same size and color as the last. The sutures are distinct, and the flat whorls are marked by a few strong spiral bands and many minute cross-ribs.

The list of these graceful but inconspicuous creatures is not yet complete, for, closely following, we have *Evalea tenuisculpta*, Cpr., E-va'-le-a ten-u-i-sculp'-ta, with its white, few-whorled, nearly smooth shell, a little over one-eighth of an inch long; and its sister, *Evalea graciliente*, Cpr., gra-sil-i-en'-te, which is very minute, whitish, few-whorled and lightly cancellated.

For examining such shells a good lens is quite indispensable, but in the hands of more advanced students the minute specimens are full of interest.

To determine the features and differences of the several genera of these microscopic mollusks, one should consult some recent work on conchology; while to make sure of the correct specific name, the most satisfactory way is to compare them with authentic specimens in some good museum, or send send them for determination to some one who has such a collection at hand.

We will now leave these slender, spire-shaped shells and consider the Odostomias. The shells of this genus are white, and are less slender in form than those of the last group. They have few whorls, and on the columella is a fold like a tooth, on account of which they received this name, which is derived from the Greek words for tooth and mouth. They are frequently found nestling upon large shells like those of the oyster and the abalone.

Odostomia inflata, Cpr., O-dos-to'-mi-a in-fla'-ta, has a minute white shell composed of four whorls, and is about one-eighth of an inch in length.

Odostomia Gouldii, Cpr., is similar to the last species, and is probably only a variety. It is very small and has "a gently-rounded base" (Cpr.).

Odostomia gravida, Gld., grav'-i-da, has a shell minute, thin, and somewhat more slender than that of the last mentioned. It is made up of five whorls.

Odostomia nuciformis, Cpr., nu-si-for'-mis, comes next with a shell white, solid, and having a large body

whorl.   Sometimes the shell grows to the length of
one-fourth of an inch or even more.

Odostomia satura, Cpr., sa-tu'-ra, is shown in
Fig. 34. The shell is beautifully white and
pure, and less solid than that of the last species.
Fig. 34. The sutures are very distinct, and the whorls
are checked with a microscopic network of extremely fine lines.   It is one-fourth of an inch long.

Obeliscus variegatus, Cpr., the shell of which is
shown in Fig. 35, is now believed to be identical
with the *Pyramidella conica* of C. B. Adams,
Py-ram-i-del'-la con'-i-ca. Both names savor of
ancient Egypt.   It has a perfectly conical,
tapering shell, composed of about ten whorls.
There is a fold on the columella as in the Odos-
Fig. 35. tomias. The color is brownish, somewhat
clouded, and the length is half an inch.   It is found
in southern waters, but is quite rare even there.

Mumiola cincta, Cpr., Mu-mi-o'-la sink'-ta.   Shell
minute, white, few-whorled, having the surface distinctly sculptured or cancellated.   Most of the similar
species are smooth.   This completes our list of these
minute shells.

We turn now to a very distinct and well-marked
species, *Conus Californicus*, Hds., Ko'-
nus Cal-i-for'-ni-cus. Fig. 36 shows the
appearance of a large specimen.   This
is our only representative of the great
Cone family which has so many beautiful examples in the tropical waters of
the Pacific and the Indian oceans.

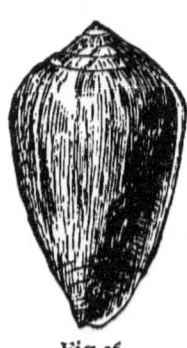

Our little species is very humble,
being about an inch in length, of a
Fig. 36.   chestnut color, with a smooth surface,

though it may occasionally be found covered with a hairy epidermis. Living shells are rare, but dead ones may frequently be found, particularly on the southern coasts.

There is a little black shell named *Mitromorpha filosa*, Cpr., Mi-tro-mor'-fa fil-o'-sa, and this name tells us that it has the form of the Miter Shells, and that its surface is threaded. Please look back to Fig. 22 and you will find its shape, pointed at both ends and largest in the middle; and if you examine it with a lens you will see that it is distinctly marked by many spiral lines. Its length is only a quarter of an inch.

Mitromorpha aspersa, Cpr., as-per'-sa, is even smaller than the above, but it has a brownish surface marked with a very distinct, sieve-like network of fine lines.

Mangelia striosa, C. B. Adams, Man-je'-li-a stri-o'-sa, is a rare southern species with less sculpture than the next, but otherwise resembling that shell, which is known as *Mangelia merita*, Gld., mer'-i-ta, and which is shown in Fig. 37.

The whorls are six in number, the aperture long, and the surface of the shell is marked by high cross ridges and fine spiral lines. Notice the notch in the outer lip where it joins the body whorl. Color, white; length, from one-fourth to one-half of an inch.

Fig. 37

Mangelia angulata, Cpr., an-gu-la'-ta, is similar to the last, but is of a brown color, with broad and angular whorls.

Three larger shells next present themselves for our examination. Each of them is slender and spindle-shaped, and each has a notch in the outer lip.

The first one is the Pencilled Drillia, *Drillia peni-cillata*, Cpr., Dril'-li-a pen-i-sil-la'-ta. A picture of this graceful shell is shown in Fig. 38. The spire consists of eight slender whorls; the aperture is long, and the surface is smooth, brownish, and marked by very delicate cross-lines of color. Length, an inch and a half; southern.

Drillia torosa, Cpr., to-ro'-sa Fig. 39, is found farther to the north. It is rather less grace-ful than its southern relative, and is somewhat smaller, also.

Fig. 38.

The surface is almost black, but each whorl is marked by a spiral row of lighter-colored knobs.

Fig. 39.

The third species, *Drillia mœsta*, Cpr., me'-sta, resembles the last, but the whorls have cross-ribs instead of knobs. The body-whorl, however, is nearly smooth. Color, brown or olive; length, one inch; southern. Said to be found under stones, between tides.

Myurella simplex, Cpr., My-u-rel'-la sim'-plex, Fig. 40, is another southern mollusk, having a very pretty, slender, conical shell. The spire winds grace-fully upward, and ends in a sharp point at the apex; while at the other end of the shell the aperture is small, and ends in a short, recurved canal. Following the sutures is a spiral thread of beads, which adds much to the attractiveness of the shell. The length is an inch or more, the whorls are about twelve in number, and the color is whitish or

Fig. 40.

brown.

Fig. 41 (Frontispiece) represents one of the rarest as well as one of the most beautiful of all the marine species of our West coast. The specimen from which this figure was drawn was obtained from deep water in Monterey bay.

The shell is spindle-shaped, with a conical spire which slopes with the utmost grace to the apex, a long aperture, and an outer lip which has the characteristic notch near its junction with the whorl. The shell is marked with many fine lines of growth, each of which retains the peculiar notch. The color is a rich, brownish yellow, diversified by several narrow bands of reddish brown. Its entire length is nearly three inches. Lastly, its name is *Surcula Carpenteriana*, Gabb, pronounced, Sur'-cu-la Carpen-te-ri-an'-a. I sincerely trust that many of my readers may some day see and admire one of these beautiful shells ; but even from the figure, you will notice its peculiar gracefulness of form. When we see one of these rare and pleasing creations which has been brought up from the depths of the ocean, how forcibly the lines of Gray come back to us :

"Full many a pearl, of purest ray serene,
The dark, unfathomed caves of ocean bear."

CHAPTER IX.

ON February 1st, 1864, Dr. Newcomb described a little shell which, up to that time, had been found in but very small numbers. The name which he then applied was *Pedicularia Californica*, Newc., Pe-dik-u-la'-ri-a Cal-i-for'-ni-ca. An enlarged repre- sentation is shown in Fig. 42, from which you will see that the aperture and the outer lip are greatly 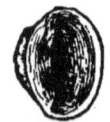 extended, and that the spire is completely hidden. The inside of the shell is smooth and glossy, but the outside is slightly rough. By the aid of a microscope, one is greatly pleased to see a fine system of minute lines and meshes.

Fig. 42.

Its color is peculiar for our shells, being a rich, rosy pink, far more beautiful than that of the famous "Peach-blow Vase." During the past twenty years a considerable number of these little red shells have been found, but they are still rare, and are gathered almost wholly from corals and sea-fans which are brought up from tolerably deep water. When fully grown the shell is nearly half an inch in length.

Another fine shell of our coast is the Brown Cowry, shown in Fig. 43. Its scientific name is *Luponia*

spadicea, Gray, Lu-po'-ni-a spa-dis'-e-a.   So distinct
is it from all other species, that it would
surely be recognized by one who is at
all familiar with its form and color.
In fact, it is our chief representative
of the great genus *Cypræa*, which is
so finely represented in the warmer
oceans.   Most of the Cowries live in
the South Pacific and Indian oceans,
and some of the smaller species are used
as money by the natives of adjacent

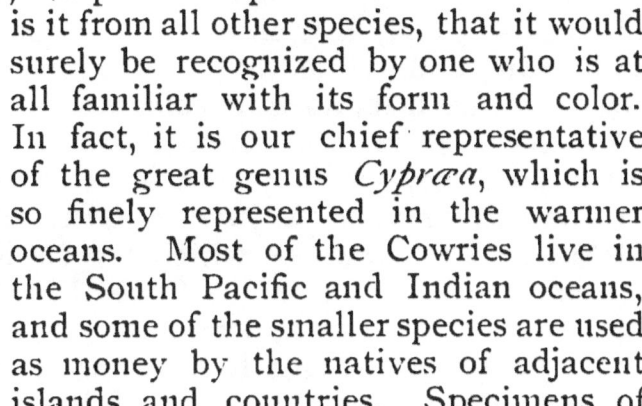

Fig. 43.   islands and countries.   Specimens of
the large spotted Tiger Cowry may be found in
almost every house in our country, and what well-
bred baby has not enjoyed playing with a Cowry-
shell?

When young, the Cowries have thin, conical shells,
with a short spire and a large aperture.   As time
goes on, the outer lip increases in size and thickness,
while the spire often becomes completely hidden
under the advancing whorls.

Our Cowry has a slightly curved aperture as long
as the shell, and the lips are set with numerous teeth.
These lips are white, but the back of the shell is
marked with a ring of dark brown, while the central
part is of a lighter shade.

Live shells of this species are bright and glossy,
while dead ones are dull and lustreless.   By live
shells are meant those which were gathered when the
living animal was inside, and from which it has been
removed by artificial means.   These are always more
perfect than dead specimens, by which we mean the
empty shells that we pick up along the shore, and
which are usually somewhat defaced.

Full-grown specimens of our Cowry are two inches in length. They live chiefly on the coast of southern California, and while they are quite rare as a rule, they have been found in considerable numbers, living with the large mussel, *Modiola modiolus*, which is of a similar color, and may thus serve as a protection.

The little *Trivia Californica*, Gray, Triv′-i-a Cal-i-for′-ni-ca, two views of which are shown in Fig. 44, is sometimes known as the Coffee-bean shell, and its size and appearance warrant this name. On one side it is flat, while the other side is very plump and full. The surface is marked by about a dozen sharp ribs, and the long, narrow aperture is set with many small teeth. The general color of the shell is a reddish chocolate, though the interior is white.

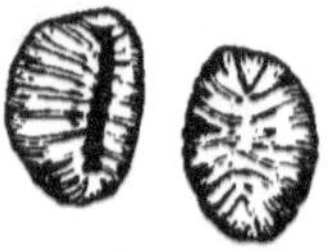

Fig. 44.

These shells are quite rare, but may occasionally be picked up on the beach. They are so highly prized that they are sometimes worn as jewels. The length of a shell is from one-fourth to one-half of an inch.

Trivia Solandri, Gray, is found on the shores of Lower California, and reaches as far north as the vicinity of Santa Barbara. It resembles the last species, but is twice as large, and is marked by a deep longitudinal channel on the back of the shell.

Fig. 45.

Somewhat resembling the Cowries, but more pear-shaped, are the Eratos, of which we have two species. The larger one is named *Erato vitellina*, Hds., E-ra′-to vit-el-li′-na, and its shell is shown in Fig. 45. It is about half an inch in length, quite smooth, and has a large aperture and a thickened outer lip. The short spire is almost concealed by the strong body-whorl, which is chestnut-brown along the back, but white near the toothed margin of the aperture.

Dead shells of this species may occasionally be found along the shore, and if one is very watchful, he may sometimes find a specimen, also, of the little *Erato columbella*, Mke., col-um-bel'-la, shown in Fig. 46. It is so small and delicate, however, that one may be pardoned for over-looking so minute a shell. As shown in the figure, it has a visible, though very short spire, and a long aperture with finely-toothed margins ; its length is not more than one-fourth of an inch. The lips are white, and the back is olive. It has been dredged from a depth of from twenty to forty fathoms.

Fig. 46.

Still more rare along the shore, but occasionally brought up by the fishermen from deep water, is the peculiar shell represented in Fig. 47, and whose name is *Ovulum formicarium*, Sowb., O'-vu-lum for-mi-ca'-ri-um.

In appearance it is unique, looking more like a roll of shell than like a spiral whorl, and tapering almost equally toward either end. The aperture is very long, the outer lip thickened, the spire concealed, and the sculpturing microscopic. The color is pink, and the length is rather less than an inch.

Fig. 47.

Now we must turn for a few minutes and examine a few very small shells, one of the smallest of which is *Diala marmorea*, Cpr., Di-a'-la mar-mo'-re-a. Its shell is minute, conical, six-whorled, solid and glossy. It is of a brownish color, clouded with red, and the aperture is nearly circular. The length is only one-eighth of an inch.

Diala acuta, Cpr., is similar, but has a flattened, sharply-angled base. Both of these species live in the sea.

Truncatella Californica, Pfr., Trun-ka-tel'-la, lives about salt marshes, though it may also be found upon sea-weed and under stones. The shell is less than one-fourth of an inch long, and is nearly cylindrical, with distinct sutures between the whorls. The aperture is small and circular, the operculum horny, the color light brown, and the surface smooth.

Similar to this, but having a more solid shell, is *Truncatella Stimpsonii*, Stearns. The whorls of this shell are crossed by numerous fine ridges.

Valvata sincera, Say., Val-va'-ta sin-se'-ra, is a fresh-water species. And thus we turn away from the sea and all its abounding life, to the lakes and rivers. Sometimes, as in this case, we shall travel far inland; for the specimen before me came from Franklin, Idaho. It is a minute, flattened, spiral shell, one-eighth of an inch across, consisting of three whorls, which circle around a distinct umbilicus. The aperture and the operculum are circular, and the color is greenish.

Valvata virens, Tryon, vi'-rens, is shown in Fig. 48. It is turban-shaped, bright green in color, and its breadth is less than one-fourth of an inch. The specimen from which the figure was drawn came from Clear lake, California.

Fig. 48.

Fig. 49 represents the shell of *Fluminicola fusca*, Hald., Flu-min-ick'-o-la fus'-ka. This name, translated into English, means the Tawny River-dweller.

Fig. 49.

The shells of this species are about the size of peas, quite solid, and have a short, three-whorled spire. The aperture is oval, the outer lip sharp, the operculum horny, and the color is greenish. The specimen before me came from Malad river, Utah.

Fluminicola Hindsii, Baird, is similar in size to the last. The spire is short, and is frequently eroded by the acids found in river water. Without, the shell is of a dark brown color, but it is a bluish white within. From the Willamette river, Oregon.

Fluminicola virens, Lea, is similar to the last, and is found in Oregon. The shell is remarkably thick, the aperture ovate, and the whorls rather inflated.

Fluminicola Nuttalliana, Lea, is represented in Fig. 50. Longer and more slender than the last species, few whorled, and often with the spire eroded at the top. Greenish brown without, whitish within; operculum thin. The shell is from one-fourth to one-half an inch in

Fig. 50. length. The variety *Columbiana*, Hemphill, is more rounded, with a shorter spire. This species is found in the rivers of Oregon and Washington.

Potamiopsis intermedia, Tryon, Po-tam-i-op'-sis in-ter-me'-di-a, has a minute shell, resembling the last figure, but more slender, and is less than one-fourth of an inch in length; the aperture is nearly circular. The specimen was collected at White Pine, Nevada.

Amnicola longinqua, Gld., Am-nik'-o-la lon-gin'-qua. This shell comes from Utah. The shell is thin and umbilicated, the body-whorl full, the spire short, and the suture distinct. The color is greenish, and the length is only one-eighth of an inch.

CHAPTER X.

AWAY from the ponds and rivers, and back to the
ocean's rocky shore we must now hasten, and take
out our magnifying glasses once more; for we are now
to look for some of the smallest shells that are to be
found anywhere.

Perhaps we shall be fortunate enough to find a big
Abalone or Haliotis, as we ought to call it. It has a
broad, flat shell, larger than your hand, and on the
back of this shell are growing tufts of coralline, sea-
weed, and fringes of moss. Now we will search
more carefully, and in the little crevices of the shell
and among the bits of seaweed we may find a colony
of little mollusks, having simple, conical shells, about
one-eighth of an inch in length. They are quite
slender, of a brownish color, few-whorled, and have
only a small aperture. Following Dr. Carpenter, to
whom we owe so much for his investigations on the
shells of this coast, we will call this little mollusk
that seems to love the Haliotis, *Barleeia haliotiphila*,
Cpr., Bar-lee'-ya hal-i-o-tif'-i-la.

Another similar shell from San Diego is named *Barleeia subtenuis*, Cpr., sub-ten'-u-is. It is somewhat larger and less slender, and is sometimes found on grass.

Alvania æquisculpta, Cpr., Al-van'-i-a e-qui-sculp'-ta, has a shell, minute, slender, and coarsely cancellated. The spire is five-whorled, and the aperture is circular and entire. Its color is white, and its length is only one-eighth of an inch.

Rissoa acutelirata, Cpr., Ris'-so-a a-ku-te-li-ra'-ta, resembles the last species, but is even smaller. It is brownish and very beautifully marked by numerous fine ribs and lines, which are clearly brought out by a lens.

Rissoina interfossa, Cpr., Ris-so-i'-na in-ter-fos'-sa, has a slender, sharply conical shell. The seven or eight whorls are cut into squares by a few bold, spiral ridges, which are crossed by numerous ribs. The aperture is quite small, oval, and notched at the base. The shell is white, and its length is over one-fourth of an inch.

Clathurella interclathrata, Cpr., is smaller and more slender than the last. The brown surface is cancellated, and the aperture is distinctly notched.

Isapis obtusa, Cpr., I-sa'-pis ob-tu'-sa, has a roundish little shell, less than a quarter of an inch in length. The aperture is oval, and the outer lip is marked by scallops, while the general surface is diversified by shallow spiral grooves. The spire is small and few-whorled ; the color is light brown.

Isapis fenestrata, Cpr., fe-nes-tra'-ta, much resembles the last, but is marked by sharp spiral ridges.

Three little shells next engage our attention, and call for a brief explanation of their common name.

The first one, shown in Fig. 51, is *Lacuna unifasciata*, Cpr., La-ku'-na u-ni-fas-si-a'-ta. This somewhat lengthy name may be freely translated, the One-banded Chink-shell. It is a very

Fig. 51. little thing, about one-sixth of an inch in length, and consists of but few whorls. It is brown and glossy, with the color broken into dots on the keel of the body-whorl. The aperture is semi-lunar, and the flattened columella has a small umbilical fissure, from which circumstance it is called the *Lacuna*, or Chink-shell. It is worth looking for, and can often be found on sandy beaches.

Lacuna solidula, Lov., so-lid'-u-la, is a northern species, and has a shell sometimes half an inch in length, though often it is of less size. It is three-whorled, strong, smooth, with small umbilicus, brown surface and white columella.

Lacuna porrecta, Cpr., por-rek'-ta, resembles Fig. 51, but is broader and more compact. It is found on kelp.

Paludinella Newcombiana, Hemphill, has four distinct, rounded whorls. The shell is thin, smooth, and is covered by a brown epidermis. The aperture is nearly circular. The length is one-fourth of an inch or less. My specimen is from Humboldt bay.

Assiminea Californica, Cooper, As-si-min'-e-a Cal-i-for'-ni-ca, has a shell rounded, thin and brown. The spire is short and conical, and the whole shell is less than one-eighth of an inch long. This species may be said to be almost amphibious, living much of the time out of water. Specimens have been gathered near Oakland, California.

Such an array of minute, uncommon shells as the past few pages have presented may make the timid

student lose heart, and say that the study of mollusks
is too difficult a subject to be engaged in by any one
who is not an enthusiast or a prodigy. Shells only
an eighth of an inch in length, and rare at that, are
hardly worth the seeking, I fear some one is saying.
Well, do not be discouraged, nor leave off the study
on this account. All these little creatures live in the
great ocean, and all deserve mention ; for some one
will find them and wish to know what they are. If
from this book you can learn the probable names, the
larger works will give you information respecting the
genera, and will enable you to study their relation-
ships and affinities.

But if you neither have time to look up the little
shells, nor opportunity to study about them in the big
books, you can surely find some of the shells which
I am about to describe.

When you went to the seacoast, and climbed among
the rocks where the waves were throwing up their
spray as the tide came in, you surely saw numbers of
dark-colored shells about the size of peas. You found
them in the cracks of the rocks, along their sides,
and concealed in every little nook and cranny. Their
shells are dull—somewhat like the rocks themselves ;
the apertures are closed with horny opercula, and the
animals seem to be asleep. But put some of them
into a jar of sea-water, and in a little while the little
black snails come creeping out, and begin to work
their way up into the air again.

These little Littorines, as we will call them, are
the first mollusks we meet as we go down to the
shore. The upper part of the beach is known as the
littoral region, so you see how the mollusks get the
name of Littorine. They live out of the water most

of time, and, except at high tide, they can always be found upon the rocks along the shore. Each of the little shells has a small spire of a few whorls, an entire aperture, a sharp outer lip, and a thin, horny operculum.

Our first species, *Littornia scutulata*, Gld., Lit-to-ri-na sku-tu-la'-ta, is shown in Fig. 52. The com-

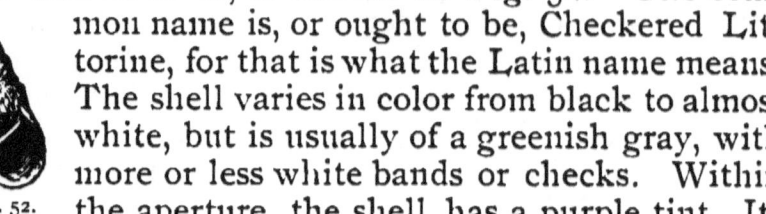

mon name is, or ought to be, Checkered Lit-torine, for that is what the Latin name means. The shell varies in color from black to almost white, but is usually of a greenish gray, with more or less white bands or checks. Within the aperture, the shell has a purple tint. Its length is from one-fourth to one-half of an inch, and sometimes you find specimens even larger.

Fig. 52.

Littorina planaxis, Nutt., plan-ax'-is, Gray Littor-ine, is shown in Fig. 53. This species has a some-

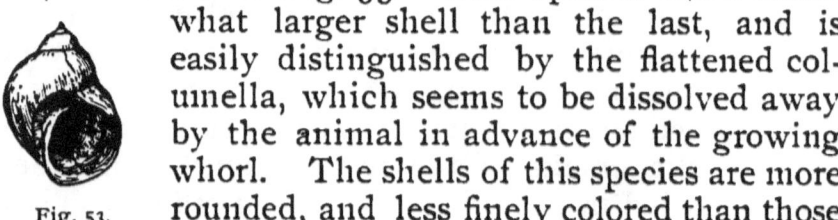

what larger shell than the last, and is easily distinguished by the flattened col-umella, which seems to be dissolved away by the animal in advance of the growing whorl. The shells of this species are more rounded, and less finely colored than those of the last species, but the two are often found closely associated.

Fig. 53.

The third Littorine, which is found in northern waters, is named *Littorina rudis*, Don., ru'-dis, or Rough Littorine. The shell of this bold northener, in form and size, greatly resembles a large pea. It is easily distinguished from *planaxis* by its rounded columella, while its general surface, instead of being nearly smooth, as in the last two species, is marked by a good number of more or less developed spiral ridges. Its color varies from white to black, but it is usually of a yellowish brown.

And now, since we have filled our lungs with fresh sea air, and have collected Littorines to our heart's content, we will vary our shell-gathering journey a little, by taking a hasty trip inland, and strolling along the rivers of Oregon. Here we shall find abundant specimens of the Plaited River shell, *Goniobasis plicifera*, Lea, Gon-i-ob'-a-sis pli-sif'-e-ra. A good illustration of this shell is shown in Fig. 54, in which you see the general shape, and the average size of the shell. But there are many varieties of this species, which vary slightly from one another, yet which are very similar in all essential particulars. Several of these varieties have been described under different names, but this should not puzzle the student.

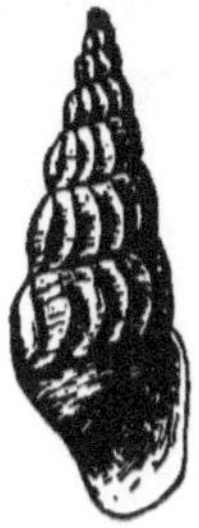

Fig. 54.

The shell of a perfect specimen is a long, slender cone, though the first whorl or two may be missing, and thus change the cone into a frustrum. The later whorls are nearly smooth, but the earlier ones are marked by folds, or plications, the presence of which suggested the name *plicifera*. The aperture is ovate and entire; the color of the shell is greenish black, and its length is an inch or less. Many specimens come from the vicinity of Salem, Oregon.

Goniobasis nigrina, Lea, ni-gri'-na, Fig. 55, is a California shell, with numerous smooth, rounded whorls. It is rather smaller than the last species, but is of the same color.

Goniobasis occata, Hds., ok-ka'-ta, is from the San Joaquin river. In general form, as well as in size and color, it resembles the preceding species,

Fig. 55.

but the whorls are marked by many sharp, roughened spiral ridges. The Latin word *occata* means harrowed, hence the application of the term to this shell is evident.

Several shells of similar shape, but which abide in salt water, will be considered in the next chapter.

CHAPTER XI.

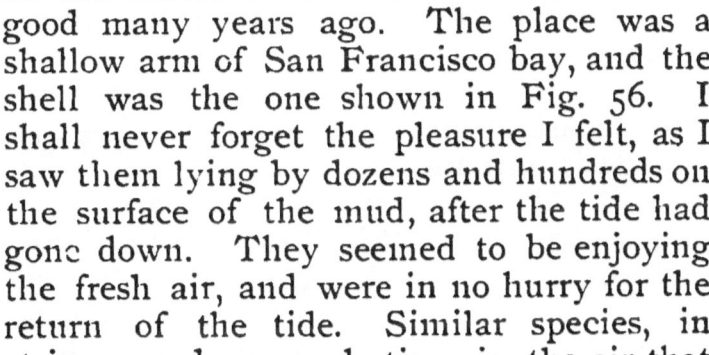

Fig. 56.

MY first opportunity to gather any of the shells which are described in this book occurred a good many years ago. The place was a shallow arm of San Francisco bay, and the shell was the one shown in Fig. 56. I shall never forget the pleasure I felt, as I saw them lying by dozens and hundreds on the surface of the mud, after the tide had gone down. They seemed to be enjoying the fresh air, and were in no hurry for the return of the tide. Similar species, in other countries, spend so much time in the air that they have been mistaken for land shells.

As they were my first shells, and I was ignorant of their name, I sent a few to the Smithsonian Institution to be identified. The name proved to be *Cerithidea sacrata*, Gld., Se-ri-thid'-e-a sa-cra'-ta. In common words we may call them Horn Shells.

But I was as ignorant about the proper care of the shells as concerning their name, and a pretty source of trouble they were to me. The animals soon died, and my crude attempts to remove them from the shells were instructive, if not entertaining. To prevent any other young collector from getting into the same troubles, I would advise that after prompt boiling, all the soft parts be removed by a pin or bent wire. In shells of this shape, a complete removal of the perishable parts is often very difficult. In such cases, remove all that you can, and then securely plug the hole with cotton, and attach the operculum to the cotton by a drop of glue.

This shell is commonly an inch or more in length, and consists of about ten strongly ribbed whorls. The outside is dull and black, but the inside is of a glossy brown. The aperture is entire and nearly circular, and is closed by a thin, brown operculum.

Bittium filosum, Gld., Bit-ti-um fi-lo'-sum, is shown in Fig. 57. Unlike the last species, which seems to delight in the brackish water of salt marshes, the little Bittiums live in the ocean, and may be found alive at low tide, by turn-

Fig. 57. ing over stones and searching carefully for their small shells. The dead shells are often inhabited by the Hermit Crabs, and are quite abundant in many places, where little shells are apt to be found. This shell is shaped like a short, stout thorn, and varies in length from one-fourth to one-half an inch. The whitish or brownish whorls are eight or ten in number, and are marked by slight spiral grooves.

Bittium quadrifilatum, Cpr., quad-ri-fil-a'-tum. As indicated by its name, the whorls of this shell have four equal spiral threads, which coil over slight cross-ribs. In shape, it is a regular but very slender cone; its color is dark; its length is from one-fourth to one-half an inch; southern.

In Fig. 58, we have a picture of the Tower Shell, *Turritella Cooperi*, Cpr., Tur-ri-tel'-la Coop'-er-i, which is likewise a southern shell, found, according to Mr. Hemphill, on the sandy beach, between tides. The shell can hardly be said to have a body-whorl, but consists wholly of a slender, tapering, many-whorled spire. The sutures are distinct, the aperture circular, and the outer lip sharp and thin. The color is yellowish, somewhat spotted with brown; length, two inches. It can hardly be mistaken for any other shell.

Fig. 58. *Mesalia tenuisculpta*, Cpr., Me-sa'-li-a ten-ui-sculp'-ta, is like a minute specimen of the last, and is found on mud flats. Its whorls are rounded, and feebly sculptured by cross-lines. The usual length is less than one-fourth of an inch.

The next species is wholly different from any that have gone before. It has a shell about one-eighth of an inch long, looking like a minute, slightly-curved tube. Under the microscope it is seen to be composed of very numerous and closely-crowded rings. Its color is white or yellowish, and its name is *Cæcum Californicum*, Dall., Se'-kum Cal-i-for'-ni-cum.

Cæcum crebricinctum, Cpr., kre-bri-sink'-tum, is a species having a shell twice as large as the last, marked by exceedingly fine rings, which are often quite indistinct. Both of these species are found chiefly in the South.

Spiroglyphus lituella, Morch., Spi-ro-gly'-fus lit-u-el'la. This singular mollusk has an irregular, tubular shell, which becomes attached to the side of a stone, and twists itself into an ill-shaped, flattened cone.

Several specimens are frequently found near one another. The shell is often angular and roughened ; the aperture is circular, and is one-eighth of an inch or less in diameter. The color, as in several of the following specimens, is a dingy white.

Serpulorbis squamigerus, Cpr., Ser-pu-lor'-bis squam-i-je'-rus. Very irregular ; frequently many specimens grow together upon a rock, and look like a heap of contorted snakes. The shell is marked throughout its length by transverse, scaly ridges. The aperture is circular, one-fourth of an inch across. The tube, if straightened, would measure some four inches or more in length ; it has a circular operculum. I found a few living specimens of this species at Monterey ; but it is rare so far north. Many of these more uncommon species may be found by wading into the water at low tide and turning up stones, or bringing them out to dry land for closer examination. A pair of long rubber boots will be found very convenient on such excursions.

There is a series of shells, dead specimens of which are abundant, which present a puzzling aspect, and which vary greatly in outward appearance. They are not spiral, but appear like hollow cones more or less flattened, with the apex to one side of the center. Some of them are singularly like a horse's hoof in shape, hence they have received a name, derived from the Greek, which has that meaning.

The number of true species which belong to this coast is somewhat uncertain, on account of the variable nature of the shell. I will mention two, which will probably include all our common specimens. The first one is named *Hipponyx antiquatus*, Linn.,

Hip'-po-nyx an-ti-qua'-tus, the Horse-hoof shell. Fig. 59 gives a side-view of a flat specimen, showing

the apex near one side, and part of the interior. The shell is very variable, but in general it is hoof-shaped, with an internal muscular impression shaped like a horse-shoe. The lines of growth

Fig. 59.

give it a more or less scaly appearance. Sometimes it is nearly flat, but in other specimens it is obliquely conical. The color is white, and the diameter is half an inch. Occasionally live specimens may be found at low tide on the surface of rocks.

Hipponyx tumens, Cpr., tu'-mens. Smaller and more regular than the last species. Apex recurved ; lower part of the shell sometimes bearded. Radial lines of sculpture run from the apex, and are crossed by concentric lines of growth.

The Slipper-shells next invite our attention. They are easily recognized by the deck which runs across the back part of the shell, forming a chamber which contains some of the internal organs of the little inhabitant, and which, when the shell is empty, reminds one of the toe of a Chinese slipper.

The most common species is *Crepidula adunca*, Sby., Cre-pid'-u-la ad-un'-ca, Hooked Slipper-shell,

shown in Fig. 60. The apex is strongly recurved, giving the shell a hooked appearance. Its color is brown, but the deck is white. Living specimens

Fig. 60.

may often be found growing upon rocks or upon other shells. Common length from one-half to three-fourths of an inch ; abundant.

Larger and more flattened than the last shell, is

that of the next species, *Crepidula rugosa*, Nutt., ru-go'-sa. The surface is somewhat roughened and shaggy, and the apex is on the very edge of the shell. The color of the outside is light brown, sometimes marked with narrow stripes, while the inside is dark brown, except the deck, which is white. The length is sometimes more than an inch.

Crepidula navicelloides, Nutt., nav-i-sel-loi'-des, is the White Slipper-shell, and is shown in Fig. 61. This species has a pure white shell, and may easily be recognized by its color, its flattened shape, and by the very thin and delicate deck, which is shown in the engraving.

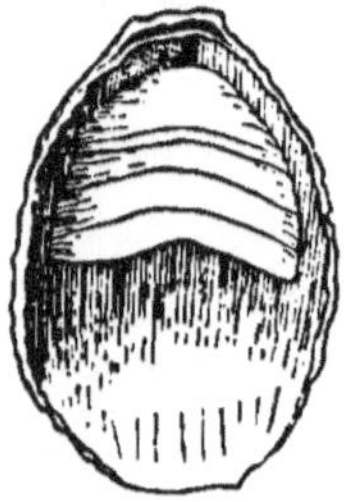

Fig. 61.

Sometimes this mollusk makes his home upon the rock, and the back of his shell becomes rough and discolored; again, live specimens may be found within the aperture of a dead spiral shell, and then the Crepidula is smooth, curved, elongated, and almost transparent. The common length is less than an inch.

A small species of this extensive genus is named *Crepidula dorsata*, Brod., dor-sa'-ta; It is nearly circular in outline, with a small, curved, partly detached deck, and a more or less wrinkled shell, about half an inch in diameter. The color is brown and white, sometimes mottled, and the shell is thin and flat.

Crepidula aculeata, Gm., a-ku-le-a'-ta, is a small southern species, with a low apex, curved to one side. The yellowish white shell is marked by many irregular, radiating ridges. It occurs "around the world." (Cpr.)

Closely resembling the Crepidulas, but containing a triangular cup instead of a shelly deck, comes the

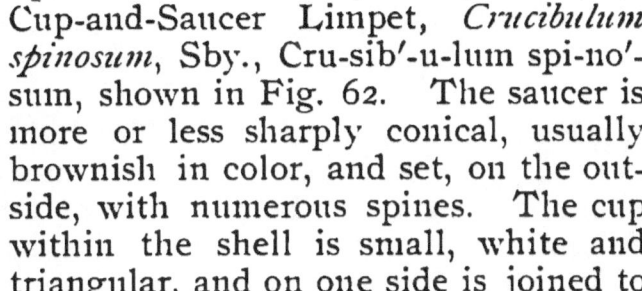

Cup-and-Saucer Limpet, *Crucibulum spinosum*, Sby., Cru-sib'-u-lum spi-no'-sum, shown in Fig. 62. The saucer is more or less sharply conical, usually brownish in color, and set, on the outside, with numerous spines. The cup within the shell is small, white and triangular, and on one side is joined to the saucer. This species assumes many forms, and the shell varies in color from brown to almost white; sometimes it is quite free from spines. Diameter from one-half an inch to three times that size. Its home is to the south of Monterey bay.

Fig. 62.

CHAPTER XII.

Turban-Shells and Top Shells—Mother-of-Pearl—
The Little Shells—The Beautiful Caliostomas—
Brown, Black, Golden, and other Turbans—Pachy-
poma and its Neighbors—The Leptonyx of Linnæus.

WE have now reached the Trochidæ, a great family, which includes the Turban-shells and Top-
shells, and to which belong some of the most beautiful and interesting of all our mollusks.

We shall find little ones and big ones; shells black
as night, and shells red as bricks; some shells with
little beauty, and others composed of brilliant pearl,
and marked with richly colored stripes; some thick
and heavy, made for the sport of the waves, and others so thin and delicate that you can crush them with
your fingers. The inner layer of these shells is
nacreous, that is, composed of that rainbow tinted
substance called mother-of-pearl. All the mollusks
of this great family may be classed with the vegeta-
ble-eaters.

The first species that I shall mention is named
Margarita pupilla, Gld., Mar-gar-i'-ta pu-pil'-la, and
its shell is represented in Fig. 63. This pretty
little Turban is a northener, living in and
about Puget Sound, but sometimes coming
further south. Its whorls are four, marked
with spiral ridges; its umbilicus distinct, and its

Fig. 63.

aperture nearly circular. It is yellowish brown in color, and is about the size of a small pea.

Margarita acuticostata, Cpr., a-cu-ti-cos-ta'-ta is like the last, but much smaller. It is a southern shell, and its surface is marked with a few sharp ridges and some clouded painting.

Margarita helicina, Mont., hel-i-si'-na, is a third species, and may be briefly described as follows: Spire low, few-whorled, aperture circular, umbilicus small, whorls smooth, color whitish. It is less than one-fourth of an inch in diameter, and its home is in the far north, on the shores of Alaska. It is widely distributed, and is described as circumboreal.

Gibbula parcipicta, Cpr., Gib'-bu-la par-si-pik'-ta, has a turban-shaped shell, marked with small ridges.

The outside is dark or spotted, but the interior is of beautiful green pearl. Its diameter is about one-eighth of an inch. It is a northern species.

Gibbula succincta, Cpr., suk-sink'-ta, has a very small shell, marked with delicate ridges, and brown, spiral pencilings.

Calliostoma annulatum, Mart., Cal-li-os'-to-ma an-

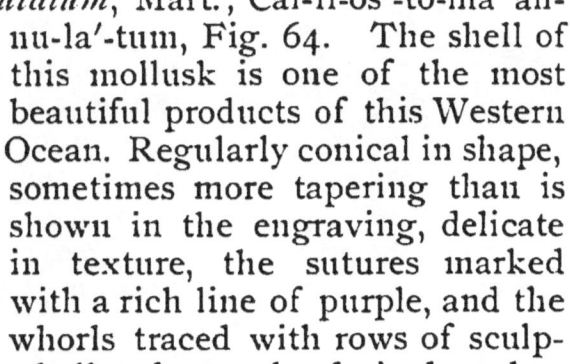

nu-la'-tum, Fig. 64. The shell of this mollusk is one of the most beautiful products of this Western Ocean. Regularly conical in shape, sometimes more tapering than is shown in the engraving, delicate in texture, the sutures marked with a rich line of purple, and the whorls traced with rows of sculp-

Fig. 64.

tured points, it is a shell to be much admired, and to be highly prized.

It is seldom found on the beach, but is obtained from the seaweed, at some distance off the shore.

In bright weather, the mollusks crawl up the stems of the seaweed and rest near the surface of the water. At such times the collector goes out in a boat, hauls a quantity of the weed over the rail, and easily captures a quantity of these beauties. Should he go out in the wrong part of the day, or when the sky is dark, it is probable that the seaweed will be found quite deserted, and that our pretty friends will be enjoying themselves down below the waves. Too delicate to bear the beating of the surf upon the rocks, their home is in deep water, where they cling to the long seaweeds, and sway to and fro; or, when the weather is too rough, sink to more quiet abodes.

The color is yellowish or reddish brown, striped with violet. The aperture is somewhat angular, and the edge of the lip is sharp and thin. Its length is seldom more than one inch.

Fig. 65.

Quite similar in general form and habits, is another Top-shell, named *Calliostoma canaliculatum*, Mart., can-al-ik-u-la'-tum, and shown in Fig. 65. This shell is larger than that of the last species, though the engraving represents quite a large specimen. Its shape is conical, and the whorls are girdled with deep spiral channels, between raised ridges. The surface is light brown, or ash-colored, though the shell is rainbow-tinted within. The thin exterior layer may readily be removed by a weak acid, if one wishes to bring out the pearly interior.

Fig. 66 presents to us another shell, *Calliostoma costatum*, Mart. This species is smaller than either of the preceding members of the genus, and lives nearer the shore. Hence we would naturally expect to find that it had a thicker and stronger shell than either of the others, and in this we are not disappointed.

Fig. 66.

It has four rounded whorls, marked with fine spiral ridges. The thin, reddish brown outer coat is readily removed, showing the blue pearly shell underneath.

I have found very fine living specimens, hanging upon the roof and walls of some rocky grotto which had been left by the early morning tide. I have also gathered them from the long seaweeds which grow near the rocky shore.

The length of one of these shells is about three-fourths of an inch; the operculum is thin and perfectly circular; the aperture of dead shells is often inhabited by a thin variety of the White Slipper-shell.

The above mentioned three species are the most common representatives of the group, but there are several others, some of which are not less beautiful, though they are more rare. The names given to them indicate their special characteristics.

Among them we find *Calliostoma gemmulatum*, Cpr., jem-mu-la'-tum, in size like the last, but more acute in form. Each whorl has two principal rows of granules, with some smaller markings. The whorls of this southern species are very distinct, and its color is gray, with dark cross-stripes running down from the apex.

(6)

Calliostoma tricolor, Gabb., tri'-co-lor, is shown in Fig. 67. The shell is conical, its five whorls little raised, but marked with delicate spiral sculpturing. The back-ground of yellowish gray is ornamented with fine spiral threads of color, broken into alternate joints of purple and white, thus giving it the three-colored aspect.

Fig. 67.   It is a southern shell, and is obtained by dredging. The figure represents a large specimen.

Another rare southern species is named *Calliostoma supragranosum*, Cpr., su-pra-gran-o'-sum. It resembles the last figure, but is more conical, and has more flattened whorls. The interior is white, but the outside is of a light reddish-brown color, with a chain of dark circular dots along the sutures and the angle of the body-whorl. Good specimens have been found at Monterey. (Mrs. Estabrook.)

Calliostoma splendens, Cpr., splen'-dens. Small, the size of a pea ; whorls marked with slight spiral ridges; base flattened and glossy; color yellowish chestnut. It is a rare shell, and is found at low water, or is dredged.

Turcia caffea, Gabb., Tur'-shi-a caf'-fe-a. A little larger than the last, with whorls flattened, and sutures deep and bearded. Thin, brown, and very rare.

Leaving the Top-shell, with their sharply conical form, so suggestive of that toy which every boy delights to spin, we pass on to the more rounded Turban-shells, which put you in mind of Bible-stories, and the turbaned heads of the men of the East.

Our first species is shown in Fig. 68, and its scientific name is *Omphalius fuscescens*, Phil., Om-fa'-li-us fus-ses'-sens.

It has a strong, solid, turban-shaped shell, whose rusty brown whorls are banded with raised spiral lines. These lines are broken or beaded, and sometimes are dotted with black, giving the shell a very characteristic appearance.

The operculum, as in nearly all of this group, is thin, horny and circular.

Fig. 68.

The umbilicus is large and distinct, the aperture circular, and marked below with rounded knobs. The length of the shell is from half an inch to an inch.

Chlorostoma Pfeifferi, Phil., Klo-ros'-to-ma fi'-fer-i. In shape the shell of this rare species resembles the one shown in Fig. 64. It is conical, with whorls perfectly flat ; the base is likewise flat and circular, and the umbilicus is large. Its color is light brown ; its length is sometimes more than an inch, and its breadth is the same.

In Fig. 69 we have the representation of a more common Turban, or Chlorostoma, which name means Green-mouth, and refers doubtless to the greenish nacre within the aperture.

This species is named *Chlorostoma brunneum*, Phil., brun'-ne-um, and we will call it the Brown Turban. When found alive, as it may be, on the rocks at very low tide, or on the kelp if you have a boat,

Fig. 69.

this mollusk has a handsome, rich brown shell, with a portion of white around the aperture. The base is flattened, the umbilicus is closed, and the lines of growth are very oblique; while the edge of the outer lip is very sharp.

Even the dead and worn shells preserve their brown

color remarkably, and can easily be told from those of the more common Black Turban. Old and over-grown specimens, an inch and a half long, are sometimes found, but one-half that length is more common.

Chlorostoma aureotinctum, Fbs., au-re-o-tink'-tum, Gilded Turban.

The shell of this species is similar in shape to Fig. 69, but the whorls, instead of being nearly smooth, are banded by a few very heavy, rounded spiral ridges, and wavy crossings. The shell is gray or nearly black; the umbilicus is large and marked with a bright yellow stain, which gives the species its name. The shell is about an inch long.

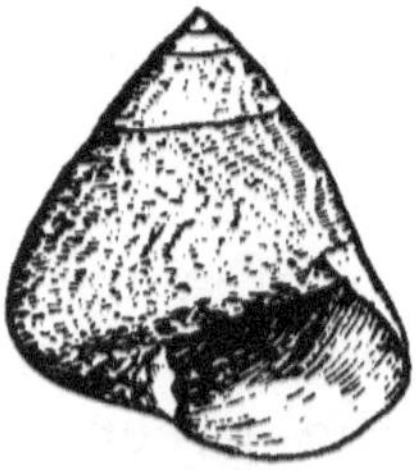

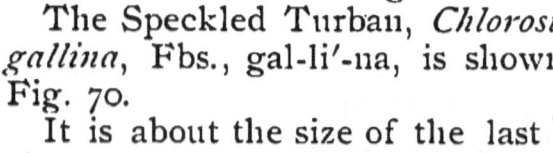

The Speckled Turban, *Chlorostoma gallina*, Fbs., gal-li'-na, is shown in Fig. 70.

It is about the size of the last spe-cies, and has a solid shell, mostly black in color, but finely mottled with a lighter shade, like the feathers of a speckled hen or *gallina*, as it is in Latin.

Fig. 70.

The outer lip is thin, black, and lined with white nacre, and there is no umbilicus. This species belongs to the south; one of its varieties, named *tincta*, has a yellowish shell. But most of the specimens are black, and sometimes greatly resemble the exceedingly common Black Turban, or *Chlorostoma funebrale*, A. Ad.; fu-ne-bra'-le, shown in Fig. 71.

Fig. 71.

This is the old friend that is so ready to greet us whenever we set foot upon the rocky shore. Protected by a firm and solid shell, well fitted to resist the buffeting of the waves, it clings to the rocks which are daily left bare by the retreating tides. Immense numbers of these little creatures lie at the base of the cliffs; in some cases I have seen the rocks almost black with them, of all ages and sizes.

On my first visit to the seaside, I wanted them all, and I gathered and cleaned them for hours. Two very natural results followed; first, that there remained apparently as many as before; and second, that on subsequent visits I gathered very few. But whether we collect them, or merely watch their movements and study their habits, still they soon become like old friends to anyone who has learned the pleasant art of putting himself in sympathy with the lower animals.

When in the water, the little black animal with its short head and lively feelers may be seen briskly moving about; but when out of water he evidently feels that the inside of his shell is the safest spot for him to rest, and into it he withdraws, and closes the doorway with his circular operculum.

The color of the shell is dark purple, almost black on the outside, with greenish white pearly layers beneath. The whorls are four in number, and the uppermost ones are often eroded, so that the shell appears more flattened than is shown by the engraving. The body-whorl is puckered near the suture; the umbilicus is nearly closed, and the columella is set with two little white knobs, near its base. The common length of the shell is less than an inch, but sometimes specimens are found which are considerably longer.

Ethalia supravalata, Cpr., and its variety, *invallata*, Cpr., are exceedingly minute creatures, having flattened, spiral shells, about the size of a pin's head.

The former has a furrow and keel near the suture, while the variety has neither; southern.

Liotia fenestrata, Cpr., Li-o'-shi-a fe-nes-tra'-ta, has a small, flattened, whitish shell, cut into numerous little square pits, by the crossing of ribs and lines. Its diameter is one-eighth of an inch.

Liotia acuticostata, Cpr., a-cu-ti-cos-ta'-ta, is smaller, less flattened, and is marked with sharp, spiral ridges, but without cross-lines; whitish.

Fig. 72 represents a fine shell which is common on

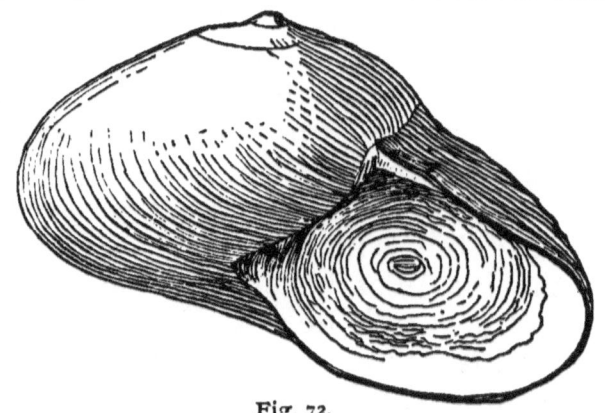

Fig. 72.

the southern coast.   Notice its flattened form, small spire, deep umbilicus, ample aperture and shaggy operculum.   The name is *Trochiscus Norrissi*, Sby., Tro-kis'-kus Nor-ris'-si.

The shell is quite smooth, and of a rich, brown color; the rim of the umbilicus, curiously enough, is tinted with bright green. The diameter of the shell of this very distinct species is two inches or less, hence our engraving represents a large specimen.

A big, strong, brick-red shell, considerably resembling Fig. 75, is frequently picked up along the shores of central California, though, in fact, it has a much wider range.   It is the shell of the *Pachypoma gib-*

berosum, Chem., Pack-i-po'-ma gib-ber-o'-sum, a mollusk that is seldom found alive. The shell is broadly conical; its whorls are quite rough, and its flat base is marked with five or six deep, concentric furrows. As the shells are usually dead and somewhat broken, it is seldom that you find the operculum in place. This operculum is quite different from any which we have noticed before, and is of an oval shape, and is made up of a plate of horn for the inside, and a solid bulge of shell for the outer part. They may frequently be picked up along the beach, and are puzzling objects to those who have never seen them in place. The shell is usually from two to three inches in breadth across the base, and of about the same height.

A much smaller shell, but similar in some respects, is that of *Leptonyx sauguineus*, Linn., Lep'-to-nyx san-guin'-e-us, shown in Fig. 73. The largest specimens are of the size of a pea, but many smaller ones will be found. The whorls are few, marked with fine, distinct, spiral ridges; operculum solid and shelly. The color is reddish, sometimes faded or banded.

Fig. 73.

This species may be found at low tide, living upon rocks; but the Hermit Crabs bring up many empty shells. You notice that the name of this species was given by the great Linnæus. Probably he never saw a specimen from the Pacific; but ours is considered identical with the Mediterranean species to which he gave the above name.

Leptonyx bacula, Cpr., back'-u-la, is another species. In shape it is like the last shell, but it is smaller, being only about one-eighth of an inch in diameter. It is nearly smooth, dark or ashy; southern.

CHAPTER XIII.

RESULTS OF THE AGASSIZ SOCIETY—THE WAITING WORLD
—CONSIDER—THE PHEASANT SHELL—THE HALIOTIS OR
ABALONE—ITS CHIEF SPECIES—THE CONTRIBUTION
SHELL—THE BLACK ABALONE—LIMPETS—THEIR ANAT-
OMY—KEY-HOLE LIMPETS—THE VOLCANO SHELL—FIS-
SURE SHELLS.

SOME years ago I read in a newspaper an account
of a lot of happy children, who were out on the
beach looking for shells. Presently one of the party
picked up a little thing, not more than a quarter of
an inch long and at once she began to dance with
joy, and to shout, "I've found a real Pheasant
shell!" "A Pheasant shell," asked the observer,
"what is that, and how do you know its name?"

"Oh," was the reply, "Mr. K. told us about it at
our Agassiz Society meeting; and see those beautiful
red stripes, and all these pretty little markings!"

I never knew who wrote the article, but I do
know that there are thousands of children, all over
this great western region, who would be better and
happier if they understood the interesting and beautiful objects of nature which lie about them in such
profusion. How many insects, birds, and other animals there are; how many flowers, trees and mosses;
what interesting rocks and minerals under foot, and
brilliant stars overhead; and each with a name, a

place and a history, and all waiting, as in a perpetual exposition, to be seen, admired and loved.

"When I consider the heavens," says David,—and if parents and teachers and kind friends will teach the children to "consider" the works of nature, they will very likely come to conclusions similar to those of the psalmist king.

"Consider the lilies," said our Savior, and we all know the happy inference which followed. And so I shall greatly rejoice if this little book leads a great many children, of all ages, to consider these humble yet beautiful inhabitants of the shore, the wood, and the stream.

But this has led me away from our little Pheasant shell, *Phasianella compta*, Gld., Fas-i-an-el'-la komp'-ta, shown in Fig. 74. The dead shells may often be picked up on sandy beaches, and when magnified by the aid of a lens, they

Fig. 74. appear very beautiful. The outline is smooth and symmetrical, and the surface is gaily marked with zigzag stripes of red, brown and white, while the operculum is shelly and rounded.

Sometimes the little mollusks are found alive on seagrass, but the epidermis obscures the beauty of the naked shell. Its length is from one-eighth to one-fourth of an inch.

Pomaulax undosus, Wood, Po-mau'-lax un-do'-sus, is a southern species, which sometimes grows to a great size. Fig. 75 represents an average specimen.

It is broadly conical, with a long, triangular aperture. The outer lip is thin, the whorls marked with numerous wavy ridges, and the base ornamented with beaded circles. The shell is of whitish pearl, covered with a brown, fibrous epidermis. The operculum is very peculiar; it is horny within, shelly without, and strengthened by two heavy curved ribs. The breadth of the shell is from two to four inches.

Fig. 75.

We have now come to the Abalone shells, as they are called on this coast, though the name is a local one. Off the coast of England, they are known as "Ormers," while the translation of the true name makes them "Sea-ears." Fig. 76 represents our most beautiful species, *Haliotis splendens*, Rve., Hal-i-o'-tis splen'-dens.

The shells of this genus are spiral, but are extremely flattened, and the diminutive spire is almost concealed at one end of the body-whorl, while the oval aperture is nearly as long and broad as the shell itself.

Near one edge of the shell is a series of holes, which serve as outlets for the water which has passed over the animal's gills, together with any waste particles which may be thrown off from the various organs. As the shell increases in size, some of these holes become closed from the inside, while new ones are formed at the edge of the growing shell.

Now, if we look within, we shall find the most highly colored portion of the shell near the center, at the spot where the huge muscle which controls the foot has been detached. This huge foot can cling to a rock with surprising force, and the animal must be taken unawares if an easy conquest is expected.

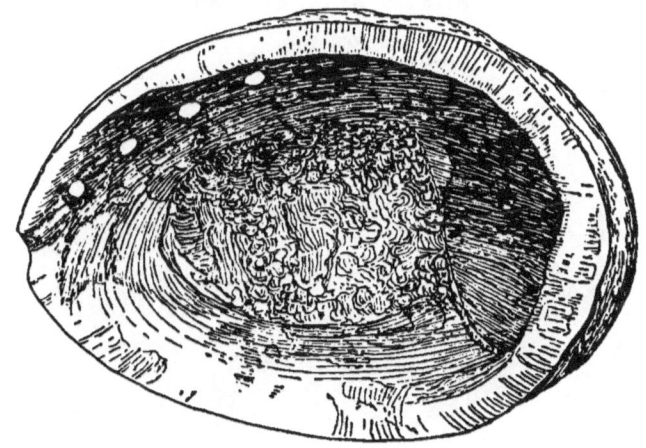

Fig. 76.

The internal organs are very interesting for dissection, particularly the mouth with its long, ribbon-like tongue, thickly set with flinty hooks or teeth. By means of these teeth the animal rasps its vegetable food into fine shreds fit for swallowing. This lingual ribbon in a good-sized specimen is one-fourth of an inch wide, and three inches long.

Haliotis splendens is a southern species. I once dissected a single specimen which was found living near Moss beach, at Monterey; but they are seldom found so far north.

The shell is quite thin, and is diversified externally by low, spiral ridges, of a dark and dull color.

Within, a whole rainbow is condensed in one of these magnificent shells, though the shades of green are most conspicuous. The coloring in the center is particularly fine, resembling a peacock's tail. There are about six open holes near one side of the shell, and its length is about the same number of inches.

Haliotis rufescens, Swains., ru-fes'-sens, Fig. 77, is the common Red Abalone of commerce. The beauty of these shells has caused them to be very

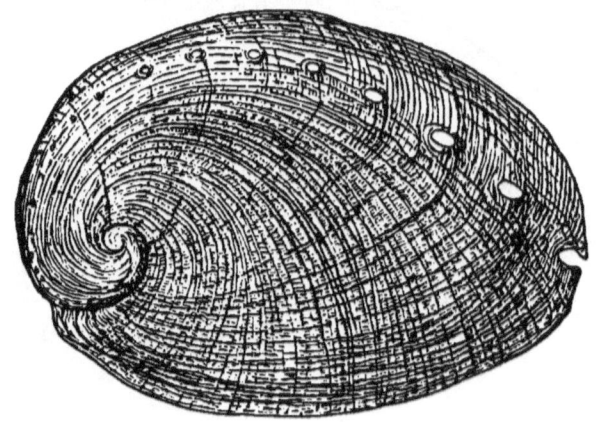

Fig. 77.

widely distributed, and though their abundance makes us somewhat careless of them, still, they are among the most beautiful objects ever gathered from this coast.

In the Eastern States they are commonly called California shells, and are highly prized as mantle ornaments.

My earliest recollection goes back to a quarterly children's meeting, at the close of which the big shell was utilized as a contribution plate, and into its broad, pearly aperture, we dropped the big copper cents, which went to establish schools for heathen children. Shell of blessed memories! I would love to see it again.

The outer layer of the shell projects over the pearly inner layer, and makes the fine red edge so much prized in perfect specimens. The back is somewhat roughened, and is overgrown with vegetation. The holes are large, usually three in number, and the muscle impression is prominent. The shell sometimes grows to a length of nine inches.

All parts of this mollusk are valuable. The Chinese dry the meat and use it for food; and it must be confessed that the muscular foot makes a most delicious soup. The shells are largely exported to Europe, and are made into buttons, and used for various kinds of inlaid work. The persistent warfare waged against this species by the Chinese gatherers has greatly reduced their numbers; but a temporary turn of fashion has caused the dealers to call for fewer shells, and it is to be hoped that they will be allowed to increase once more.

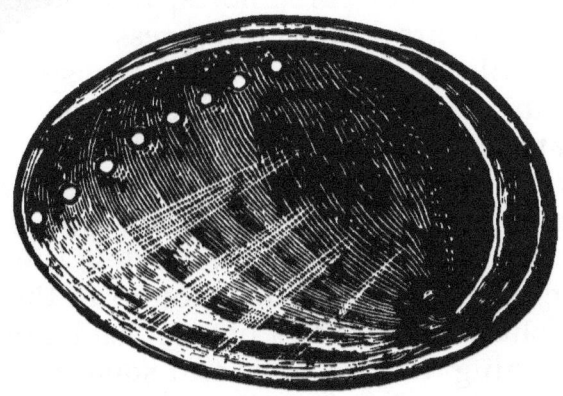

Fig. 78.

The Black Abalone, *Haliotis Crachcrodii*, Leach., Crach-e-ro'-di-i, is shown in Fig. 78.

It is smaller and more abundant than the last species. The back is quite smooth, marked only by lines of growth. The spire is very short; the holes five to nine in number, and the color is greenish black without, and pearly within. Live specimens, varying in length from one-fourth of an inch up to six inches, may be found at low tide, clinging to the rocks, particularly in the most inaccessible cracks, and under heavy boulders.

When examined in a jar of sea-water, as all of these animals should be if there is opportunity, a living specimen presents many interesting points for study, particularly its broad foot, its fringed and sensitive mantle, its stalked eyes and slender tentacles.

Haliotis corrugata, Gray, Hal-i-o′-tis cor-ru-ga′-ta.

As its name indicates, this species has a roughened or corrugated shell. In size and color it resembles *H. rufescens*, but its shell is nearly circular, thick, high arched and corrugated.

It has only two or three holes, but these are quite large, and the central muscle impression is quite wide and very brilliant. It is a southern species and is usually found below the low-water mark.

A variety of this species named *assimilis*, Dall., as-sim′-i-lis, is smaller, less roughened, has more holes, and is marked by a furrow, running parallel with the line of holes, and just below them. Deep water specimens are sometimes found in the stomachs of large fishes. There has been considerable discussion concerning this variety, and some regard it as a distinct species. Specimens of it are found further north than the simple *corrugata* is known to have been gathered.

The Pacific seacoast abounds in Limpets. They are harmless, vegetable-eating mollusks, which cling to the rocks, and are protected by shells shaped like inverted saucers. Many of them seem to have permanent habitations, and though they make frequent short excursions, they come back to roost on the old spot, which becomes worn and scarred by their constant presence. The anatomy of these animals is similar to that of other mollusks. There is a mantle lining the free parts of the shell, a broad, muscular foot, a head with a pair of eyes and feelers, a mouth fitted with a crescent-like jaw, and a long tongue set with flinty hooks. There are gills for the purification of the blood, a liver, a heart, and other organs of digestion, circulation and secretion. A few species have an opening in the top of the shell, which serves the same purpose as the holes of the Haliotis.

By far the largest of the Key-hole Limpets, as they are called, is named *Lucapina crenulata*, Sby., Lu-ka-

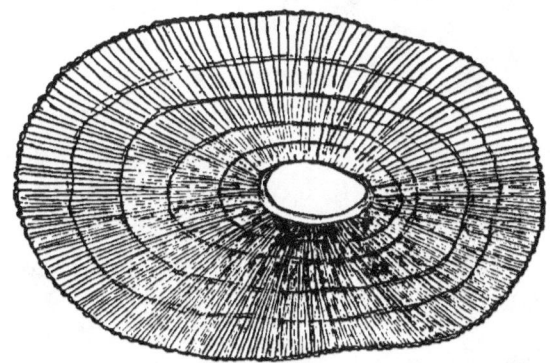

Fig. 79.

pi'-na cren-u-la'-ta. A small figure of the shell is shown in Fig. 79. Though this shell is often some four inches long, the animal is much larger, and somewhat resembles a brick, both in shape and size.

It has a huge yellow foot and a black mantle, which nearly conceals the white shell which rests upon the animal's back.

This shell is marked by many radiating ribs, and concentric lines of growth; it has a large, oblong hole to one side of the center, around which, internally, is a thick rim of enamel. The crenulated or scalloped edge of the shell is a marked feature, and suggested the name.

Internally, the shell is of a pure, glossy white, but the outside is somewhat dingy. This mollusk is not very abundant, and is seldom found alive near the shore.

Glyphis aspera, Esch., Gly'-fis as'-pe-ra, Fig. 80,

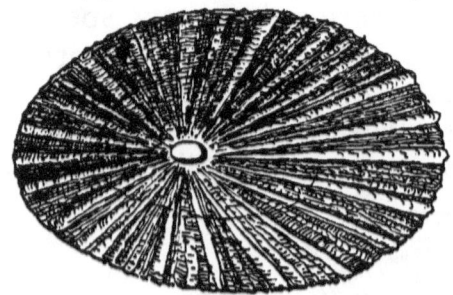

Fig. 80.

has a rough shell, more sharply conical than the last, with a small oval hole at the top, quite different from the narrow, oblong slit of the next shell. This shell has a wrinkled edge, a white interior, and a gray or striped outside. Its common length is an inch and a half, though I once found a fine live specimen of twice that length.

Fig. 81 represents the shell of our most common Key-hole Limpet, *Fissurella volcano*, Rve., Fis-su-

Fig. 81.

rel'-la vol-ca'-no. The dead shells are abundant, and living specimens, with yellow foot and red-striped mantle, may often be found on the rocks at low tide.

The shell is about an inch in length, and is oblong conical in form, while the red stripes, running down from the small, oblong hole at the top, suggest streams of red hot lava issuing from the crater of a volcano. The coloring appears plainest on dead shells; the live ones are darker, smoother, and less brilliant.

Glyphis densiclathrata, Rve., den-si-clath-ra'-ta, is smaller, more delicate, and has closer and finer sculpturing. Length about half an inch, color white or gray, hole circular; below tides.

Fissurellidæa calliomarginata, Cpr., Fis-su-rel-li-de'-a cal-li-o-mar-gin-a'-ta, is a small, deep-water species. Its shell is low-arched, with a large, oblong hole, and roughened rays. The margin is crenulated and the inside is white.

Fissurellidæa bimaculata, Dall, bi-mak-u-la'-ta, is the long name of the little shell shown in Fig. 82.

Fig. 82.

Dead shells may frequently be found, and occasionally a live one may be gathered from the sea-weed or the rocks. The shell is about one-fourth of an inch in length, oblong, with rounded corners and external sculpturing. The hole in the center is shaped like the shell. The color is white, but there is a dark, triangular spot on each side, which gives it the name *bimaculata*, meaning two-spotted.

(7)

CHAPTER XIV.

GADINIA—THE OWL SHELL—THE WHITE CAP—A LARGE
FAMILY OF LIMPETS AND THE MEANING OF THEIR
NAMES; CHANGEABLE FORMS—SEA-WEED LIMPETS, OR
NACELLAS.

IN the preceding chapter we have considered a number of mollusks whose shells have a slit or fissure
at the apex; in this one, let us note those which have
a solid shell.

The first one on our list is named *Gadinia reticu-
lata*, Sby., Ga-din'-i-a re-tik-u-la'-ta. (*Gadinia
radiata*, Cpr.) The natural size of the
shell is shown in Fig. 83. It is low-arched,
entire, and has a nearly central apex, from
which run radial ridges to the edge of the
shell. These rays are crossed by deep lines
of growth, giving the shell a nettled or reticulated
appearance. Its color is white, and it is half an inch
in diameter. I have found a few specimens living
on a mussel-bearing ledge, near low-water mark.

Of the many species of true Limpets which are
found on the west coast of the United States, the
largest is the Owl-shell, shown in Fig. 84, and whose
true name is *Lottia gigantea*, Gray, Lot'-ti-a
gi-gan'-te-a.

On the outside the shell is usually rough, brown, and unsightly; within, it is very dark and lustrous, and has a bluish white center marked with brown. In some specimens, the part within the horse-shoe shaped muscle scar greatly resembles a horned owl sitting upon his perch. The shell is rather flat, and the apex is near one end. The length of the shell is sometimes as much as three inches, though commonly it is much less.

Fig. 84.

Fig. 85 represents a very pretty shell, commonly known as the White Cap. Its name is *Acmæa mitra*,

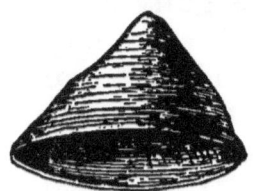

Esch., Ak-me'-a mi'-tra, though it was once thought to belong to the genus *Scurria*. Everybody who walks along the beach picks up this pleasing white shell, with its smooth surface and conical form. Even if you have a hundred in your cabinet

Fig. 85.

already, you wish for every new one which you see, and it is so white and pure and graceful that you don't wonder the ladies sometimes wear them attached to their ear-rings. You may occasionally find a living specimen, but the most of them dwell below the tide mark, and furnish us nothing but their empty shells. Stony vegetables often thrive upon these shells, and you often find one covered with knobby nullipores, or adorned with a tuft of jointed coralline. The common length of the shell is one inch.

Acmæa spectrum, Nutt., spek'-trum, is a very distinct species.   It lives high up on the rocks along the

seashore, and from its gray color it looks like a scale of granite. Its shell is very variable, but is generally low conical, with the apex near one end, as shown in Fig. 86, and it is marked by large, rough rays, which render the edge very irregular, as is well shown in Fig. 87.

Fig. 86.

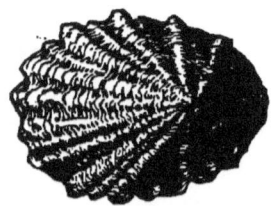

The interior is of a chalky white, dotted with various colored spots, which sometimes bring out "the owl" very distinctly.   The usual length is less than an inch.

The shell of the little *Acmæa rosacea*, Cpr., ro-sa'-se-a, is very small and delicate.   Its white cone is gaily marked with lines and dots of yellow and pink.   Its length is only one-fourth of an inch, or less, and it is rare at that.   Still you may be on the lookout, and in some good hour you may wish to turn to this page and refresh your memory.

Fig. 87.

Most of the Limpets live near the shore, between high and low water marks.   They are easily collected by suddenly lifting them from the rock, by means of a broad-bladed knife; but if they have been previously startled, they will cling so tenaciously that their shells may be broken before they yield.

In some countries they are eaten, and vast numbers are also gathered for the fishermen as bait.   Notice carefully the broad foot, the mantle and gills, and the short head with its tentacles.   After the animal has been removed from the shell, observe the horse-shoe shaped muscle scar.

One of the most common of the limpets is named *Acmæa patina*, Esch., Ak-me'-a pat'-i-na. Fig. 88 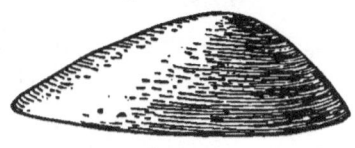 shows the form. It is oval, flattened, with a nearly central apex ; from this radiate fine lines or striæ, sometimes quite indistinct. The outside

Fig. 88.

is of a dark color; internally there is first a dark ring around the edge, then a broad, bluish-white lining, and a patch of brown near the center. The details of the coloring vary greatly, and some young specimens are very prettily checked with green and brown. The common length of the shell is from an inch to two inches. Mr. Dall considers this species as identical with the common *Acmæa testudinalis*, Fb. and Han., which abounds on both sides of the North Atlantic.

Acmæa scabra, Nutt., ska'-bra, resembles the last species in general form, and I once thought it was only a variety. But an examination of many specimens has shown me that the head and mantle of this species are of a dark color, while in *patina* they are always white.

The shell is low-arched, and is covered with scaly, radiating ridges, which give it the appearance and feeling of a fine-cut file. It is usually whitish or light-brown in color, though sometimes it is darker. The average length is one inch. I have seen a few very large and thick shells, which had belonged to aged specimens, and which proved their identity only by their white color.

Acmæa pelta, Esch., pel'-ta, Fig. 89, is more conical and pointed, and the outside of the shell has

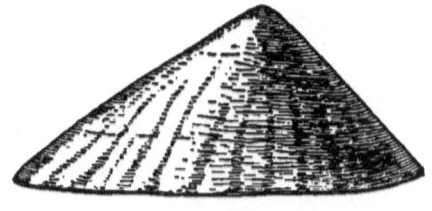

about twenty-five blunt, radiating ribs. The outside is gray or striped, and is sometimes very beautiful; the inside is mainly white, though there is generally a dark thread

Fig. 89.

around the edge and a brown spot in the center. A strange form is sometimes found in which the early growth of the shell seems to have been formed on a different plan from that of the ordinary specimen, for it is smooth, brown, and has almost perpendicular sides, like a *Nacella;* after this it suddenly changes to the ordinary form. It is probable that this was caused by a decided change in the abode of the Limpet, perhaps from the sea-weed to the rock.

A small, black, conical shell, supposed by Carpenter to be an abnormal growth of the young of this species, is now known as *Acmæa Asmi*, Midd. It is usually found living on the shells of the Black Turban. Its length is one-fourth of an inch, while the ordinary shells of *pelta* are an inch long or more.

Acmæa persona, Esch., per-so'-na, is shown in Fig. 90. What a variety of names our Limpets offer to us,

and how significant they are! *Spectrum*—the spectre, with its pale, ghostly ribs; *patina*—the dish or pan, with its saucer-like shell;

Fig. 90.

scabra—the rough Limpet, with a shell like a fine rasp; *pelta*—the shield; and now, for the last one, *persona*—the mask.

This shell may be distinguished by the position of the apex, which is situated very near one end, making nearly all the slope come upon one side like the roof of an old-fashioned farm-house. The ribs on the slope of the shell are prominent but irregular. The outside is gray or mottled, and the inside has varying amounts of brown and white. This shell is high-arched, but it seldom grows to the length of an inch.

Besides these Limpets which may be gathered from the rocks, there are several species which are found upon the stems of sea-weeds. The largest of these Sea-weed Limpets, as they are called, is named *Nacella instabilis*, Glk., Na-sel'-la in-stab'-i-lis. The shell is limpet-shaped, narrow, compressed at the sides, smooth, brown on the outside and white within. Its length is three-fourths of an inch and its breadth is a little less.

Nacella incessa, Hds., in-ces'-sa, Fig. 91. This is

Fig. 91.

the common species, and may be found on the flat central ribbons of the olive green seaweeds, which are so conspicuous near the rocky shore. The sides of the shell are flattened and nearly smooth, and the apex is rounded. The shell is of a dark brown color throughout, and looks as if it were made of horn. It is about half an inch long and is of the same height.

Two other species I will briefly describe. The first is named *Nacella depicta*, Gld., on account of its painted appearance. Shell very narrow, with straight, flat sides. White, with fine brown stripes radiating from the apex. One-fourth to one-half an inch in length. Southern; on grass at low tide.

Nacella palcacca, Gld., pal-e-a′-se-a. This shell resembles the last one, but is still narrower. It is brownish, without stripes, and is one-fourth of an inch in length. *Nacella triangularis*, Cpr., is probably a variety of the last.

Now we will turn to a droll lot of creatures, whose bodies resemble the Limpets, but whose shells are decidedly peculiar.

CHAPTER XV.

A Disturbed Family—The Chitons—How to Prepare Specimens—Description of the Common Species—The Mossy Chiton—Katherina—Butterfly Shells—Less Common Species of the Coat-of-Mail Shells.

THERE are very odd creatures under the stones which lie along the rim of the ocean. If you go down at low tide and turn the rocks over, one by one, you will be surprised at the number of singular beings which stare up at you in blank amazement, and then rush away into obscure places, as fast as their ten or fourteen legs will carry them. Others cannot run, but in sheer helplessness wait for your kind decision to do them no harm, and their very inertness appeals to your sympathies. While the saucy crabs waste no time in ceremonies, and the sea-worms creep away as fast as possible, the poor mollusks can only cling to the rock for protection, or curl themselves into the smallest space and the most secure condition which their instinct can dictate.

When you visit the seaside you will want to see all these harmless little inhabitants of the ocean, and among them you will probably find some specimens of our next group of mollusks, the *Chitons*, Ki'-tons. The anatomy of these animals is similar to that of the Limpets, but they seem less highly developed, are more sluggish, and commonly live under stones, away from all scenes of activity.

But the peculiar feature which distinguishes them from the Limpets, is the fact that the shell of the Chiton consists of eight parts, instead of a single shield. These parts or valves run across the body and overlap one another, like shingles on a roof. They are highest in the center, and they end in a leathern mantle which runs around the body, and which is highly contractile. This being the case, the Chiton shells can not be preserved with the same ease as those of the Limpets, for the mantle must be dried while the valves are in their natural position.

Probably the best way to prepare fine specimens is to bind the living animal, as it rests in a pan of sea-water, upon a flat stone or a bit of shingle. It can then be placed in warm fresh water, when, after the lack of salt has destroyed life and the muscle has lost its contractility, the animal may be unbound, the viscera removed with a sharp knife, and the parts to be preserved placed in a flat position to dry.

We have a good many species of which the principal ones are the following.

Tonicella lineata, Wood, Ton-i-sel'-la lin-e-a'-ta, Fig. 92, Red-lined Chiton.

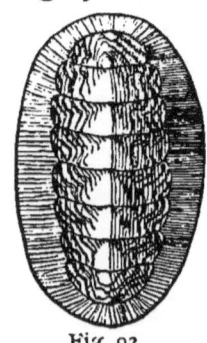
Fig. 92.

This species is a beautiful representative of this singular group of mollusks. The valves or parts of the shell are smooth, moderately arched in the center, and are of a yellowish brown color. This back-ground of color is crossed by wavy or zigzag lines of orange, red or green, making the fresh specimen an object of great beauty. The mantle-border is smooth, thin, delicate, and of a yellowish brown color. The common length of the animal is one inch.

Chætopleura Hartwigii, Cpr., Ke-to-plu'-ra Hart-wig'-i-i, is about the same size as the last species, but the exterior is not polished, and is of a dull drab or an olive green. The inside of the valves is smooth, and of a lively, pea-green color; southern.

Fig. 93 shows us the appearance of a lean Chiton, for that is signified by the first part of its long name, *Ischnochiton regularis*, Cpr., Ish-no-ki'-ton reg-u-la'-ris. The last name signi-fies, moreover, that it is of a very regu-lar form, and this is true. Its width, which is constant, is half its length, and the ends are semi-circles.

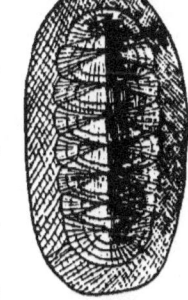

The valves are sharply arched, and are marked with very fine sculpturing. By the aid of a lens the mantle-border is seen to resemble fine

Fig. 93.

bead-work. The color is dark olive-green, and the length is an inch and a half or less.

Stenoradsia Magdalensis, Rve., Sten-o-rad'-si-a Mag-da-len'-sis, Fig. 94.

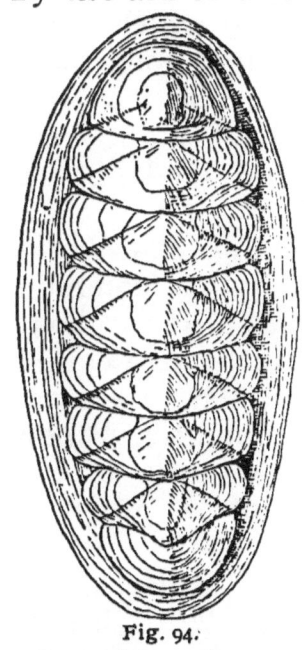

This large and very common Chiton may be found under rocks at low tide, and may at once be recognized by its worn or roughly sculptured, low-arched valves, which are white internally, and of a light ash-gray color on the outside. The hairless mantle-border is of a similar neutral tint, but the foot is yellow. When

Fig. 94.

taken from the rock it has a habit of curling itself up

into a ball. Its common length is two or three inches.

Mangerella conspicua, Cpr., Man-ger-el'-la con-spik'-u-a, resembles the above, and is considered by Mr. Hemphill as merely a variety of that species. The mantle-border is roughened by numerous short, tubular hairs. Large; southern.

Placiphorella velata, Cpr., Pla-sif-o-rel'-la ve-la'-ta, Round Chiton, is shown in Fig. 95. This singular

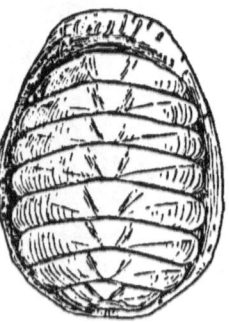

" coat-of-mail" shell is more nearly circular than any of its relatives. As shown in the cut, the muscular mantle in which the valves are inserted is considerably prolonged at one end, forming a kind of veil or awning, quite different from that of any other species with which I am acquainted. The mantle-border and the veil are set with a few stiff bristles. The valves are low-arched, of a dull reddish brown without, but white within. Its length is an inch or an inch and a half.

Fig. 95.

Nuttalliana scabra, Rve., Nut-tal-li-an'-a ska'-bra, is shown in Fig. 96. This species is rather common

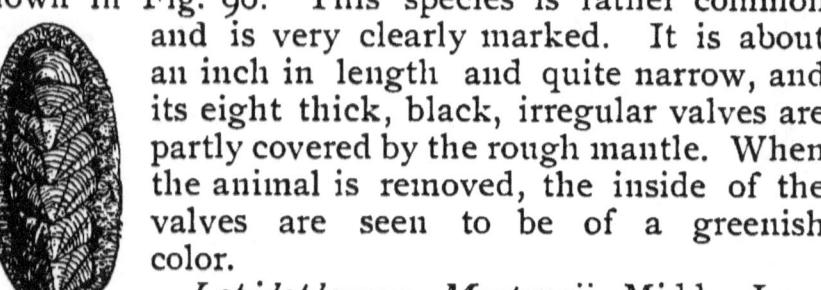

and is very clearly marked. It is about an inch in length and quite narrow, and its eight thick, black, irregular valves are partly covered by the rough mantle. When the animal is removed, the inside of the valves are seen to be of a greenish color.

Lepidopleurus Mertensii, Midd., Lep-i-do-plu'-rus Mer-ten'-si-i, Red Chiton.

Fig. 96.

Brownish red, regular in outline, sharply arched,

richly sculptured. The raised triangles on the valves
are adorned with rows of rounded knobs, and the
interspaces with ribs and frets. They are very beautiful when examined with a lens. The mantle-border
is covered with fine, rounded scales. Length, one
inch; northern.

The large Chiton shown in Fig. 97 is named
Mopalia lignosa, Mo-pa'-li-a lig-no'-sa. It differs
from the last species in many respects. It grows

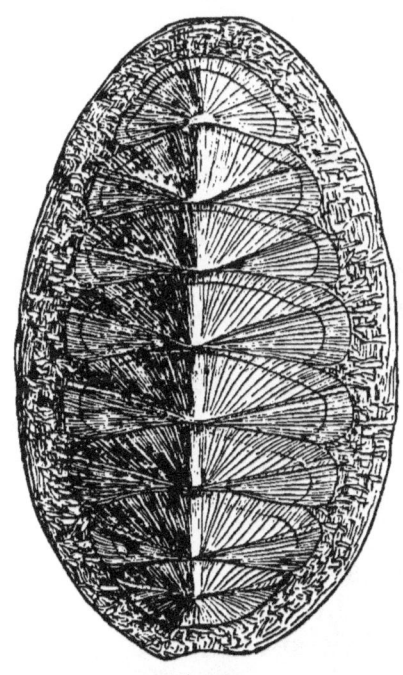

to a much larger size, and
its smooth valves are quite
sharply arched. These
valves are of a light green
color within, but on the
outside they vary from almost white to dark green.
They are also marked with
narrow brown lines, which
slant from the apex of each
valve. The mantle-border
is generally quite rough,
especially in large specimens, but sometimes we
find it nearly smooth. The
cut represents a large-sized
specimen; ordinary ones are
less than two inches in
length.

Fig. 97.

Mopalia Wosnessenskii, Midd., Wos-ness-en'-ski-i,
is the ponderous name of another species. Though
the Chinese are called Celestials, the ending " ski "
refers us at once to the Russians, and we shall find
names of this origin occasionally coming to light in
the list of our shells.

Though this species has such an exalted name, still it is somewhat flattened, and the valve area increases from the narrow point to the wide center. The valves are sculptured, and though of a greenish color, they are sometimes marked with patches of red. The mantle-border is wide, more or less roughened, with a slit back of the last valve. The length is from an inch to two inches. This species is found along the coast of California, and also in the more northern waters of the Pacific.

The mossy Chiton, *Mopalia ciliata*, Sby,, sil-i-a'-ta, is shown in Fig. 98. Under this head belongs *M. muscosa*, Gould, now considered as only a variety of *ciliata*.

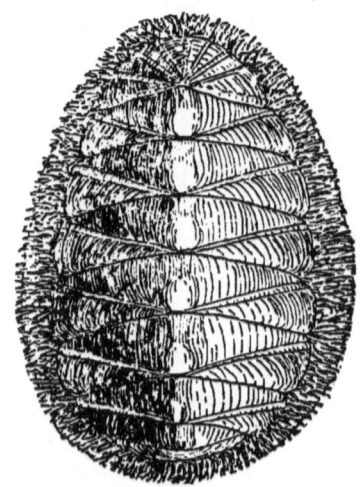

Fig. 98.

This species can readily be told by its hairy mantle border, which resembles the outside of a chestnut-bur. The outside of the valves is sculptured, but they are often overgrown with corallines or mosslike polyzoans so that the sculpturing is obscure. The outside is dull and varies from green to black, but the inside of the valves is light green. This species is common along a great stretch of the Pacific coast. The specimens are an inch or two in length.

And now comes the Giant Chiton, *Cryptochiton Stelleri*, Midd., Cryp-to-ki'-ton Stel'-ler-i. When found whole it is a huge affair, six inches in length and three in breadth. In the last species we saw that the mantle had encroached upon the valves and had

nearly concealed them, but in this species the work is
completed. The whole back of the animal is covered with a hard, gritty, reddish brown mantle, which
wholly conceals the eight white valves, one of which
is shown in Fig. 99.

These single valves are found much more often

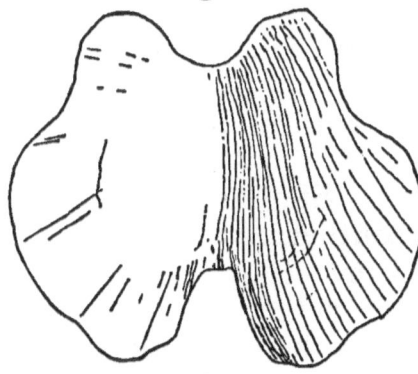

than the complete animal,
and from their peculiar
shape they are called Butterfly shells. Perhaps
many who gather them
are at a loss to know their
origin, but a study of this
very singular "butterfly"
of the sea will reveal all
the mystery. These
valves are pure white and
are about an inch and a half in breadth.

Fig. 99.

In Fig. 99, we have the picture of a small specimen of the Black Chiton, *Katherina tunicata*, Sby.,

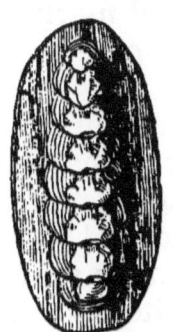

Kath-e-ri'-na tu-ni-ca'-ta, which was
named in honor of Lady Katharine
Douglass, who first sent a specimen to the
British Museum. The outline is elliptical, and the small white valves are nearly
covered by the thick black mantle. This
singular arrangement of the parts is so
striking that it cannot be mistaken for
any other species. Think of a smooth
black skin, rounded like a whale's back,
and set with eight little shelly plates, and you will
get the idea. The foot is of a reddish color, and the
common length is two or three inches. It is especially
abundant far to the north.

Fig. 100.

Less common Chitons include the following briefly described species:

Leptochiton rugatus, Cpr.   Minute, smooth, reddish; southern.

Chætopleura gemma, Cpr.   Small, narrow, highly sculptured, reddish brown.   It is sometimes found at Monterey.

Ischnochiton Cooperi, Cpr.   Regular, richly sculptured, especially on the first valve.   Sharply arched, brownish without, light green within; length an inch and a quarter.

Ischnoplax pectinatus, Cpr.   Similar to the last, but with a rougher mantle; southern.

Callistochiton decoratus, Cpr.   Small, regular in shape, quite sharp along the ridge, valves richly sculptured, each raised triangle being divided into two or more parts.   Reddish or yellowish brown; less than an inch in length; southern.

Callistochiton palmulatus, Cpr.   Small, high arched, valves marked with raised sculpturing.   One of both of the end valves are greatly thickened and marked with radiating grooves.   Length somewhat over half an inch; dark brown; southern.

Callistochiton fimbriatus, Cpr., is another southern species, similar to the last in form and size; sharply arched, narrow, end valves not much thickened, rare.

Mopalia Hindsii, Gray.   Low arched, marked with faint sculpturing, mantle border covered with minute scales.   Nearly black on the outside but white within. Length from an inch to two inches.   The specimens before me were collected at Bolinas, Cal.

CHAPTER XVI.

The Tooth Shell—Indian Money—The Violet Snail—
Siphonaria—Fresh-Water Limpets—Carnifex New-
berryi—The Helisomas—The Physas of the Brooks
—Sinistral Shells in Variety.

A STRANGE little shell is that shown in Fig. 101,
and a fairy tale could it tell of the life of its
little inhabitant. Shaped like the tusk of an elephant, pure white, slightly curved, and open
at both ends, it differs widely from all the
shells which we have so far considered.

The name of this little creature is *Dentalium pretiosum*, Nutt., Den-ta'-li-um pre-shi-
o'-sum, and it is found chiefly in the vicinity
of Puget Sound. The species has also been
named *Indianorum*, Cpr.; we will call it the Precious
Tooth-shell.

Fig. 101.

The mollusk is not so highly organized as some of
its neighbors, and it spends its life in the sand. The
large end of the shell opens downward, and from its
aperture projects the foot, with which it is able to dig.
From the small end which projects above the sand, it
can throw out little tenacles, which ensnare the infu-
soria and other minute animals upon which it feeds.

In olden times the Indians used these shells as
money, stringing them upon long threads, and they
were highly prized. This fact explains both the

(8)

names which have been attached to the species, *preti-osum*, meaning precious, and Iu-di-an-o'-rum, meaning "of the Indians." They gathered the shells with a rude instrument, shaped like a comb with few teeth, fixed to the end of a spear. While his squaw slowly rowed the boat along, the brave Indian plunged his comb-like spear into the sand; if he made a successful thrust there would be one or more of these creatures caught upon the teeth of the comb; after the expedition they were prepared for stringing. This was the primitive way of "making money" on the Pacific coast. The shells vary from less than an inch to a considerably greater length.

Dentalium hexagonum, Sby., hex-ag'-o-num, is a southern species, having a shell white, delicate, angled, slightly curved, and about an inch long.

Ianthina trifida, Nutt., Yan'-thi-na tri'-fi-da, Violet Snail. This little creature has habits very different from those of the Dentalium. Instead of burrowing in the sand, it lives far out in the open ocean. It is kept at the surface by a singular raft which it secretes, and it feeds upon small jelly-fishes.

The shell is small and is shaped much like that of the land-snail. It is thin and delicate, and has a deep notch in the outer lip. The color is a deep violet, quite unlike that of any other shell. Though it usually lives far out at sea, sometimes shells get washed to the shore, but they are comparatively rare on our coast.

Siphonaria peltoides, Dall, Si-fo-na'-ri-a pel-toi'-des, has a Limpet-shaped shell, small, thin, and low-arched, with the apex a little to one side of the center. The color is light brown with more or less darker rays, and its length is one-fourth of an inch or more.

The interior muscle scar is divided on one side by a siphonal groove, but this mark is not always very distinct. This little mollusk lives upon rocks, between tides, and is quite rarely found. When disturbed, it gives out a milky fluid.

Now we will turn from the saltwater for a little while and study the similar mollusks which live in the lakes and rivers.

The first one we meet is very small, only one-eighth of an inch across and one-fourth of an inch long. It is the fresh-water Limpet, *Ancylus fragilis*, Tryon, An-sy'-lus frag'-il-is. The shell is Limpet-shaped, narrow, thin, and of a light brown color. From Portland, Oregon.

Ancylus subrotundus, Tryon, sub-ro-tun'-dus. Similar to the last, but more oval in outline. From The Dalles.

Acroluxus Nuttalli, Hald., Ac-ro-lux'-us Nutt-all'-i,

Fig. 102. The shell is Limpet-shaped, nearly circular in outline. Brown, thin

Fig. 102. and translucent, one-fourth of an inch or more in diameter; associated with the last species.

Gundlachia Californica, Rowell, Gund-lak'-i-a Cal-i-for'-ni-ca. Very minute, limpet-shaped, with a small shelf across part of the aperture. It is found on the stems of plants growing in stagnant ponds.

There are mollusks in almost every brook and pond in the country. Every boy will be sure to find them if he carefully turns over the stones and examines the old sticks and leaves which have fallen into the water.

They feed almost wholly upon vegetable matter; some of them eat the green *confervæ*, that is, the slimy vegetation which abounds in stagnant water.

Others gnaw out the pulp of fallen leaves, and thus manufacture those leaf skeletons which we find in the brooks. They creep along the bottom, or up the stems of plants, and occasionally they come to the surface to breathe.

The members of this family are called the *Limnæ-idæ*, which means the marsh mollusks. The first of this numerous family which we shall consider, is named *Pompholyx effusa*, Lea, Pom-fo'-lyx ef-fu'-sa. The first name means a bubble, hence we might expect to find that it has a thin, globular shell, as we really see in Fig. 103.

The spire is exceedingly short, and the aperture is nearly circular and very large. The length and breadth of the shell are

Fig. 103. each about one-fourth of an inch. The shell is horny, and sometimes it is ribbed. It is found in Oregon and Nevada, and there are several varieties which differ slightly in appearance.

A very distinct and characteristic shell is shown in Fig. 104, and bears the name of *Carnifex Newberryi*, Binn., Car'-ni-fex New-ber'-ry-i.

The whorls are few and are flattened at the top; both above and below they are terminated by sharp angular keels. Um-

Fig. 104. bilicus large, shell thin and horny, one-fourth of an inch in breadth; from lakes.

Gyraulus vermicularis, Gld., Ji-rau'-lus ver-mik-u-la'-ris. This little species has a flattened shell, consisting of about three rounded whorls, and is only one-eighth of an inch in diameter. My specimens are from Oakland, Cal. The generic name is interesting because it was originated by Agassiz, in the year 1837. The specific name was given by Dr. Gould.

Gyraulus parvus, Say, par'-vus. Shell very flat, consisting of a coil of the fine, horn-like shell-tube. Whorls about four in number, and the whole only one-eighth of an inch in diameter. From Oregon and California.

Menetus opercularis, Gld., Men'-e-tus o-per-cu-la'-ris. This species, likewise, has a flattened, coiled shell, sometimes nearly plane above, with an oblique aperture and a conspicuous umbilicus; it is about one-fourth of an inch in diameter.

Helisoma ammon, Gld., He-li-so'-ma am'-mon, is shown in Fig. 105. The shell of this fresh-water mollusk, which is found in the San Joaquin river, is

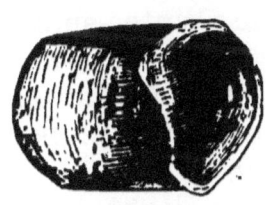

in the form of a flattened tube, coiled horizontally so that a cup-shaped depression is left on either side. As the animal grows it winds its shell round and round in the same plane, and does not build in the spiral form like most of the mol-

Fig. 105.

lusks. The aperture is large and ear-shaped. The outside of the shell is of a rich, yellowish brown color, but it is white within the aperture.. The lines of growth are very distinct, and mark the shell in a pleasing manner. Its breadth is from half an inch to an inch.

Helisoma bicarinatus, Say, bi-car-i-na'-tus, resembles the last but is much smaller. Whorls with a sharp angle or keel, both above and below the suture. The specimens before me were collected in Portland, Oregon.

Now we come to a fresh-water mollusk that is very widely spread, and many of its varieties have

received special names. They are, however, essentially alike, and may all be included
under the name *Helisoma trivolvis*,
Say, tri-vol'-vis, the general form of
which is shown in Fig. 106. The shell
tube is wound in a coil, consisting of
about four whorls. The color is light

Fig. 106.

brown, and the aperture is irregular. The diameter
of the coil is from one-fourth to three fourths of an
inch. Some of the names of the varieties are given
for the convenience of those making exchanges.
They are *corpulentus*, *fragilis*, *occidentalis*, *fallax*,
tumens and *Oregonensis*.

In the brook which runs past Mills College I have
caught many specimens of the little Water-snail,
Physa heterostropha, Say, Fi'-sa het-e-ros'-tro-pha,
shown in Fig. 107. It is common in brooks
and streams over much of the Pacific Slope,
as well as east of the Rocky mountains. The
shell is thin and delicate, of a light horn
color, with a small spire, a sinistral (left-
handed) aperture, and commonly is about
half an inch in length. The animal is black or
nearly so, and when the shell is inhabited it appears
much darker than when it is empty.

Fig. 107.

It is amusing as well as instructive to put some of
these little creatures in a jar of water and watch their
movements. Sometimes they will quietly remain at the
bottom, eating the pulp of an alder leaf which you
have given to them; then they will rise to the surface
to take a breath of fresh air and slowly sink back
again, or perhaps they will crawl along, shell downward, apparently clinging with their foot to the surface of the water—an apparently impossible feat, but
they do it nevertheless.

They make little nests of transparent jelly, filled with minute eggs, and attach them to the side of the jar, where you can easily watch the development of the embryos. In my jar the little things came out after twenty days, each with a perfect shell, and began life on their own account. Suppose you put such a jar in your school-room.

This species, as well as the last, has many varieties—as *ancillaria, propinqua, diaphana* and *virginea.*

Physa politissima, Tryon, from Oregon, has a brilliant shell with a dark line near the edge of the outer lip. I should consider it but a variety of the wide-reaching *heterostropha.*

This last name is the Greek for "turning-the-other-way," though all the Physas have sinistral shells and may thereby be recognized at the first glance.

Physa costata, Newc., cos-ta'-ta, has a very small, thin shell, with a somewhat ribbed or corrugated surface. From Clear Lake, California.

Physa Gabbi, Tryon. Spire small, consisting of three or four minute whorls. Body whorl large, aperture large also, outer lip broad and full. Specimens from Portland, Oregon, are light horn-colored, and from one-half to a whole inch in length.

Physa Carltonii, Lea, Carl-to'-ni-i. Body whorl full and round, horn-colored; outer lip marked internally with stripes of dark brown; length, three-fourths of an inch. From near Antioch, California. Named in honor of its worthy discoverer, Mr. H. P. Carlton.

Physa Cooperi, Tryon, Coop'-er-i, named for another eminent conchologist, has a small, slender shell, which somewhat resembles a very small grain of wheat. From Santa Barbara, California.

Quite resembling the Physas, but with a longer spire, comes *Bulinus hypnorum*, Linn., Bu'-li-nus hyp-no'-rum, Fig. 108. The minute apex is rounded, the sutures distinct and oblique, the whorls six or seven in number, and the aperture of moderate size. The color is light brown, and the surface is very smooth and glossy. The length is three-fourths of an inch. The specimen illustrated came from Box Elder county, Utah.

Fig. 108.

Physella Columbiana, Hemphill, Fi-sel'-la Co-lum-bi-an'-a, is the last in this instructive group. It has a pretty little sinistral shell, consisting of a short spire and a very round and full body whorl, with an ample aperture. It is of a brown color, but the curved columella is often white. Its length is half an inch, and it lives, as its name indicates, in the Columbia river.

CHAPTER XVII.

DEXTRAL SHELLS AGAIN — SPECIES OF LIMNOPHYSA — A BROTHER'S TRIBUTE — THE TWO GREAT LIMNÆAS — EAR-SHELLS — CARYCHIUM AND MELAMPUS — TORNATINA AND THE BARREL-SHELL — BUBBLE-SHELLS — SEA-SLUGS AND THEIR BEAUTY — FAREWELL TO THE OCEAN HOME.

LEAVING now the left-handed Physas, let us examine their dextral neighbors, which also live in lakes and streams, and are similar in their habits to those we have studied. Nearly all fresh-water shells are covered with a greenish brown epidermis, and where this becomes broken, as it frequently does, near the apex, the shell becomes eaten or eroded by the weak acids which are usually present in the waters of lakes and streams.

Of the species which we are to notice, the first is named *Leptolimnæa Kirtlandiana*, Lea, Lep-to-lim-ne′-a Kirt-land-i-an′-a, and a view of it is given in Fig. 109. The shell is dextral and somewhat cylindrical; the spire is long and five-whorled; the aperture is rather small and oval, and the columella is marked with a fold. The cut is somewhat magnified, as the natural size is from one-half to three-fourths of an inch. From near Logan, Utah.

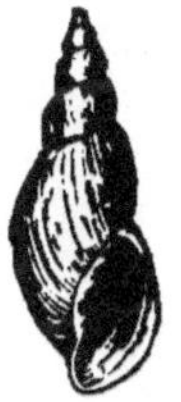
Fig. 109.

Limnophysa desidiosa, Say, Lim-no-fi′-sa de-sid-i-o′-sa, has a slender, dextral shell, with a conspicuous spire of rounded whorls, which are separated by deep sutures. Aperture oval; umbilicus small, under the recurved lip; length, one-half an inch. From Washington territory.

Limnophysa bulimoides, Lea, bu-li-moi′-des. The first whorls are small, but the later ones increase rapidly in size, giving the shell a robust appearance. Aperture small, oval; length, half an inch. From Idaho.

Limnophysa humilis, Say, hu′-mi-lis, has a small and thin shell, the body-whorl of which is full, while the aperture is half the length of the shell. The latter is only a quarter of an inch long. It comes from southern California.

Limnophysa catascopium, Say, cat-a-sko′-pi-um. This species is very widely distributed, extending from New England westward. Spire distinct, whorls rounded, body-whorl full, shell very thin, half an inch in length. Specimens from near Oakland, Cal.

The variety *Adelinæ*, Tryon, from the vicinity of San Francisco, is considered by some as a distinct species. It was named for Miss Adeline Tryon, by her learned brother.

Fig. 110 represents a large specimen of *Limnophysa caperata*, Say, ca-pe-ra′-ta. The spire consists of five rounded whorls, the aperture is oval, and the outer lip is slightly reflexed. The shell is horn-colored, and is half an inch or more in length. The specimens before me were collected in Idaho and Utah, but the species ranges over a large part of North America. The variety *Binneyi* belongs to this species.

Fig. 110.

Limnophysa proxima, Lea, prox'-i-ma. Spire rather long and slender, lip reflexed, body-whorl partly divided into small, flattened squares, like hammered silver. The shell is nearly an inch in length. The specimens described came from near Ogden, Utah. It is also found near San Francisco, and elsewhere in California.

The next species, shown in Fig. 111, is named *Limnophysa* (or *Limnæa*) *palustris*, Müll., pa-lus'-

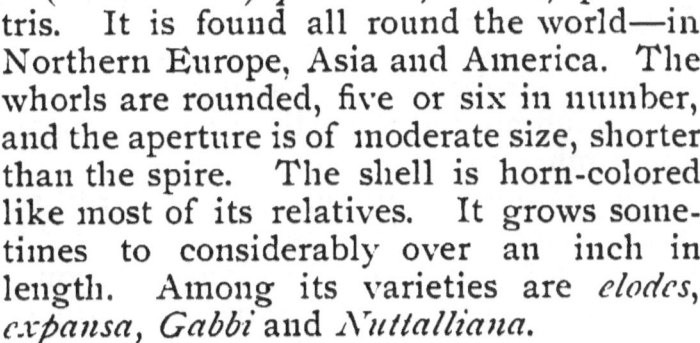

tris. It is found all round the world—in Northern Europe, Asia and America. The whorls are rounded, five or six in number, and the aperture is of moderate size, shorter than the spire. The shell is horn-colored like most of its relatives. It grows sometimes to considerably over an inch in length. Among its varieties are *elodes*, *expansa*, *Gabbi* and *Nuttalliana*.

Fig. 111.

Limnæa stagnalis, Linn., Lim-ne'-a stag-na'-lis, Fig. 112, is the largest of this class of fresh-water mollusks, and is universally distributed, both in this country and in the Old World. It is a very distinct species, and can instantly be recognized. Spire very slender, body-whorl and aperture very large; shell thin and delicate. It grows sometimes to the length of nearly two inches. This mollusk inhabits lakes and rivers, and is found on the Sierras, in Utah, and in many other localities.

Fig. 112.

Limnæa ampla, Mighels, has a small, very thin shell, nearly globular in shape, and one-fourth of an inch in length, as shown in the specimens from Sonoma county, California; but it grows to a very much larger size in Maine, where it was discovered in 1842.

The *Auriculidae* or Ear-shells inhabit salt marshes and seem to love brackish water. They have strong shells with short spires, and narrow, ear-shaped apertures.

The first of our species is named *Alexia myosotis*, Drap., A-lex'-i-a my-o-so'-tis. Its shell is brown, spindle-shaped, similar in size and form to a small grain of wheat. There is a distinct fold on the columella. Probably it was imported from Europe, as it is found around the Atlantic seaports, and also near San Francisco.

Carychium exiguum, Say, Ka-rik'-i-um ex-ig'-u-um, is another little creature scattered through the east, and found also at Portland, Oregon. The shell is minute, whitish, with a distinct spire, consisting of five rounded whorls. The aperture is nearly circular and there is a distinct tooth on the columella. The length of the shell is about one-sixteenth of an inch. It is found about wharves and on stones which are sometimes covered by the tides.

Melampus olivaceus, Cpr., Me-lam'-pus ol-i-va'-se-us, is shown in Fig. 113. This species has a

pretty little pear-shaped shell, with a short spire, an aperture long, narrow, and rounded at the base, and a columella marked by two folds. The color is dark brown, with lighter stripes and bands. Length, half an inch; southern.

Fig. 113.

Pedipes unisulcata, Cooper, Ped'i-pes u-ni-sul-ka'-ta. Spire short, body-whorl large and full, columella marked with very large and peculiar white folds.

General surface light brown; length one-fourth of an inch or less.

The remaining species mentioned in this chapter inhabit the sea and are mostly carnivorous.

Tornatina harpa, Dall, Tor-na-ti′-na har-pa, has a white shell with a short spire, a cylindrical body-whorl, and an aperture which is long, narrow, and curved at the base. The length is less than one-fourth of an inch.

Tornatina inculta, Gld., and *Tornatina carinata*, Gld., closely resemble the preceding species. They are found in the south, on mud flats between tides.

Fig. 114 represents the shell of *Tornatina culcitella*, Gld., cul-si-tel′-la. It resembles the former three species in shape, but is much larger, sometimes growing to a length of nearly an inch. The color is brownish, and fresh specimens are banded with numerous microscopic striæ.

Fig. 114.

A pretty little shell is occasionally found upon the beach, having the form shown in Fig. 115. On account of its cylindrical shape and dark bands it commonly called the Barrel-shell. Its scientific name is *Rhextaxis* (or *Tornatella*) *puncto-cœlata*, Cpr., Rex-tax′-is punk-to-se-la′-ta.

Fig. 115. Its length is about half an inch, and its form is oval. The whorls are few, and there is a fold on the columella. Its surface is pure white, crossed by two series of narrow black bands.

Amphisphyra subquadrata, Cpr., Am-fis-fy′-ra sub-quad-ra′-ta. Minute, thin, spire depressed, body-whorl short and full. Whitish; one-eighth of an inch in length.

Haminea virescens, Sby., Ha-min'-e-a vi-res'-sens. Shell very thin, bubble shaped; spire apparently wanting; aperture very large. It is of a greenish white color, and is half an inch long. It is found on mossy rocks along the coast of southern California.

The White Bubble-shell shown in Fig. 116 is named *Haminea vesicula*, Gld., ve-sik'-u-la. The

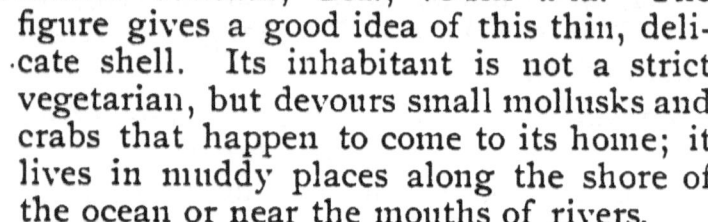

figure gives a good idea of this thin, delicate shell. Its inhabitant is not a strict vegetarian, but devours small mollusks and crabs that happen to come to its home; it lives in muddy places along the shore of the ocean or near the mouths of rivers.

Fig. 116.

It has a powerful gizzard armed with teeth, to crush any hard morsels which it may have swallowed. The shell is nearly white, and is an inch or less in length. You will notice that the aperture is extremely large, the spire depressed, and the whole shell quite like a bubble.

And now in Fig. 117, we have our beautiful Cloudy Bubble-shell, *Bulla nebulosa*, Gld., Bul'-la neb-u-lo'-sa. It is a thin, polished, mottled shell, resemb-

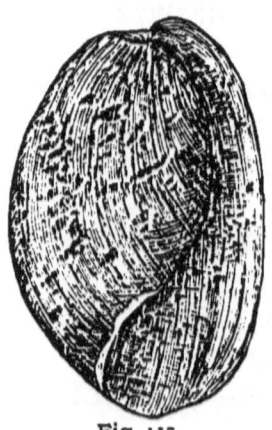

ling a large bird's egg. The spire is depressed, leaving a hole; more properly speaking, the body-whorl is elevated above the original spire. The shell is sometimes wholly brown, but in the finest specimens it is mottled with white and yellow clouds. Length, from an inch to two inches; southern; sometimes found in great numbers.

Somewhat similar in their anatomy to the last few species, come a

Fig. 117.

group of naked mollusks, or sea-slugs. They have no ornamental shells to attract our attention, but their bodies are often very brilliantly colored, so that when alive and swimming they are among the most beautiful objects of the sea.

You will find some of them on sea-weed at low tide, looking like little lumps of soft tissue, without form or beauty; but when put into a jar of sea-water, they will extend their tentacles and expand their flower-like gills, and display their fine colors in all their glory. Some are white with scarlet trimmings, others are yellow with brown rings, while others have brilliant fringes of various hues.

They are mostly small, even when extended, and measure but an inch or two in length. They cannot be preserved except in alcohol, and then their beauty is destroyed; hence they can be satisfactorily studied only at the seaside.

And now, turning away from the great ocean home with its millions of creeping things, and from the lakes and streams and marshes with all their inhabitants, come with me to the land; let us search the fields and the groves, for there, too, we shall find our humble shell-bearing friends, patiently awaiting our coming.

CHAPTER XVIII.

LAND-SHELLS — AMBER-SNAILS — THE PUPAS — LA BRILLANTE—NATURE OF THE HELICES—EUPARYPHA—ARIONTA—THE MONTEREY SNAIL—THE COAST SPECIES—ISLAND SNAILS.

NOW that we have left the water, both salt and fresh, and are setting out for explorations on the dry land, we will approach our new field of operations rather gradually, and will first examine those mollusks which lurk in damp places, though they seldom venture into water. The very nature of mollusks renders them fond of moisture, and during our dry summers they are obliged to suspend active operations, and either retire into their shells and close up the opening, or else bury themselves in the earth and wait for the welcome winter rains. They breathe by means of a simple lung or air-sack, which usually opens on the right side of the body, as is plainly shown in the picture of the slug, Fig. 135.

We will begin with an Amber-snail, *Succinea Haydeni*, W. G. Binney, Suk-sin′-e-a Hay′-den-i, Fig. 118.

The Amber-snails are rather small mollusks, which love moisture, though they do not often enter the water. The amber-colored shell of this species is long, thin and few-whorled. The aperture is very large, and from its base you can look inside the shell to its very apex. The spire is small and consists of about three delicate whorls. The length of the whole shell is three-fourths of an inch. From near Salt Lake, Utah.

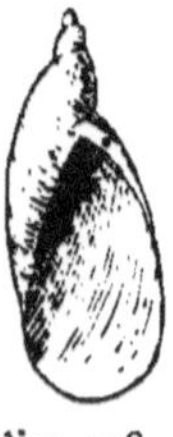

Fig. 118.

Succinea Nuttalliana, Lea, Nut-tal-li-an'-a. Whorls somewhat more rounded than those of the last, and the aperture wider in proportion to its length. Shell light horn-colored, with distinct lines of growth, and a little smaller than that of the last species. The specimens were collected in Weber cañon, Utah, but it is said to occur also in California and Oregon.

Succinea Sillimani, Bland, Sil-li-man'-i. The spire of this shell, which was gathered near Stockton, California, is extremely short, and the aperture is very large and does not narrow near the base. The shell is so very thin that it is nearly transparent, and it has but a trace of color. Its length is about half an inch.

Succinea Oregonensis, Lea, Or-e-go-nen'-sis. Shell yellowish, spiral whorls few and well rounded, body whorl wide, aperture a perfect oval. Length about half an inch. From near Los Angeles, but found in other parts of California and in Oregon.

Succinea Gabbii, Tryon, is somewhat smaller. Specimens from Brigham City, Utah, are considered by Mr. Binney as a variety of the last species.

Succinea Stretchiana, Bland, Strech-i-an'-a, has a yellowish or greenish horn-colored shell, with few whorls and a rounded aperture. The whole shell is also quite full and rounded, and its length is less than half an inch. It is a mountain species, the specimens studied having been collected near Elko, Nevada.

Fig. 119 shows the form of the little *Succinea avara*, Say, a-va'-ra. The shell is horn-colored, and very thin and delicate. The three spiral whorls are rounded, the body-whorl of moderate size, and the aperture is ovate. The length is a quarter of an inch or more. Specimens before

Fig. 119. me are from the Salmon River mountains of

(9)

Idaho, also from near Los Angeles, California. It also occurs in the east.

The Pupas, which we are next to consider, belong to a very ancient family, for the fossil shell of a little Pupa which was found in the coal mines of Nova Scotia, is the oldest land-shell that has ever been discovered. They take their name, evidently, from their resemblance to the pupa-case of an insect.

The shells of all our species are small, some of them being so minute that they would not be noticed except by experienced eyes.

The first one, shown in Fig. 120, bears the name *Pupa Californica*, Rowell, Pu'-pa Cal-i-for'-ni-ca. Although the cut is small enough, still it gives a greatly enlarged view of the shell, and even the cross is too long to tell the truth. The shell is nearly cylindrical, with about five whorls, Fig. 120. and a small aperture on the sides of which are four very minute white teeth. The color of the shell is brown. It has been found near Lone Mountain, in San Francisco, also in southern California, and it doubtless exists in other localities.

Pupa Arizonensis, Gabb, Ar-i-zo-nen'-sis, is similar in form to its California relative, but it is larger, being one-eighth of an inch in length. It has been found in Arizona, Nevada and Utah.

Pupa Rowelli, Newcomb, Row-ell'-i, is a minute species, apparently but slightly different from *Californica*, but more conical. It has been observed in several places in California, particularly near the city of Oakland, among rocks.

Pupa Blandi, Morse, occurs in Dakota, Colorado, and also in Utah, near Logan. Its shell is composed of six distinct and rounded whorls. Its shape is cylindrical, the apex is rounded, the aperture small, with little teeth on the walls far inside the opening. Yellowish horn-colored; length, one-eight of an inch.

Pupa corpulenta, Morse, cor-pu-len'-ta, is a minute species, having a shell of four whorls, and an aperture set with four teeth. Length, one-tenth of an inch. From Washoe county, Nevada, also from Utah and Colorado.

Pupa muscorum, Linn., mus-co'-rum, is a circumpolar species, and is found in Nevada and Colorado. Whorls six or seven, rounded; aperture small; color dark chestnut; length about one-eighth of an inch.

Ferussacia subcylindrica, Linn., Fer-rus-sa'-si-a sub-sil-in'-dri-ca, Fig. 121.

Fig. 121.

The little creature to which this shell belongs lives chiefly in forests, concealing itself under leaves and the bark of dead trees. The shell is about the size and shape of a grain of wheat, thin, dark horn-colored, very bright and glistening. There are five or six rounded whorls and a rather small, elliptical aperture. The specimen from which this figure was drawn came from Weber cañon, but the same species exists in the east, and also in Europe. Owing to the great luster of the shell, it is known in France as "la brillante."

The generic name for most of our land snails is *Helix*, He'-lix. They live in all countries, and the number of species is very great indeed. In general we may say that the Helix has a spiral shell and a soft body, which it can withdraw into the shell when it wishes to be concealed. The eyes are fixed upon long stalks, the tongue is set with minute, flinty hooks or teeth, and the creeping disk or foot is crossed by many muscular fibres. When they move they leave a train of mucus behind, which dries into a glistening scale. Their motions are slow, and they are more active in the night than in the daytime.

They love moisture and must have it; hence the dry summers of California would be fatal to them if they had no means of withdrawing themselves from active life during the rainless season. Even at the best they are not very abundant on our coast, and those which do live here are to be sought for chiefly under trees and bushes.

Their food consists strictly of vegetables, and they prefer soft leaves, like those of the lettuce and cabbage. All true snails have shells, but there are many naked slugs which greatly resemble the true snails, both in their habits and their structure.

On account of the great number of species included under the genus Helix, many subdivisions have been made, based upon differences not very apparent to the the ordinary observer. In treating of our species, therefore, I shall give the old name, Helix, and also place in parenthesis the modern generic name, or the name of the section to which each species belongs.

And first we have in Fig. 122, a good representation of *Helix* (*Euparypha*) *Tryoni*, Newcomb, Eu-par'-i-fa Try-o'-ni. The shell is strong and solid, globose conical, with a rounded apex and five regular whorls. The surface is reticulated or cut into fine checks by the crossing of spiral threads and the lines of growth. The color varies from white to brown, and the whorls are often

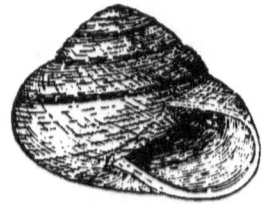
Fig. 122.

banded, while the upper half of each whorl is usually darker than the corresponding lower half. The animal is said to be black. The shell is about one inch in diameter. This species lives chiefly on Santa Barbara Island, off the coast of southern California.

Helix (Arionta) intercisa, W. G. B., A-ri-on'-ta in-ter-si'-sa, is similar, in both size and shape, to the last species. The aperture is oblique and shaped like a horse-shoe; the umbilicus is small and partly concealed by the white, reflected lip. The surface is reticulated, and in some specimens the lines of growth are very conspicuous. The color is white or brown, and sometimes the whorls are obscurely banded. Chiefly from San Clemente Island, California.

Helix (Arionta) Kelletti, Fbs., Kel-lett'-i. Shell consisting of six whorls, spire rather low, umbilicus nearly closed, aperture horse-shoe shaped. Shell smooth, color varying from whitish to brown, usually mottled, with a brown band around the center of the body whorl. Diameter about an inch. From Santa Catalina and San Clemente Islands.

There are numerous varieties, as *castaneus, minor*, and *Stearnsiana*, Gabb. The last one is more globose, and is of an ashy color. It is found chiefly in Lower California, but it exists around San Diego. It is considered by Mr. Binney as a distinct species.

Helix (Arionta) Nickliniana, Lea, Nik-lin-i-an'-a. This species has a fine, yellowish horn-colored shell, with a distinct band of dark brown. Spire moderately elevated, whorls six in number, lip white within, somewhat reflexed at the base, umbilicus distinct, but not large. The diameter is an inch or less. This species is found near the coast of central California, and by some authorities it is considered as but a variety of the following, shown in Fig. 123, and named *Helix (Arionta) Californiensis*, Lea, Cal-i-for-ni-en'-sis.

The original specimens from which this species was named, came from Monterey, and it is in that

Fig. 123.

region that it grows to perfection. Such a specimen has a nearly globular shell, quite unlike that of any other of our snails. The shell is rather thin, of a light horn-color mottled with yellow, and is girdled by a narrow brown band. The surface of the shell is cut up into fine, microscopic granules. Mr. Binney states that this species extends as far north as Mendocino county, and that it embraces many forms less globular than the original.

I have found a few living specimens at Point Cypress, and it is said that it may be found concealed at the base of the shrubby Lupine (*Lupinus arboreus*), which abounds at Monterey. The diameter is three-fourths of an inch or less.

Helix (Arionta) ramentosa, Gld., ra-men-to'-sa, is considered by Mr. Binney as one of the above mentioned varieties, though it seems quite different from the Monterey form.

The specimens before me were collected in Alameda and San Mateo counties, and I have recently discovered a colony of them living near my house, around an old oak-stump. They resemble the last species in respect to the surface of their shells, for these are cut into innumerable checks, which are shown by a lens to consist of little oblong grains, arranged parallel to the lines of growth. The shell is more depressed and less globular than Fig. 123, and the umbilicus is small. The color is from light to dark brown, and a dark band runs around the whorls, but the rim of the lip is white. I have seen living specimens from a garden in the City of Alameda, and from the hills back of Oakland. The diameter is less than an inch. The epidermis of the young ones is studded with little bristles.

Helix (*Arionta*) *Diabloensis*, J. G. Cooper, Di-ab-lo-en'-sis, has a flattened shell consisting of six whorls. Its surface is thickly marked with little depressions, like the dents caused by the blows of a small hammer. The aperture is oblique, the umbilicus distinct, and the peristome or rim around the aperture is white and reflexed. The shell is horn-colored, with a darker band. Its diameter is less than an inch. It is a species of the Coast range of central California, being named from its occurrence near Mt. Diablo. By some it is considered as but another variety of *Californiensis*.

Helix (*Arionta*) *arrosa*, Gould, ar-ro'sa, Fig. 124, is a noble species living along the California coast, from

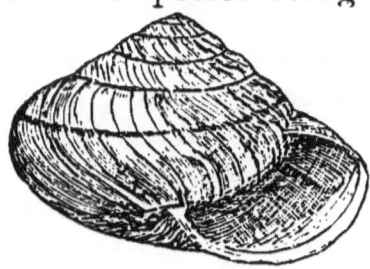

Santa Cruz to Mendocino. The shell frequently grows quite large, an inch and a half in diameter, and is moderately conical in form. The seven whorls, which are from light to dark brown in color, are banded with still darker

Fig. 124.

brown. The umbilicus is distinct, and partly covered by the reflexed peristome.

I once found fine specimens of this species enjoying their summer sleep under the fallen leaves of some Buckeye trees, which grew on the hillsides, just east of Bolinas.

There are several varieties, some of which are smaller than the cut. One of these varieties is usually classed as a distinct species, under the name of *Arionta exarata*, Pfr., ex-a-ra'-ta. It has a yellow-ish, roughened shell, about an inch in diameter, and is circled by a very distinct, dark chestnut band. The umbilicus is large and distinct, and the peristome is white. It is found in San Mateo and Marin counties, California.

Helix (Arionta) tudiculata, Binney, tu-dik-u-la'-ta. Shell large, rather thin, marked by numerous small indentations; umbilicus nearly or completely closed, peristome white, thickened near the umbilicus. The six whorls are of an olive brown color, and a rather wide band with a lighter space above and below it encircles the body whorl. Diameter from an inch to an inch and a quarter. This is a southern species, being found about San Diego, also ranging northward through Tulare and adjacent counties to the Sierras.

Helix (Arionta) Townsendiana, Lea, Towns-end-i-a'-na, Fig. 125.

This distinct species is a northerner, being found chiefly in Oregon and Washington Territory. The specimen from which the engraving was drawn was collected near K a l a m a, Washington.

Fig. 125.

Shell strong, five and one-half whorled, spire but little elevated, color yellowish or brownish, sometimes mottled; peristome turned outward and resembling a white horseshoe; umbilicus large and distinct. The surface is marked by very many microscopic, spiral lines, which are crossed by roughened ridges. Diameter one inch or more.

A smaller variety, named *ptycophora*, B r o w n, ti-kof'-o-ra, is found in Idaho and Eastern Oregon. The shell is thin, nearly smooth, and is of a light horn-color, but it has the regular markings and the broad white peristome of the normal specimens.

Helix (Arionta) ruficincta, Newcomb, ru-fi-sink'-ta. This species has a small, smooth shell with a low spire. The whorls number five or six, the umbilicus is distinct, and the peristome is white, rounded, and conspicuous. The shell is of a light horn-color, with a distinct, reddish brown band. It lives on Santa Catalina Island.

Quite similar to the above but smaller, is *Helix (Arionta) Gabbi*, Newcomb, from the three islands taking their names from the three saints, Santa Barbara, San Clemente and San Nicolas. I have seen a little Helix, called the "Holy Snail," because it lived its little life in Palestine; but if names are good indications, what an odor of sanctity there ought to be around our little *Helix Gabbi*. But alas! even a holy name does not change the one who receives it, and so with these islands and the mollusks which live upon them.

The shells of this species are about the size of large peas, being nearly smooth, with a more or less elevated spire and a rounded peristome. The shade varies from white to horn-colored, and a brown band is generally present.

Helix facta, Newcomb, is but a variety of the same species, and Mr. Hemphill considers them all but varieties of *ruficincta*.

Helix (Arionta) Ayresiana, Newcomb, Ayrs-i-an'-a, is a species from three other islands with similar sacred names—Santa Rosa, San Miguel and Santa Cruz. The shell is quite strong, six-whorled, and has a considerably elevated spire and a distinct umbilicus. The outer lip is sharp and is but slightly reflected at the umbilicus. Microscopic striæ may be traced upon the shell. It is of a brown or chestnut color, and is usually girdled with a broad dark band. Its diameter is three-fourths of an inch.

Helix (Arionta) Traski, Newcomb. This is a coast species found in the vicinity of Los Angeles. Whorls six, spire but little elevated, apex flattened, umbilicus distinct, peristome but little widened except near the umbilicus. Shell horn-colored, girdled by a dark chestnut band edged with yellow. The interior is white, but it shows the dark band. The surface is usually marked with microscopic striæ. Its greater diameter is one inch.

Arionta Carpenteri, Newcomb, is probably a variety of *Traski*, but it has a more delicate shell. It comes from Coronado Island and Mexico.

CHAPTER XIX.

CYPRESS POINT is a projection of land, a few
miles south of Monterey, which looks out boldly
upon the broad Pacific ocean. The huge waves come
rolling in and beat themselves into spray against its
rugged cliffs, and the sweet breath of the ocean pours
over the tree-tops and then rushes on across the hills,
carrying health and vigor to the parched interior of
the State. There is no more delightful spot on this
beautiful earth than this same Point of the Cypress
Trees, and whoever visits it carries away a picture of
mingled wildness, sublimity and beauty.

It is well named, for here, within the compass of
a few score of acres, is the diminishing home of the
cypress trees of California. From this little spot
came the seeds which have developed into hundreds
of miles of beautiful hedges, and tens of thousands
of beautiful trees.

The parent-trees are venerable specimens, blown
by the strong sea-breezes into the most fantastic
forms. Here is one on the very edge of the bluff;
its trunk is horizontal, and its thick-leaved top slants

up from the ground like the moss-covered roof of an ancient farm-house. Here stands another, grim and solitary, with a gnarled and twisted trunk upholding a close-reefed sail of bright green foliage. And there is a little group of them, kneeling together toward the east—like penitent pilgrims—yet showing by their defiant limbs, which are bent and knotted like the arms of wrestling giants, that although the proud west wind has brought them to their knees, still their spirit is not bent, and that they continually throw back his challenge, and will never yield their ground till the last green leaf has withered on their scant and flattened tops.

In the midst of all this mingling of the beautiful and the picturesque is the home of a very humble but very interesting mollusk, the Point Cypress snail, *Helix (Arionta) Dupetithouarsi*, Desh., Du-pet-i-thou-ar'-si, shown in Fig. 126. During the summer

months I have sought them under the old cypresses, and have found them quietly sleeping under old logs, behind

Fig. 126.

pieces of loose bark, among the twigs forming a wood-rat's nest, and in other out-of-the-way places. Many empty shells also I found, to my great regret, for each one had a hole in the side or near the apex, showing that the occupant's life had been violently taken. For this act of vandalism the blue-jays were evidently responsible, and even while I was collecting my few specimens, these saucy birds stormed and scolded in the trees, as if I, and not they, was the real robber. I verily fear that these reckless marauders will speedily rob Cypress Point of one of its chiefest attractions.

However, I took away quite a number of dormant specimens of the snail, as well as a good number of the best shells which the jays had dared to desecrate, and after a long summer's sleep I placed some of the former in a fernery, and sprinkled them with water. After a few hours they slowly pushed themselves out into the open world and became quite lively, for snails, and seemed to enjoy their state of captivity to a very reasonable degree. One of these captives sat for his picture one fine day, and you see the result in the engraving.

The shell is umbilicated and seven-whorled; the spire is low conical, and the outer lip but slightly thickened. The peristome is whitish, but the shell is dark chestnut, with a still darker band, which is edged with equal stripes of light yellow. The animal is slate-colored, and its surface is covered with numerous little elevations. The diameter of the shell is three-fourths of an inch, sometimes larger.

Helix (*Arionta*) *Mormonum*, Pfr., Mor-mo'-num. The shell of this species, as shown in Fig. 127, has a

Fig. 127.

flattened spire, a recurved lip, and a large umbilicus, and is marked by a dark band with whitish edges. Whorls six— flattened; aperture oblique; color from reddish brown to almost white.

This species inhabits the Sierra Nevada mountains, the first specimens having been found on Mormon island, in the American river; hence the name. They do not live in Utah, as one would at first suppose. The diameter of the shell is an inch or an inch and a quarter.

A shell has been sparingly found somewhat similar to the last, but whose whorls are ornamented with a spiral keel and numerous cross ribs. It was named *circumcarinata*, sir-cum-car-i-na'-ta, by Dr. Stearns, who considers it as only a variety of the last species, though it seems to have specific differences.

Helix (*Arionta*) *sequoicola*, Cooper, se-quoi'-co-la, meaning, "inhabiting the Sequoias, or redwoods." The shell of this species resembles the last figure in size and general form, but it has a more elevated spire. It is of a glossy chestnut color, and is marked by one dark and two light bands. The upper whorls have many microscopic granulations. It is found in the vicinity of the coast, near Santa Cruz.

Helix (*Aglaia*) *fidelis*, Gray, A-gla'-ya fi-de'-lis, Fig. 128.

Fig. 128.

This noble species is found in Northern California, Oregon and Washington, and it extends as far east as the Cascade mountains. The shells vary much in size and color, but the larger ones have a diameter of an inch and a half.

Whorls seven, umbilicus partly concealed by the reflected peristome, surface marked by fine lines of growth. The color is always dark beneath, but the spire is sometimes lighter and marked by rich bands of black and yellow or light brown.

To the south of the region occupied by this species, along the coast of California to the north of the Golden Gate, lives the variety *infumata*, Gould, formerly considered as a distinct species, but now regarded as only a variety of *fidelis*. It is quite flat, and the body whorl has a sharp, angular edge. The shell has a peculiar cloth-like surface, and is of a nearly black color throughout. The umbilicus is distinct, and the aperture is very oblique. The diameter of large specimens is an inch and a half.

Of a shape similar to the last, but smaller, lighter colored, and beaded within the aperture, is the rare *Helix Hillebrandi*, Newcomb, Hil-le-brand'-i. This is a Sierra species, and is found in the counties of Calaveras and Tuolumne.

Fig. 129.

Fig. 129 gives us a basal view of a shell found in Southern California, particularly around San Diego. The picture represents a small specimen, however, for large ones grow to a diameter of an inch and a half. Its name is *Glyptostoma Newberryanum*, W. G. Binney, Glyp-tos'-to-ma New-ber-ry-a'-num. The spire is flattened and the umbilicus is very large, distinctly showing the coil of rounded whorls. The lip of the aperture is thin and acute, the whorls six in number, and the color of the shell is nearly black.

Helix (*Pomatia*) *aspersa*, Müll., Po-ma'-shi-a as-per'-sa, is a European species which has been introduced into this country on a limited scale, as an article of food. I have specimens from San Jose, California, where a small colony of them have lived in a sheltered spot for many years.

The shell is large, sub-globose, and without an umbilicus. The whorls are four or five in number, the spire obtuse, and the aperture large. The shell is rather thin and its surface is marked by small

wrinkles and lines.   Color dark gray, with various
bands of chestnut, crossed by threads of yellow.
The diameter and height are about equal, an inch
or more. As is well known, these creatures are highly
esteemed in France and other countries of Europe by
lovers of good things. The time may come when
they will be abundantly raised in California for the
same purpose.

Gonostoma Yatesi, Cooper, Go-nos'-to-ma Yates'-i,
is a little species found in Calaveras county, California.   The shell is very peculiar from the fact that the
spire, instead of being elevated as in most shells, is
considerably depressed. The whorls are wound round
and round one another in a horizontal plane, and as
the shell-tube grows larger and larger it leaves a hollow both above and below. Whorls seven, aperture
crescent shaped, color yellowish brown, diameter one-
fourth of an inch.

Polygyrella polygyrella, Bland, Pol-y-gy-rel'-la, is
the singular name of a little snail, having a many-
whorled spire but slightly elevated, an aperture
guarded by a white tooth on the inner wall, and an
umbilicus large and open. A curious feature of this
shell is that one or more sets of little white teeth may
be seen inside the body-whorl through the transparent, horn-colored shell. Its diameter is less than half
an inch. It is found in Idaho, on the Cœur d'Alene
Mountains, especially in spruce forests.

Polygyra Harfordiana, Cooper, Pol-y-gy'-ra Har-
ford-i-a'-na, has an umbilicated, flattened shell of four
whorls, with an aperture guarded by three teeth, one
on the inner wall and two on the white, reflected peristome. The shell is horn-colored. It is found on
high elevations in Fresno county, California.

Triodopsis loricata, Gld., Tri-o-dop'-sis lor-i-ca'-ta.

The shell of this little creature is only a quarter of an inch in diameter, but it is a perfect five and a half whorled spiral, having an open umbilicus and a slightly raised spire. The aperture is irregular, with a white tooth on the columella and two white, thickened spots on the outer lip; the surface of the shell is light horn-colored. It is found near Oakland, California, and in other parts of the state.

An Oregonian species, which we will now consider and which may be easily recognized by its peculiar features, is named *Mesodon devius*, Gould, Mes'-o-don de'-vi-us. The shell is yellowish horn-colored, solid, and six-whorled; the umbilicus is partly covered, and the peristome is white, wide, and bent back at right angles to the walls of the aperture. There is a distinct white tooth on the inner wall of the aperture, and sometimes one or more waves on the peristome. There are several varieties which range in diameter from a half to a whole inch.

Mesodon Columbianus, Lea, Co-lum-bi-a'-nus. Fig. 130.

Fig. 130.

The shell of this little snail greatly resembles some varieties of the last species. Its spire is more acute, and the epidermis on the upper whorls is set with short, stiff, microscopic hairs, making the shell feel rough. Whorls six, umbilicus small, peristome wide, reflected, whitish, aperture ear-shaped. In some varieties, as shown in the cut, there is a small white tooth on the inner wall of the aperture. The shell is of a light horn-color, and its diameter is over half an inch. It is found chiefly in Oregon and Washington, but it extends into California, and even into Alaska. (10)

Microphysa Lansingi, Bland, Mi-cro-fy'-sa Lan'-sing-i, has a minute, flattened shell, consisting of five or six horn-colored, shining whorls, without an umbilicus. The aperture is long and narrow, the outer lip sharp and thin, and the diameter of the whole shell is less than one-eighth of an inch. It is found among damp leaves in the vicinity of Portland, Oregon.

Mycrophysa Ingersolli, Bland. The shell of this species is white, very thin, and almost transparent. The umbilicus is distinct, the spire greatly flattened, the whorls five and a half in number, the aperture crescent-shaped, and the outer lip thin. The greatest diameter of the shell is a quarter of an inch. It is found in eastern Oregon and in Colorado.

Vallonia pulchella, Müll., Val-lo'-ni-a pul-kel'-la. This is another little mollusk, whose shell consists of four rounded whorls, arranged in a flattened spiral form. The umbilicus is large and open, the aperture nearly circular, the peristome white, reflected, and forming a nearly complete circle. The shell is white, thin, and in our variety it is usually marked by cross ribs. Its diameter is barely an eighth of an inch. The species is very widely distributed, being found in northern countries all round the world. The specimen described was found in Logan cañon, Utah. It is found also in Nevada, Idaho and Arizona.

Helix (*Patula*) *striatella*, Anthony, Pat'-u-la stri-a-tel'-la. The specimens of this shell were collected near the same locality as those of the last, and its American range is also similar. It resembles the last in general shape, having four whorls, a large umbilicus, a circular aperture, and low cross ribs;

but it is horn-colored, has a thin and sharp lip, and is about three-sixteenths of an inch in diameter.

Patula Cronkheitei, Newcomb, is slightly larger than the last, but is very similar, and may be but a variety. From northern localities.

Helix (*Patula*) *solitaria*, Say, sol-i-ta'-ri-a. This species is essentially an eastern one, being particularly abundant near the Ohio river; nevertheless it is found in Idaho, Oregon, and Washington Territory. The specimens before me were collected at Walla Walla, Washington Territory. The shell is low conical, has five whorls, a large, circular umbilicus, and a sharp outer lip. It is of a yellowish brown color and the whorls are marked by two dark brown bands with a lighter stripe between them. Its diameter is three-fourths of an inch or more.

Helix (*Patula*) *asteriscus*, Morse, as-te-ris'-cus. This is a very small snail, being about one-sixteenth of an inch in diameter. Spire low, whorls four, umbilicus large, lip thin, whorls marked by many minute, sharp cross ridges; color brown. Widely distributed, the specimens studied having been collected among grass roots at Bolinas, Cal.

CHAPTER XX.

THE most abundant snail found between the Rocky and Sierra Nevada mountains bears the name *Helix* (*Patula*) *strigosa*, Gould, Pat′-u-la stri-go′-sa. It assumes very many forms, one of which is shown in Fig. 131. Another variety has a smooth surface, and in general form closely resem-

Fig. 131.

bles Fig. 127, on a previous page. The shell has a broad umbilicus, a nearly circular aperture, and a sharp lip. The whorls are five in number, and in most specimens the spire is low. The whorls of some varieties are crossed by distinct ribs, in others, as shown in Fig. 131, they are banded by raised, spiral ridges, while the shells of many specimens are almost smooth. The whorls of many of the shells are marked with two brown stripes, but some are quite destitute of this ornament. The average diameter of the shell is rather less than an inch, though some specimens are much smaller.

The fine set of specimens of this greatly varying species, belonging to the cabinet of Mills College, were mostly collected from different parts of Utah by Mr. Henry Hemphill, whose investigations upon this species have been of the greatest value to science, and for whose help in various ways I would express sincere thanks. I will not attempt to describe the numerous varieties, but will simply mention by name—*Cooperi*, *Haydeni*, *Newcombi*, *Hemphilli*, *Gabbiana*, *Wasatchensis*, *Oquirrhensis*, *Gouldi*, *Binneyi*, *albofasciata*, *castanea*, *Utahensis* and *multicostata*. In one of Mr. Hemphill's published letters he significantly remarks, "The field is very large, * * * and no doubt many more varieties of *strigosa* are just waiting for the catcher."

Helix (*Patula*) *Idahoensis*, Newc., I-da-ho-en'-sis, is shown in Fig. 132. Shell small, strong, white.

Fig. 132.

Spire elevated, consisting of five whorls, which are crossed by many blunt ribs. Umbilicus small, aperture nearly circular. The shell as a whole is nearly spherical in shape, its diameter being equal to its height, which is only half an inch. Even this species is now considered as an extreme variety of *strigosa*. As its name indicates, it is an inhabitant of Idaho, the one from which this figure was drawn coming from the Salmon River mountains.

Several species of the genus *Zonites*, Zo-ni'-tes, now follow in our train of study. They are all small, having spiral shells, usually with rounded whorls and an open umbilicus.

Zonites arboreus, Say, ar-bo'-re-us, has a spire of four or five whorls, so much flattened that the shell appears nearly like a circular disk. Shell smooth, amber-colored, very thin and almost transparent. Diameter somewhat over an eighth of an inch. This species which hides under leaves and among bushes, inhabits all North America. The specimen described was collected at Los Angeles. A variety, *Z. Breweri*,

Newc., with a somewhat thicker shell, comes from northern California.

Zonites viridulus, Menke, vi-rid'-u-lus, is similar in shape to the last, small, very thin and transparent, of a slightly greenish tinge; the animal is said to be bluish black. This species also is widely scattered, the specimens described coming from Seattle.

Zonites fulvus, Drap., ful'-vus. Shell small, thin, somewhat conical, without umbilicus; whorls five or six, narrow, suture distinct, aperture narrow and oblong, color light amber, diameter one-eighth of an inch. It is found in Europe, Asia and North America; the specimens described came from near Salt Lake.

Zonites conspectus, Bland, con-spek'-tus. Shell very small, with an umbilicus, and a moderately elevated spire of four whorls, which are marked by fine cross ribs. Horn-colored; diameter one-sixteenth of an inch. Found in Alaska, Oregon, California and Colorado. The specimens described were gathered near San Francisco.

For the further study of these minute species the best book to consult is the "Bulletin of the United States National Museum, No. 28." It is entitled, "A Manual of American Land Shells. By W. G. Binney." It is published at Washington, D. C., under the direction of the Smithsonian Institution.

Zonites Whitneyi, Newc., Whit'-ney-i. Shell thin, spire scarcely elevated, whorls four, the last one being much the largest, umbilicus small, aperture somewhat circular, diameter nearly one-fourth of an inch; from the Sierras, also from Emigrant cañon.

Zonites cellarius, Müller, sel-la'-ri-us. The shell of this little snail is thin, fragile, translucent, smooth, and of a greenish yellow color. The spire is but slightly elevated, the whorls five in number, and the umbilicus of moderate size. Diameter one-fourth of an inch. It is a European species, but has been widely distributed by commerce. Specimens were kindly sent me from Portland, Oregon, by Mr. Harry E. Dore.

Zonites milium, Morse, mil'-i-um, is an extremely small snail, not larger than the head of a pin. Whorls three, umbilicus large, shell conical, whitish, marked by cross striæ; lip sharp and thin. This minute shell is found throughout a large part of the United States. The specimens before me are from San Diego.

Do not be weary, kind reader, of the seeming repetition of characteristics, but rather rejoice in the almost endless variety of living things which the Creator has placed upon this earth, each one displaying some new peculiarity, and no one, doubtless, made in vain.

Macrocyclis Duranti, Newc., Mak-ro-si'-klis Durant'-i. Shell consisting of a small, flattened coil; whorls four, umbilicus large and open; color dull or greenish white, diameter one-fourth of an inch or less. This species is found in Lower California, on several islands, and also near the cities of San Francisco and Los Angeles.

Fig. 133 represents the shell of *Macrocyclis Voyana*, Newc., Voy-an'-a. It is similar in shape and color to that of the last, but is larger. Aperture flattened, notched near the suture; diameter about half an inch. This species inhabits the coast region of California.

Fig. 133.

Macrocyclis sportella, Gld., spor-tel'-la. Spire of five whorls, flattened, similar in general shape to the last species; lines of growth distinct, aperture somewhat oblong, with the lips bent near the suture. The color is yellowish green, and the diameter of the largest specimens is nearly an inch, though many are much smaller. The specimens described are from Freeport and Olympia, Wash. Terr.

Macrocyclis Vancouverensis, Lea, Van-cou-ver-en'-sis, Fig. 134. Spire flattened, umbilicus large, aperture nearly straight above, lip sometimes bent downward near the suture. Whorls five, quite

Fig. 134.

smooth and covered with a yellowish green epidermis. Interior of shell white, inner wall of the aperture covered with a thin, white callus. Diameter of shell about one inch, height half as much. It is found from Alaska to San Francisco, also in Idaho and Montana, where the shells are smaller than those on the coast. It is more common in Oregon and Washington Territory. The cut represents a sinistral specimen, but the ordinary form is dextral.

Macrocyclis Hemphilli, W. G. Binney, is probably a variety of the last species, smaller and with a narrower umbilicus. From the Oregon region.

Mr. Hemphill is of the opinion that all these examples of *Macrocyclis* are but varieties of only one species. The animals are snail-like, with long eye-stalks, and are said to be carnivorous.

Vitrina Pfeifferi, Newc., Vit-ri'-na Fi'-fer-i, Glass-snail. This little snail, which is found at high altitudes in California, Nevada, Utah and New Mexico, has a very thin, depressed shell, consisting of three whorls, of which the last is by far the largest. Aperture very large, oblique, rounded. Nearly transparent, greenish white, one-fourth of an inch in diameter.

Helicodiscus lineatus, Say, He-li-co-dis'-cus lin-e-a'-tus, has a minute, flattened shell, one-eighth of an inch in diameter, shaped like a depressed, circular disk. Whorls four, visible from below as well as from above. Within the outer whorl may be seen two or three pairs of white, conical teeth. The epidermis is greenish, and numerous fine lines cross the whorls. It lives in many places in the east, and is reported from Oakland, California.

There remain several mollusks which are either wholly destitute of a shell, or are only partially covered by one that is small or rudimentary. These animals are called slugs, in distinction from the snails, which bear well developed shells.

The first one on our list is named *Binneya notabilis*, Cooper, Bin'-ney-a no-tab'-i-lis. It is found on Santa Barbara Island, and also in Mexico. The body of this mollusk is whitish, with many dark blotches on its sides. The shell is about the size and shape of your little finger nail, spiral at one extremity, and open and flattened at the other. It is of a yellowish horn-color.

Hemphillia glandulosa, Bl. and Bin., Hemp-hill'-i-a glan-du-lo'-sa.

This curious little slug lives in Oregon and Washington. When extended it is about an inch long. On its back is a hump, and on the hump is a shell, brownish, flattened and scale-like, one-fifth the length of the animal. Its color is white, mottled with dark brown.

Prophysaon Hemphilli, Bl. and Bin., Pro-fy'-sa-on Hemp-hill'i.

Animal slug-like, large and thick in front, tapering behind. The body is of a smoky white color, marked with many dark lines, somewhat resembling the veins of a leaf. Under the mantle on the back is a small, thin, six-sided shell. A line separates the foot from the body. Its length is from an inch to two inches. The specimen before me is from Portland, Oregon, but it is also found down the coast into California.

Limax Hewstoni, Cooper, Li'-max Hews'-ton-i.

This slug is found in San Francisco, and a variety which is perhaps the same exists in Portland and other places. The body is two inches long or less, narrow and high, black above, paler on the sides, and whitish on the base of the foot. There is a minute internal plate on the back.

Limax montanus, Ingersoll, mon-ta'-nus, is a small, bluish gray slug, about an inch long, found in Colorado and Utah.

Ariolimax niger, Cooper, A-ri-o-li'-max ni'-jer.

The body is long and narrow, blunt in front, and tapering but little behind. When crawling, the animal is some two inches in length, but when at rest, as it may be found under old boards and in similar places, it is so contracted that it is hardly one inch long.

Its color is quite dark, sometimes being nearly black, especially on the upper surface of the body; but I have found specimens which were much lighter, almost an ashy gray. This species is common in Alameda county, California, and in the neighboring regions.

Ariolimax Hemphilli, W. G. B., is a very slender, flesh-colored slug, an inch or two long, found at Niles, Alameda county, and it probably lives in the surrounding region.

Finally, we have in Fig. 135, a representation of the huge yellowish green slug, so common in the woods and damp places along the whole coast of the Pacific states.

Fig. 135.

A short evening walk under the trees is almost sure to reveal one or more of these harmless but rather startling creatures, quietly moving over the ground, and leaving a glistening trail in lieu of footsteps. They frequently grow to the length of six or seven inches, and look as if they were exceedingly well fed.

As you would suppose, they are seen most in damp weather; for during the dry summers many of them descend into cracks or holes in the ground, though some linger in shady woods, particularly about springs and marshy places. The name of this great slug is *Ariolimax Columbianus*, Gould, Co-lum-bi-a'-nus; though there is another slug which scarcely differs externally from this one, but which is considered as a different species on account of a difference in some of its internal organs. The name of this second species, which is not so widely distributed as the first, is *Ariolimax Californicus*, Cooper.

For a careful discussion of these and other obscure points, and for directions concerning an examination of the viscera, I would again commend the student to the " Manual of American Land Shells."

CHAPTER XXI.

HOMES OF THE MOLLUSKS—GATHERING CLAMS—THE TYPI-
CAL SHELL—DESCRIPTION OF PARTS AND TERMS—THE
INTERNAL ORGANS—FOOD—THE FOOT AND ITS USES—
LAMELLIBRANCHS—THE WAY TO MEASURE A SHELL
—ANOMIA—THE OYSTER—HINNITES—THE PECTENS—
LIMA.

IN an early chapter I told of my morning visit
to Duxbury reef, and of the abundance of shells
which could be gathered on that stretch of rocks
when the tide was low. The first species, *Crysodo-
mus dirus*, we used as an illustration of the great
class of the Gasteropods, and from that beginning we
traced the creeping, one-shelled mollusks to their
various homes—upon the rocks which line the shore,
on the sea-weeds, in the streams which come down
from the hills, and the lakes which nestle among the
mountains, in the thickets, under the tall redwoods,
and upon the grass of the meadows—breathing the
salt water of the ocean by means of their gills,
rising to the surface of the stream or pond for a
breath of fresh air, or slowly creeping along the grass
and occasionally opening a simple lung to the blessed
influences of the atmosphere.

Ocean, stream, forest, and field each has its proper
molluscan inhabitants—hard-shelled, thin-shelled or
no-shelled—predaceous, carnivorous or herbivorous—
huge, medium-sized or minute—yet all having the

same general features of form and structure, and all carrying out their part in the great plan of creation.

When I was returning from the reef, I saw a man gathering clams. He had a hoe and a basket, and as he walked along the gravelly sands, every now and then he would be attracted by a jet of water which came shooting up from a little hole in the sand. A little digging at such a place would usually bring up a small, hard-shelled clam, such as are sold so freely in the San Francisco markets.

Later on in the day I found a good many other shells of similar species, and traced several of these mollusks to their homes in the different kinds of sand, mud, and clay; and when night sent me to the hotel, my genial hostess prepared me a most delicious chowder from the largest of all of the various clams. I will speak of each of these species in their proper order, but to illustrate the `subject, we will study a fine, large shell which naturally belongs a little farther on, among the Carpet shells.

Fig. 136 represents the inside of one of the shells of this mollusk, whose true name is *Tapes tenerrima*, Cpr., Ta'-pes te-ner'-ri-ma. I say one of the shells, for all mollusks of this class are protected by two shells, a right and left, which are joined together on the back by a hinge. Sometimes this hinge consists of little more than a straight line where the two valves or parts of the shell touch, and are bound together by a strong ligament, but usually there are several hinge-teeth on each valve, which fit into one another, and allow the shells to move in only one direction.

The teeth, which are grouped near the starting point of the shell are called *cardinal teeth*. You will notice three of them in the engraving, forming

a little triangle; the long, slender one to the left, is
the *lateral tooth*, and is marked *l. t.*   The point of
the shell, which is usually curved inward, is called
the beak, or *umbo* (plural *umbones*), and is marked
u, in the cut.   The two valves are drawn together
by two strong adductor muscles which run from one
to the other, and which are firmly grown to the shells.
The scars, showing where the muscles have been

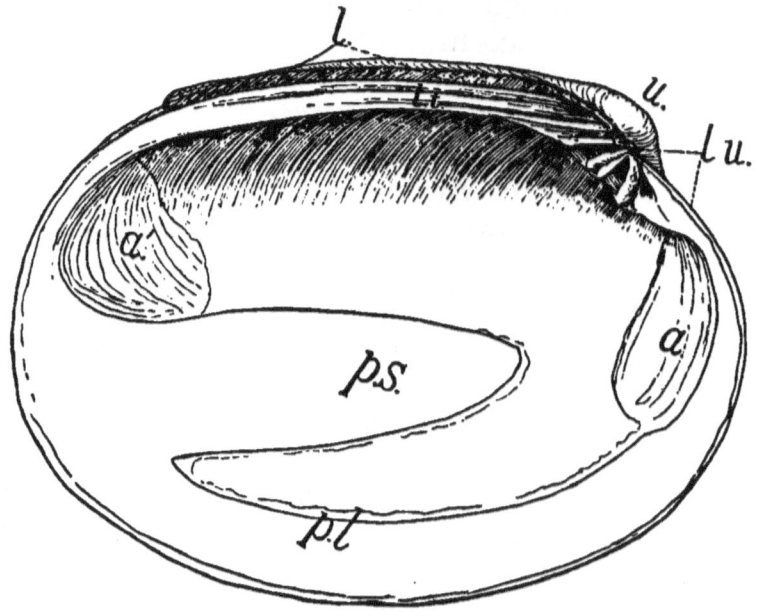

Fig. 136.

removed, are shown in the cut at *a* and *a'*, the former
being called the anterior and the latter the posterior
muscle-scar.

While these muscles can easily hold the two valves
together very firmly, there must be some provision
for opening them again.   Muscles would not answer,
for muscles can pull but cannot push; so a strong
spring is provided to act in opposition to the muscles.

This spring is called the ligament, and is composed of a dark, tough, elastic substance resembling india rubber.

In this species, the long ligament, *l*, is external. It becomes brittle when it is dried, but when the animal is alive it is strong and firm; besides acting as a spring to open the valves, it also helps to bind them firmly together.

In the living mollusk the valves are lined with a soft skin or mantle, called the *pallium*. This pallium secretes the substance of the shell, building on new matter at the edge and thickening its interior. It is firmly attached along a curved line which runs from one muscle scar to the other. In some species this *pallial line*, marked *p. l.*, makes a simple curve, but in others, as shown in the engraving, it bends back more or less deeply, making a bay or sinus, marked *p. s.*, which stands for *pallial sinus*.

Having thus briefly noticed the parts of the shell, let us now examine the structure and habits of its occupant.

Inside the mantle are the principal organs of the mollusk, which consist of the gills, liver, digestive and circulatory organs. There is no head, and the mouth is only a slit surrounded by four triangular lips, and opening directly into the gullet, which in turn leads directly to the stomach and the intestine. The heart is a simple sack-like organ; in the oyster it may easily be seen lying in a little opening just below the great central muscle. The liver is large, of a dark color, and is separated into granules. The gills are four in number, two on each side of the body, lying just beneath the mantle. They resemble thin, delicate ribbons, and are attached by their edges. They are crossed by very many tubes through which the blood circulates, and in which it is exposed to the dissolved oxygen which is contained in the water.

The gills have another function besides purifying the blood; they are the food gatherers. Since the animal has no head and no teeth it must depend for its food upon the supply which is brought to it by the surrounding water. Upon the surface of the gills are innumerable *cilia*, or microscopic hairs. These keep up a continual lashing and thus create a current. The fresh water flows into the space within the mantle, around the gills, and the old supply is constantly being driven out. This circulation accomplishes two important results; first, fresh oxygen is brought in for the blood, and carbonic acid is expelled; and secondly, hundreds of minute organisms which float in the water are caught upon the surfaces of the gills, where they are rolled into a kind of mucilaginous thread and passed on into the mouth. The food of these mollusks consists, therefore, of microscopic animals and vegetables, and is brought to them by the united action of all the little whips which cover the surface of the gills.

To give a proper direction to the currents of water, different means are employed. In those mollusks which live above the surface of the mud, as the oyster, the mantle lobes are divided, and the water currents pass freely through the open edges of the shells. But in the clams which burrow in the mud, the case is different. In these the mantle lobes are united, inclosing the animal in a bag. At the rear end of the shell the folds of the mantle are prolonged into a double tube, or two single ones, which the animal has power to protrude to a considerable length and then retract again into the space indicated by the pallial sinus.

Suppose the clam is quietly resting in his burrow, a foot below the surface of the mud; resting in peace —"as happy as a clam." At length he feels the need of communication with the outside world; so, up the small hole which reaches to the light he pushes his two tubes or siphons, and sets his whip-like pumps in action. These cilia are so arranged that they lash the water down one pipe, over the surface of the gills, and then, when both food and breath have been abstracted from it, and it has been loaded with any refuse matter that ought to be rejected, it is whipped up the other tube and mingles with the water above. With such a fine arrangement for living at ease, no wonder the proverb speaks of the happy condition of our mollusk!

After the tide has turned and the surface of the mud is left bare, our molluscan friend stops his pumps and reposes for a time. Should any footstep excite his fears, he suddenly withdraws his water-pipes, shuts the doors of his house with a bang, and out comes a jet of water from the hole in the mud, revealing the presence of life down in those dark regions.

If we are inclined to dig, we shall know just where to commence operations. But the mollusk can dig too, though his motions are usually quite slow. His spade is a muscular organ called the *foot*, which can be increased or diminished in size at the will of its owner. This foot can be projected through a slit in the mantle and extended down into the sand or mud, and then by a strong pull the shell is drawn in after it.

It is very interesting to put a clam into a jar of sea-water, with sand at the bottom, and see him instinctively try to bury his shell. Perhaps some of my little friends who live far from the coast may feel discouraged at this statement, but many of them can try the same experiment with a fresh-water mussel, which they can get from some pond or stream. In bivalve mollusks which live above the mud the foot is small or absent.

All ordinary bivalve mollusks take their name from the lamellar or plait-like form of the four gills or *branchiæ*, hence they are called *Lamellibranchs*, La-mel'-li-branks. The young are hatched from minute eggs, and usually spend their earliest days within the mantle of the parent. They are free swimming little creatures, and when breathed out into the surrounding water they sport around for a little time, become separated, and then settle down to dig a burrow, or attach themselves to some object above the mud. Their shells soon begin to grow, and they quickly take up the humdrum life of their ancestors.

The shell which I began to describe has a deep pallial sinus, as shown in the engraving, and this fact indicates that it lives a good way below the surface of the sand or mud, and that it has long siphons. The shells are rather flat and thin, and are marked externally by many fine lines radiating from the umbo, and these are crossed by small concentric ridges, which correspond to lines of growth. The cardinal hinge-teeth are near the anterior extremity of the shell, which is always opposite the pallial sinus; and the ligament is long and external.

The length of a pair of bivalve shells is the distance from one end to the other, parallel to the hinge line. The height is the distance from the hinge line to the opposite edge of the shell; and the breadth is measured at right angles to both, and is the distance from side to side, through the most bulged portion of the valves. Thus a round clam has much breadth, while a flattened one has but little. The thickness of the shell means the thickness of the solid material of each valve.

The length of this species is from three to five inches, its height is about three inches, its breadth an inch and a half, and the average thickness of the shell is one-eighth of an inch. The engraving represents the left valve, as you can see from the position of the *pallial sinus*.

Anomia lampe, Gray, A-no′mi-a lam′-pe, is a southern species, having a very thin and delicate shell, which is nearly circular in shape. It lies upon its side in the water, and the right or lower valve is much smaller than the left one, and is perforated. Through the hole runs a strong organ called the byssal plug, which attaches the mollusk firmly to some stone or the surface of another shell. The upper valve is arched, and is marked internally by

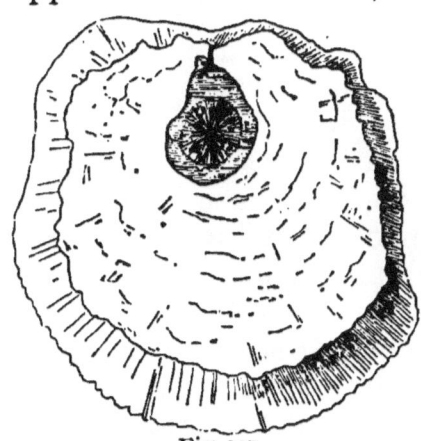

Fig. 137.

several muscle scars; color yellowish, shining; length, an inch or more. The Anomia somewhat resembles a small oyster, and in France it forms an article of food.

A more northern species, belonging to the same family, is named *Placuanomia macroschisma*, Desh., Plak-u-a-no′-mi-a mak-ro-shiz′-ma, and a view of the same is shown in Fig. 137. The form of the shell varies greatly, though its normal shape is circular. The lower valve is smaller than the upper, and as in the last species it is pierced for the strong plug which attaches the animal to a rock. Through this hole you can see the large muscle scar inside the upper valve, and can notice its curious, radiated structure.

The shells are pearly within, and are generally of a greenish tinge. The outside is marked by irregular radiating ridges. Sometimes this species grows to the size of a large oyster, but ordinary specimens are about two inches across. When the structure and the color of the pearl are once known, even a fragment of this shell can be readily recognized. This species is found along the whole coast, particularly at the north.

Ostrea lurida, Cpr., Os'-tre-a lu'-ri-da. This is the common native oyster of this coast, and is well known as distinct from the Eastern oyster, *Ostrea Virginiana*, Lister, which is brought here from Baltimore and other Atlantic ports. The young oysters, about an inch long, easily endure the seven or eight days of travel across the country, and when planted in our bays, they thrive and grow rapidly. In three or four years they are ready for the market. Although they spawn abundantly, but few of the young survive, probably on account of the coldness of the water; though occasionally a true, young Eastern oyster may be found attached to some old post, showing that at least a few of the eggs have developed properly.

The specimens of our native species, *O. lurida*, are small, with rather dark-colored shells, sometimes stained with purple. The greatest dimension of the shell is about two inches. The variety *expansa*, Cpr., is nearly circular, and is attached by the whole surface of one valve. The species is found from San Diego to Puget sound.

We come now to a notable species, *Hinnites gigantcus*, Gray, Hin'-ni-tes gi-gan'-te-us, Fig. 138. It is sometimes called the Rock Oyster, and sometimes the Winter Shell. In its early life it has a free, symmetrical shell, looking like a Pecten. Its shell is then distinguished by its very unequal ears and the

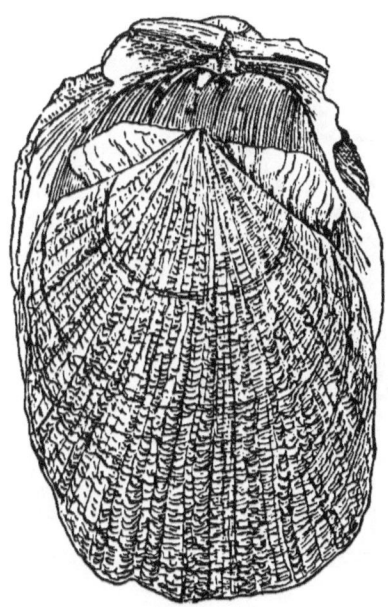

Fig. 138.

twelve prominent, serrated ribs on its upper valve. It soon settles down for life in some convenient and sheltered spot, such as the inside of an old Haliotis-shell, fastens its lower valve to this support, and yields itself up to circumstances.

It soon looses its regularity of form and becomes oyster-shaped, developing sometimes one valve and sometimes the other, as opportunity offers; twisting itself to the right or to the left, and becoming so distorted that it seems to have wholly forgotten its youthful grace. Its outside color varies from yellow to brown, while within it is pure white, except a rich purple area at the hinge-line. This purple color is very permanent, and may be seen even in the fragments of shells which are picked up along the beach. The ligament is internal, lodged in a deep, narrow pit; the muscle-scar is smooth and very large.

This species sometimes grows to the size of a large oyster, but some specimens are only three inches long. It is rarely cast up alive by storms, but dead shells are not uncommon. It is most abundant in northern waters.

Unlike the last species, the Pectens or Scallops remain free during their whole life, though they sometimes spin a *byssus*, or cable of threads, and attach

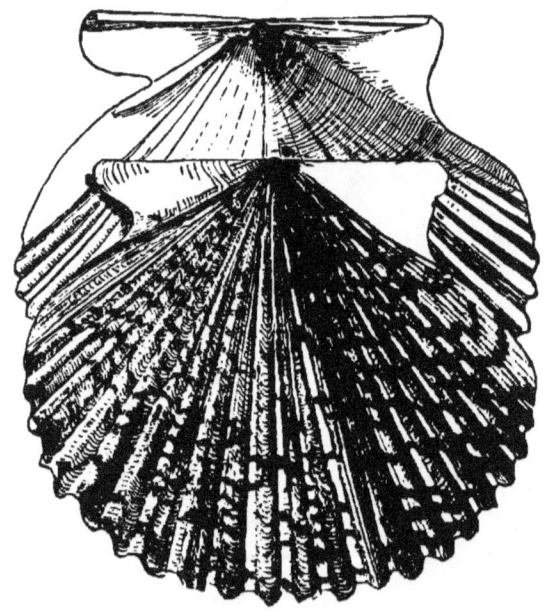

Fig. 139.

themselves to pieces of sea-weed. They swim by opening and shutting the valves of the shell, and they have small eyes along the edge of the mantle. The valves are connected, as in quite a group of similar species, by a single, large, central muscle, instead of by two, as in most of the bivalves.

The first species, *Pecten æquisulcatus*, Cpr., Pek'-ten e-qui-sul-ka'-tus, is a southern shell, and its beautiful form and markings are shown in Fig. 139.

It is quite robust, and its surface is marked by about twenty strong ribs, which are separated by deep and equal furrows. Whitish, more or less mottled and striped with reddish brown. Large specimens are three inches across.

Pecten latiauritas, Conr., lat-i-au-ri'-tas. The ribs of this shell are about twelve in number, plain and distinct. The ears, or flattened parts of the shell upon each side of the umbo, are broad, suggesting its specific name, which means broad-eared. You will notice that one of the ears of each Pecten is notched, allowing a little space for the finger-like foot to pass through without opening the shell. This foot spins a byssus of horny threads, and attaches them to some support, thus casting anchor when the animal wishes to remain fixed. The color of this southern shell is white and brown, and it is one inch in diameter.

Fig. 140 introduces us to another of the Comb-shells, *Pecten monotimeris*, Conr., mon-o-tim'-e-ris.

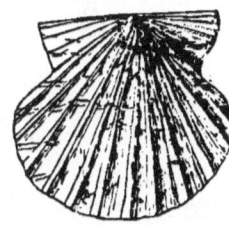

Fig. 140.

Shell very thin and delicate, ribs rounded and rather faint, ears unequal, color inclining to yellow or brown, but variously mottled with white, like the feathers of a speckled hen. Outline nearly circular; usually less than an inch in diameter.

Pecten hastatus, Sby., has-ta'-tus, Fig. 141. This exquisitely beautiful species is essentially a northern, deep-water inhabitant, though it is occasionally found quite far down the coast. The shell is thin, the ears very unequal, and the edges of the principal ribs are cut into many short and slender teeth. The valves differ from each other, both in sculpturing and in color, the lower one being nearly white, while the upper one is richly banded with concentric rings of red and pink. The choice specimen from which this

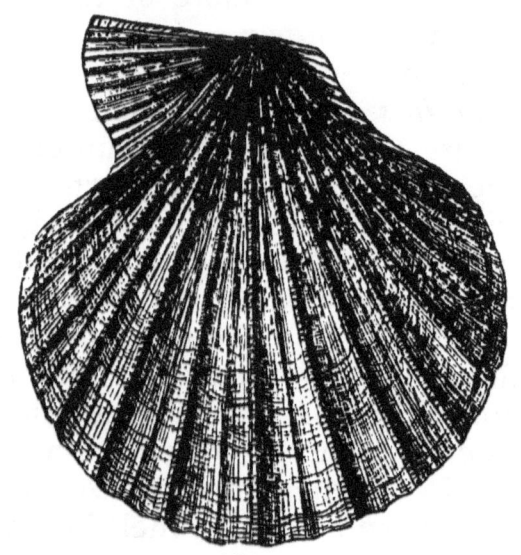

Fig. 141.

drawing was made, kindly sent from Oregon by Mr. Dore, is two and a half inches in diameter. *Pecten hericeus*, Gld., is a synonymous name.

Amusium caurinum, Gld., A-mu'-si-um cau-ri'-num, Northwest Weather-vane.

As the translation of this odd name indicates, this very large and broad shell comes from the vicinity of Puget Sound. It is a huge, flat Pecten, having unequal, circular valves, marked by twenty ribs. Edges thin, ears rather small, color white within, yellowish brown without. Diameter about six inches.

Lima orientalis, Ad., Li'-ma o-ri-en-ta'-lis, Fig. 142. Shell white, delicate, oblique, the valves gaping on one side. Sculpturing fine and straight, like the teeth of a file. It is sometimes thrown up by storms, and is found

Fig. 142. attached to sea-weed.

CHAPTER XXII.

THE family of the *Aviculidæ*, Av-i-cu'-li-dæ, which in the Gulf of California furnishes the large and beautful Pearl oyster, *Meleagrina margaritifera*, Linn., Mel-e-a-gri'-na mar-gar-i-tif'-e-ra, is poorly represented on our coast. In the vicinity of Santa Barbara there is a minute, white, oval shell, one-eighth of an inch in length, named *Bryophila setosa*, Cpr., Bry-of'-i-la se-to'-sa, which belongs to that family.

Among the Arks, which are so numerous and fine on the Atlantic coast, we also have but few.

We name first, *Barbatia gradata*, Sby., Bar-ba'-shi-a gra-da'-ta. Height much greater than its length, valves fully arched, somewhat angular, many ribbed. Breadth one-fourth of an inch or more, color, light brown; found under stones; southern.

Milneria minima, Dall, Mil-ner'-i-a min'-i-ma, resembles the last; but is smaller, curved, and marked with fewer ribs. Recurved at the base; often minute.

Axinea intermedia, Brod., Ax-in'-e-a in-ter-me'-di-a. Shell solid, white, tinged with brown, nearly circular. Inner edge finely crenulated. Pallial line entire; hinge area crescent-shaped and marked by

many small, transverse hinge-teeth.   Length about
half an inch.

The family of the mussels, or the *Mytilidæ*, My-
til'-i-de, comes next.   They have elongated, dark
colored shells, and most of them spin a byssus of
strong threads, by which they anchor themselves to a
place of safety.

A few of them are borers, as is the case with *Adula
stylina*, Cpr., Ad'-u-la sty-li'-na.   This species has a
small, peg-shaped shell, looking short and stunted.
Epidermis brown, shell half an inch to an inch long;
found in clay rocks.

Adula falcata, Gld., fal-ka'-ta, Pea-pod-shell,
Fig. 143.

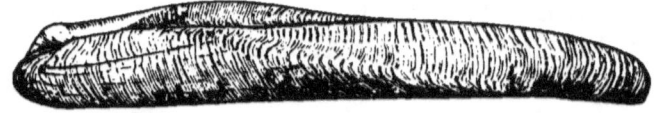

Fig. 143.

Among the difficult things to explain is the fact
that a mollusk, with a thin and flexible shell, can
bore a deep hole into hard rock.   That this is done,
however, can be proved by any one who will examine the work of this species.   The shell is long, narrow, and slightly curved.   The inside is white and
pearly, while the outside is covered with a dark chestnut epidermis, which has numerous transverse wrinkles.

I found the rocks of Duxbury Reef almost alive
with this and other borers.   The deep, narrow holes
are curved to fit the shell, and the animal also spins
a byssus, by which it attaches itself to the sides of
the burrow.   The length of the shell is two inches.

Lithophagus plumula, Hanley, Lith-of'-a-gus plu'-mu-la, has a small, cylindrical shell, rounded in front and tapering behind. It is a borer, as its name, the Rock-eater, would indicate; and it is found sometimes in rocks, and sometimes in old shells. It has a light brown epidermis, and is an inch or two in length.

Septifer bifurcatus, Rve., Sep'-ti-fer bi-fur-ca'-tus, Fig. 144. Its generic name means the Partition-bearer, and was given from the fact that a little shelly partition is stretched across a small part of the interior of each valve, near the umbo. The specific name, meaning two-forked, applies to the branching external ribs with which the surface of the valves is covered. The shell is strong, somewhat wedge-shaped, and is covered with a dark epidermis. The interior is white, pearly, and sometimes beautifully tinted with purple.

Fig. 144.

The great Horse-Mussel, *Modiola modiolus*, Mo-di'-o-la mo-di'-o-lus, is most abundant in northern waters. Shell somewhat cylindrical, very large and full; sometimes four inches in length and two in breadth. The epidermis is chestnut brown and is strongly bearded.

Fig. 145.

Modiola recta, Conrad, Straight Mussel, is shown in Fig. 145. The shell is long and narrow, thin and

delicate.   The epidermis near the hinge end is dark
brown and glossy; in front it is light brown, with
numerous chaffy hairs; internally the shell is white.
The length is three or four inches, four times its
breadth.   It is found from Puget Sound to San
Diego.

In many places along the coast the mussels are of
the kind shown in Fig. 146, named *Mytilus Californianus*, Conr., Cal-i-for-ni-a'-nus, California Mussel.

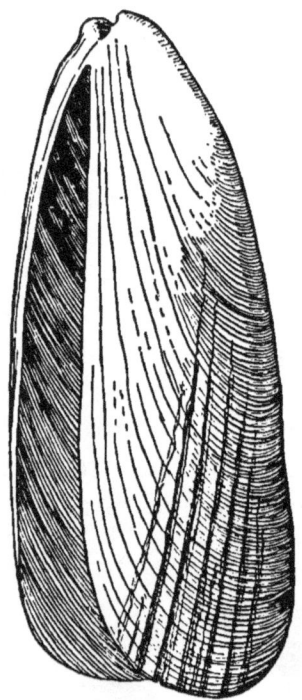

The shells of this species are
found covering the rocks over
which the breakers dash the
wildest. Moored by its strong
cable, it enjoys the rush of air
and water, and fears no danger.

This species can easily be distinguished from the last one by
its brown, glossy epidermis and
its conspicuous ribs. The shell
is purple, though its thicker portions are partly white. The
animal is orange-colored.

This shell is one of the first
on our coast that received attention in Europe. In 1789, Captain George Dixon published an
account of his voyage round the
world, and speaks of finding this

Fig. 146.   species on the northwest coast of
America, in the following words:

We saw, also, on this coast, a kind of muscle, in color
and shape much like the common eatable muscle of Europe,
but differed in being circularly wrinkled, and a great deal
larger. One valve I saw at Queen Charlotte's islands measured above nine inches and a half in length. With pieces of

these muscles, sharpened to an exquisite edge and point, the Indians head their harpoons and other instruments for fishing. They fasten them on with a kind of resinous substance.

In large and old specimens the wrinkles are seen only near the edge of the valves.

Modiola fornicata, Cpr., for-ni-ca'-ta, Arched Mussel, has a very short and full shell, somewhat wedge-shaped, having a breadth more than half of its length. The naked shell is white, but it is usually covered with a light-brown epidermis, especially near the edges. It seldom grows to a length of more than an inch. I have found it in Monterey bay, under stones, attached by a byssus.

Mytilus bifurcatus, Conr., Mit'-i-lus bi-fur-ka'-tus. The shell of this species is like that shown in Fig. 144, but it is without the internal shelf at the point of the valve. It is very wide for its length, and is somewhat curved.

Mytilus edulis, Linn., e-du'-lis. This is the purple mussel which is so abundant on the shores of the Atlantic. The shell is smooth and regular, and is covered with a dark, glossy epidermis. Within, it is of a rich purple color. It is found abundantly in San Francisco bay, as well as elsewhere, clinging in large groups to posts and wharves. Its length is seldom more than two inches.

So much for the marine mussels. Now we will turn to their relatives which live in fresh-water lakes and streams.

Of these there are but a few species west of the Rocky mountains, though to the east of that dividing ridge, in the great Mississippi valley, the species are numbered by the score and almost by the hundred. The great investigator of these mollusks was Isaac

Lea, a Philadelphia Quaker, who died near the close of the year 1886, aged ninety-four years. To this venerable man the students who live along the inland waters of our country will ever owe a debt of gratitude.

Of our few species, all of which have thin shells and slight hinge-teeth, if any, we will first study *Anodonta Californiensis*, Lea, An-o-don'-ta Cal-i-for-ni-en'-sis, Fig. 147. Shell very thin, of bluish pearl

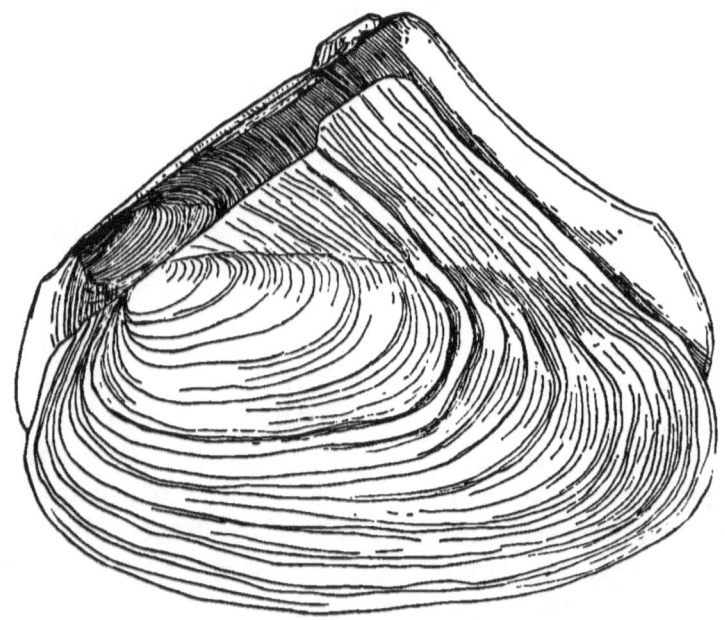

Fig. 147.

within, and covered with a greenish brown epidermis; almost transparent at the umbones. The hinge-line is prolonged obliquely upward, forming a nearly right triangle above the oval part of the shell. Its length is three inches. The specimen for the engraving was taken from the San Joaquin river.

Anodonta Oregonensis, Lea, Or-e-gon-en'-sis, has a shell oval in outline, rather thin, pearl-tinted, and covered with a dark or greenish epidermis. The oldest parts of the shell, which in this case are at the umbones, are often partially dissolved by the acids in the river-water, leaving the white shell exposed. There are no hinge-teeth. The hinge-line is nearly parallel to the base of the shell, quite different from the last species. The specimens described were gathered in the north, from the Columbia river, near The Dalles, and in the south, from the vicinity of Los Angeles.

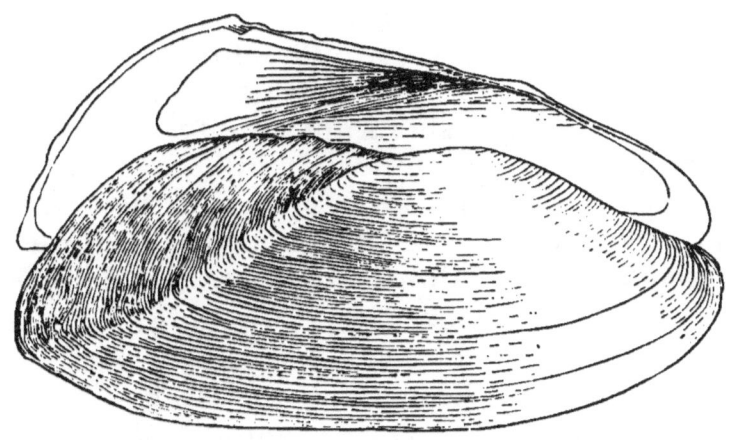

Fig. 148.

Anodonta Nuttalliana, Lea, is very similar to *Californiensis*, as is also *A. Wahlamatensis*, Lea. I consider them both as only varieties of that species.

Anodonta angulata, Lea, an-gu-la'-ta, Fig. 148, however, is distinct and has a well-marked form. It is much wider at one end than at the other, and is marked by a sharp angle running obliquely from the umbo to the corner of the shell. Epidermis dark brown; shell pearly within, somewhat flesh-colored. The length is three inches, which is twice the height.

Margaritana margaritifera, Linn., Mar-gar-i-ta′-na mar-gar-i-tif′-e-ra. This fresh-water mussel is widely distributed, being found in the eastern part of the United States, and also in Europe. The shape of its shell is oblong, somewhat bulged at the umbones. Firm and solid; hinge-teeth strong, triangular. Epidermis dark, internal color somewhat purple, length three inches. Found in the Chehalis river of Washington, and the Shasta river of Oregon.

Very much smaller than the fresh-water mussels are the following little creatures which live with them in the brooks and rivers. The first one is named *Pisidium compressum*, Prime, Pi-sid′-i-um com-pres′-sum. The bivalve shells are minute, somewhat triangular in shape, plump and full, covered with a brown epidermis. In form and size they resemble radish seeds. The length is one-eighth of an inch. Specimens from the Columbia river, near The Dalles.

Pisidium ultramontanum, Prime, ul-tra-mon-ta′-num. Still smaller than the last species. Shell thin, smooth, light brown. From Utah.

Pisidium abditum, Hald., ab′-di-tum, Fig. 149. Shell oval, thin, marked with minute lines of growth. Color light brown, length sometimes nearly one-fourth of an inch. This little species is quite widely distributed, and its name

Fig. 149.

has numerous synonyms. Its variety *occidentale*, Newcomb, ok-si-den-ta′-le, is found in a little stream running out of Mountain Lake, near San Francisco. This shell is usually about an eighth of an inch long.

A plump little river shell of pleasing outline is shown in Fig. 150, and is named *Sphærium sulcatum*, Lam., Sphe'-ri-um sul-ka'-tum. The brown epider-mis shows distinct lines of growth, and the shell is white internally. Its length is half an inch or less. From California, Oregon and Utah. These little mollusks are very active creatures, climbing about on aquatic plants with great ease.

Fig. 150.

Sphærium patellum, Gld., pa-tel'-lum. Shell very thin, resembling the last species but less robust, smoother, one-fourth of an inch in length. Speci-mens from Sonoma county, California.

Sphærium occidentale, Prime. Nearly circular in outline, shell quite smooth and firm, robust, same size as the last. Specimens from Weber Cañon, Utah.

Sphærium, dentatum, Hald., den-ta'-tum. Hatchet-shaped when viewed from the side, but bulged at the umbones and heart-shaped at the ends. Epidermis olive-green, glossy. One-fourth of an inch long. From the Chehalis river.

This completes our list of fresh-water bivalves, and we go back to the ocean side once more, to search among its sands and rocks for the mollusks which have thus far escaped our notice.

We will begin with one which scarcely differs in shape from our last picture, Fig. 150. It is called the Kelly-shell, *Kellia suborbicularis*, Mont., Kel'-li-a sub-or-bic-u-la'-ris. The Kellias are little bivalve mollusks which live in the ocean, where they hide themselves in the sheltered places among the rocks, or in other convenient retreats. This species has a minute shell, thin and light colored. It is a south-erner and hides among kelp roots.

(12)

Kellia Laperousii, Desh., Lap-er-ou'-si-i. Shell somewhat oblong in shape, thin, nearly smooth; when living it is covered with a shining, light brown epidermis. Ligament small, internal. This little nestler lives in sheltered places, like holes in the rocks; often in the deserted holes of the Piddocks or Rockborers. I once found a whole colony of them, of different ages, all living happily together within the valves of an old clam shell. Its length is half an inch or less.

Lasea rubra, Mont., Las'-e-a ru'-bra. This little mollusk, which has most of the habits of the last species, is covered by two oval valves, one-eighth of an inch in length. Reddish brown in color. It is a northern shell and is identical with the British species, of which we read that "it is viviparous, and lives as much out of the sea as in it."

Tellimya tumida, Cpr., Tel-lim'-i-a tu'-mi-da. Very minute, wedge-shaped, brownish white, northern.

A pure white shell, regularly marked with fine, concentric lines, is shown in Fig. 151. Its name is *Lucina Californica*, Conr., Lu-si'-na Cal-i-for'-ni-ca. In shape it is nearly circular, and it varies in size

Fig. 151.

from the diameter of a dime to that of a half-dollar. The cardinal hinge-teeth are small, while the lateral ones are strong. The ligament is external, and the *lunule* in this species belongs wholly to the right valve. The lunule is the little heart-shaped impression in front of and just under the beaks, In most species, when visible at all, it is divided equally between the two valves. The forward muscle scar is long and narrow, and the pallial line is entire.

The pure whiteness, symmetrical form and regular markings make this a very pleasing shell.

Lucina Nuttalli, Conr., Nut-tal'-li. The shell of this species is similar in shape to that of the last, but is more highly sculptured. The sharp, fine lines of growth are crossed by many delicate rays, making its surface look like fine basket-work. It is somewhat flattened and ridged along the hinge-line. Color white, length an inch or less; southern.

Diplodonta orbella, Gld., Di-plo-don'-ta or-bel'-la. The shell of this pretty species resembles *Lucina Californica* in size, color and surface, but the valves are greatly inflated; so much so that small specimens are nearly spherical, and resemble white marbles. It has a wide range from north to south.

Now for a neat little shell, not half an inch long, which may often be found in the sand, but live specimens of which may occasionally be discovered, fastened to the rocks in concealed places. A rather large picture of it is given in Fig. 152, and its large name is *Lazaria subquadrata*, Cpr., La-za'-ri-a sub-quad-ra'-ta. It is strong, full, and marked with fifteen rounded ribs, which seem to radiate from one corner of the nearly rectangular shell. Lunule cordate and conspicuous; liga-

Fig. 152. ment external, at the base of a broad depression. Cardinal teeth strong, three in number; pallial line entire; color brownish white, sometimes deeply stained inside with purple; edge slightly crenulated.

Crassatella marginata, Cpr., Cras-sa-tel'-la mar-gin-a'-ta. Shells minute, about the size of large pin-heads; somewhat triangular; yellowish, marked with chevrons of brown.

CHAPTER XXIII.

THE common Heart-shell or Cockle of this coast has a pleasant history. It was spoken of by Captain Dixon, in 1789, who found it at the mouth of Cook's river, in Alaska, along with mussels and other shells. He quaintly states that "half-a-dozen of them would have afforded a good supper for one person."

Its name is *Cardium corbis*, Mart., Car'-di-um cor'-bis. A beautiful end view of one of them, fully justifying the name "Heart-shell," is given in Fig.

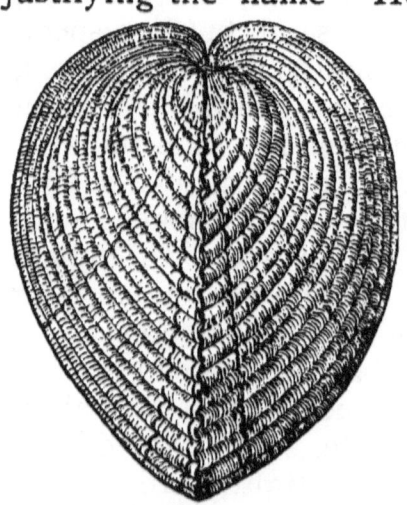

153. The shells are very full and round, the ribs about thirty in number, slightly scaly. Pallial line entire, edge of shells strongly toothed, color whitish or light brown. Portions of large, broken shells may frequently be picked up near the Cliff House in San Francisco. The diameter of ordinary specimens is two or three inches. *Liocardium elatum,* Sby.,

Fig. 153.

Li-o-car'-di-um e-la'-tum. As the last species was essentially a northern mollusk, so this one makes its home in the warmer waters of the south. It has a fine heart-shaped shell, yellowish white in color and covered with a delicate, light brown epidermis. It is nearly smooth, but is marked by about fifty small ribs, and the same number of interlocking teeth on the edge of the valves. Sometimes it grows to a great size, six inches or more in diameter. While one of these cockles would be enough for a meal, the shells would answer for bowls to contain the chowder.

Liocardium substriatum, Conr., sub-stri-a'-tum. This is a smooth little cockle, and like the last one

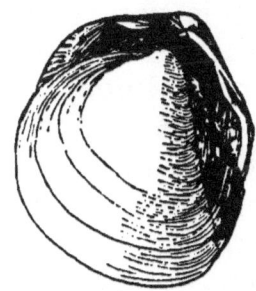

it lives in the south. Its shape is shown in Fig. 154, which gives an enlarged view, for the shell is not much more than half an inch in length. Its color is a light drab, spotted with yellow. With a glass, very fine lines of growth may be observed; from this circumstance it

Fig. 154.

takes its name, which may be freely translated, fine-lined. In shape and color it greatly resembles a sparrow's egg, and contrasts strongly with its neighbor, the giant *elatum*.

All of the Cardiums are beautiful in outline and regular in growth. They are free movers, having a strong foot, with which they can dig or jump.

Quite unlike them in all these respects is the next genus, one species of which is illustrated in Fig. 155.

The outer surface is gray or greenish, sometimes dashed with rosy red. It is very rough, being covered by many close frills, which are translucent, like chalcedony. The principal hinge-tooth is oblique and very strong, and the inside of the shell is lined with a white, opaque layer, beautifully crenulated at the edge. The general shape of the shell is circular, but it varies greatly in form, according to its surroundings. It is an inch or two in diameter.

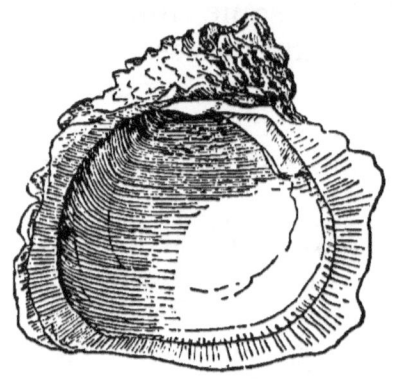

Fig. 155.

Its name is *Chama pellucida*, Sby., Ka'ma pel-lu'-si-da. It is always found firmly attached to a rock by its lower valve. So strong is the adhesion that you must break off a piece of the rock or you will sacrifice a part of your shell. It is very easy to overlook them, as they appear like ragged knobs on the rock, but when once you have collected a good specimen you will admire its peculiar beauty.

The name *Chama* is very old, having been mentioned by Pliny; the specific name, *pellucida*, beautifully refers to the pure and translucent appearance of the shell.

Chama exogyra, Conr., ex-o-gy'-ra. This is a southern species, similar in size and shape to the last, but having a coarser, more oblique shell. The chief difference, however, is seen in the curve of the umbones. If you stand a specimen of this species on its edge, with the beaks uppermost and curving towards you, the side which was attached to the rock will be towards your left hand. But if you place a specimen of *pellucida* in the same position, the rocky side will be towards your right hand.

Petricola carditoides, Conr., Pe-trik'-o-la car-di-toi'-des, as its name indicates, is a dweller in the rocks. Normally, the shell is oval, with regular sculpturing; but it has the habit of boring into a soft rock, or getting into a hole that was there before, and then growing to fit the premises. From this cause it happens that representatives of this species vary very much in their general appearance. Sometimes one is long and narrow, while its neighbor is shaped like a fat bean.

The ligament is external; the hinge-teeth and the sculpturing sometimes become nearly obsolete, and the shell becomes thick and rough. Its color is a dingy white, and it is from an inch to two inches in length. It is found in rocky places, all along the coast.

Rupellaria lamellifera, Conr., Ru-pel-la'-ri-a lam-el-lif'-e-ra, Fig. 156, is a near relative of the last

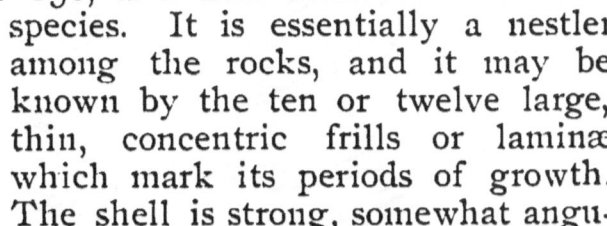

species. It is essentially a nestler among the rocks, and it may be known by the ten or twelve large, thin, concentric frills or laminæ which mark its periods of growth. The shell is strong, somewhat angular, white, and about an inch in length, though it sometimes grows larger. I have occasionally found live specimens at Monterey.

Fig. 156.

There are three species of *Saxidomi* which live in the sand and gravel along the seacoast, from British Columbia to Mexico. They resemble one another in form and habits. The beaks are placed far forward, and behind them is the large external ligament.

The first species is named *Saxidomus aratus*, Gld., Sax-i-do'-mus a-ra'-tus. The general shape of the shell is oval, and it is quite full and strong. The pallial sinus is very deep, and the shell is white, with some brown markings around the hinge-area. Radial lines are very faint, but lines of growth are fine, regular and strong. The hinge-teeth are very distinct, indicating a strong, powerful shell. Its length is from two to several inches.

Fig. 157.

Saxidomus Nuttallii, Conr., Nut-tall'-i-i, Fig. 157. The shell of this species is strong and heavy, and is marked by numerous rough, irregular, concentric ridges. The interior of the shell is white, and the thickened portion below the huge external ligament is translucent like agate. The pallial sinus is very deep, and the posterior end of the shell is slightly gaping. Color brownish white, length four inches or less. The engraving shows a reduced figure of one of these fine shells.

Saxidomus squalidus, Desh., squal'-i-dus, is considered by some as a variety of the last species. It is found off the coast of Oregon, and is sold in the markets of Portland. It is smaller than *Nuttallii*, and has a smoother shell; in other respects it is very similar. Length nearly three inches, height two inches, and breadth an inch and a half.

Tapes staminea, Conr., Ta'-pes sta-min'e-a, Fig. 158, Carpet Shell. In the markets of San Francisco may be found excellent specimens of this species, where it is sold as the "Hard-shelled Clam." Tomales bay furnishes a good part of the supply, though it abounds all along the coast. There are numerous varieties, some of which are white, while the shells of others are very prettily marked with reddish brown chevrons.

The valves of the shell are rounded, full, strong, and marked by numerous narrow, radiating ribs, which are crossed and cut by successive lines of growth. Hinge-teeth strong, ligament external, pallial sinus reaching to the middle of the shell. These mollusks burrow in stony places, and as you go along the beach at low tide, there comes up a jet of water here and there, showing that the

Fig. 158.

frisky mollusk is shutting up his door, and is waiting for the returning tide. The length of these shells varies from an inch to nearly three inches.

The variety *ruderata*, Desh., ru-de-ra'-ta, is marked by occasional concentric frills, somewhat like a Rupellaria; but it may be distinguished from that shell by the presence of radiating ribs, which its neighbor never possesses.

Tapes lacineata, Cpr., la-sin-e-a'-ta, resembles *staminea*, and perhaps is only a southern variety of that species; but its surface is covered with beautiful net-like sculpturing, quite different from the ordinary form.

The next shell on our list is *Tapes tenerrima*, Cpr., but that species has already been described in the opening chapter on the Lamellibranchs, so I will simply refer you to Fig. 136, and the accompanying description.

Psephis tantilla, Gould, Se'-fis tan-til'-la. The length of this little shell is only about one-eight of an inch, but it has some quite distinctive marks by which it may be identified. Its shape is somewhat triangular, its surface very smooth and bright, its color white or brownish, with an internal purple spot near one end. It reaches Puget sound on the north, and is probably found along the whole western coast of the United States.

Chione simillima, Sby., Ki-o'-ne si-mil'-li-ma, is a species found on the southern coast. The valves of the shell are very thick and strong, and are finely sculptured in both directions. The radial lines are rounded, while the concentric ones are sharp and thin. At the end of the shell is a conspicuous cordate lunule; on the top is a broad depression, and at the base of this is the external ligament. The cardinal hinge-teeth are three in number, the pallial line almost entire, showing that it is not a deep burrower.

The color is brownish white, deeply stained inside with purple; length two inches or less.

Chione succincta, Val., suk-sink'-ta, is a similar 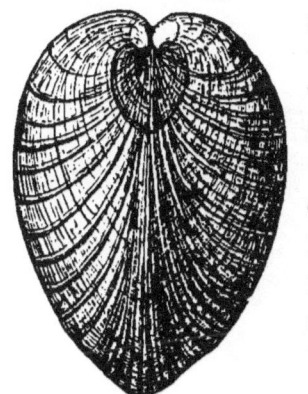 species. In Fig. 159 we have a view of the distinct, cordate lunule which is so conspicuous a mark of this shell.

In general form and size it resembles the last species, but is marked by less frequent concentric ridges. The shell is white, strong, and heavy.

Chione fluctifraga, Sby., fluctif'-ra-ga. Shell very strong and heavy, valves nearly circular when

Fig. 159.

young, and sculptured into a network. When older, the shell becomes somewhat triangular and the latter part is prolonged.

There is no distinct lunule as in the other species; the ribs and lines are rounded, and the edges are marked with fine crenulations. Externally the shell is dingy, but it is pure white within, with purple spots at or near the muscle scars. The shell is an inch or two in length; southern.

Fig. 160 represents one of the most graceful of our bivalve shells. Its name is *Amiantis callosa*, Conr., Am-i-an'-tis cal-lo'-sa. It is a pure white shell, full in the center and quite thin at the edges. Its sculpturing consists of many rounded, concentric lines, equal in size to the intervening grooves. There are no radial markings whatever. The lunule is small, set beneath the prominent umbones.

The ligament is external, the pallial sinus moderate, while the hinge has complicated cardinal teeth

and strong lateral ones. The common length of the
shell is two or three inches, but sometimes it is much
more. It is found on the southern coast.

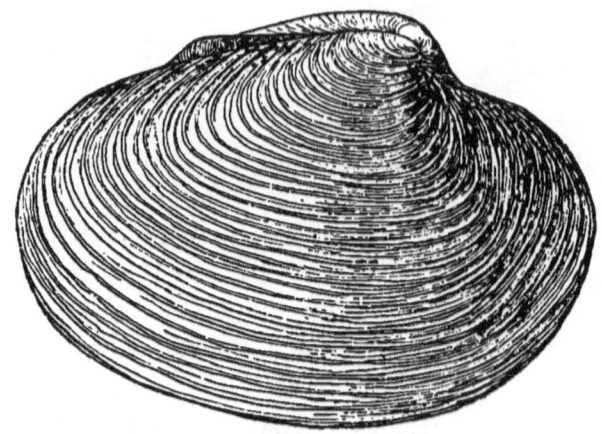

Fig. 160.

Standella nasuta, Conr., na-su'-ta. Very similar
to the next species, of which it is perhaps only a variety; shell somewhat depressed behind the beaks.
An inch or more in length.

Standella planulata, Conr., plan-u-la'-ta, is shown
in Fig. 161.

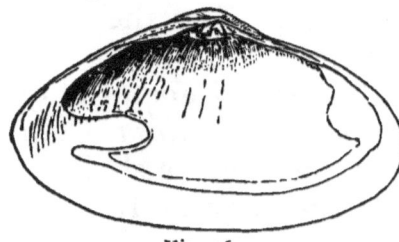

Fig. 161.

Its shape is much like
that of the last, but it is
only half as long. The
beaks are nearly equidis-
tant from the ends of the
shell, and the triangular
hinge-tooth is in front of
the ligament. Its color is white; found in southern
waters.

Standella falcata, Gld., fal-ka'-ta. Shaped like
Fig. 161, but smaller and flatter. Glossy; less than
an inch long; northern.

Pachydesma crassatelloides, Conr., Pak-i-dez'-ma cras-sa-tel-loi'-des, is the big, hard name which applies to the big, hard shell, a small picture of which is shown in Fig. 162. The pair of valves from which the figure was drawn are five and a half inches in length and weigh over a pound. They are very thick and solid, even to their edges, which are smooth and finely rounded.

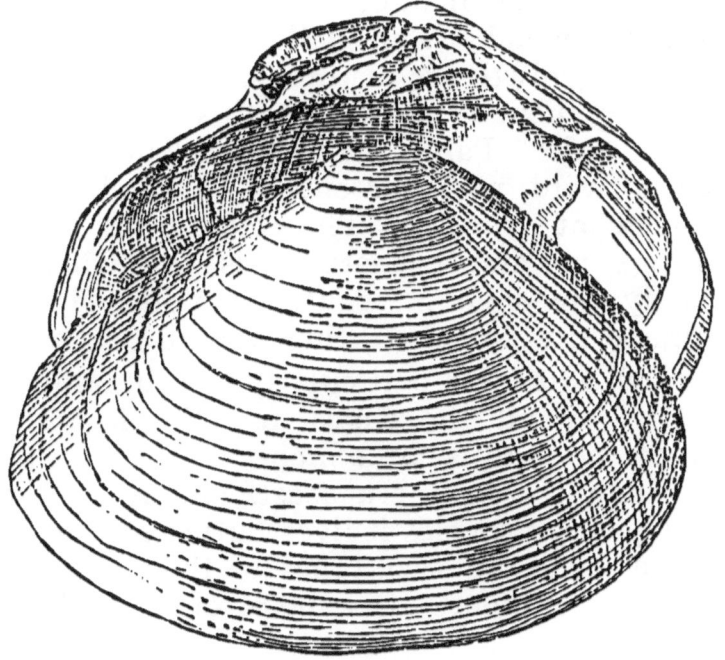

Fig. 162.

The hinge-teeth are very strong, the heavy and bulged ligament is external, and the pallial sinus is small. Externally the shell is smooth, yellowish-white in color, sometimes marked with purple rays, and it is partly covered with a glossy epidermis. The inside is pure white, with purple muscle scars.

Standella Californica, Conr., Stan-del'-la Cal-i-for'-ni-ca.   Shell somewhat oval, hollowed in front of the beaks; edges thin, surface smooth, white, covered with a thin epidermis somewhat roughened at the posterior end.   Ligament internal, lodged in a small triangular pit; pallial sinus small, U-shaped; beaks narrow and distinct, length about three inches.

Semele decisa, Conr., Sem'-e-le de-ci'-sa, has a shell nearly circular in outline, with a short straight portion at one end.   The shell is somewhat flattened, the lines of growth are distinct and somewhat rough, and the ligament is internal, with small hinge-teeth on either side.   Pallial sinus large and oval, beaks turned forward, posterior end of the shell truncated and somewhat wrinkled.   The epidermis is brownish, when present, and beneath it is the white shell. Internally the shell is beautifully polished, looking like fine white porcelain, tinged with rose or violet.

The rich tinting is particularly seen in large shells, especially around the edges and the hinge.   The length of the shell is three inches or less.   It is to be found along the southern coast, and like all of the following dozen species it lives buried in the sand or mud, and sends up two tubes to the water for purposes of respiration.   It is one of our most beautiful shells.

Semele rupium, Sby., ru'-pi-um.   Smaller, less wrinkled; white, with a pink hinge area.   Its length is an inch or more.   From Santa Catalina Island.

Semele pulchra, Sby., pul'-kra.   About half an inch in length, flat, oval; marked with closely crowded concentric ridges, with radiating lines at one end.   Yellowish white; southern.

Heterodonax bimaculatus, D'Orb., Het-e-ro-do'-nax bi-mak-u-la'-tus. Shell oval, rather flat, marked with fine concentric lines. Ligament external, hinge-teeth small and central, pallial sinus half the length of the shell. Color white or purple, length less than an inch, southern.

The rather large, thin, glossy shell shown in Fig. 163 bears the name *Macoma secta*, Conr., Ma-ko'-ma

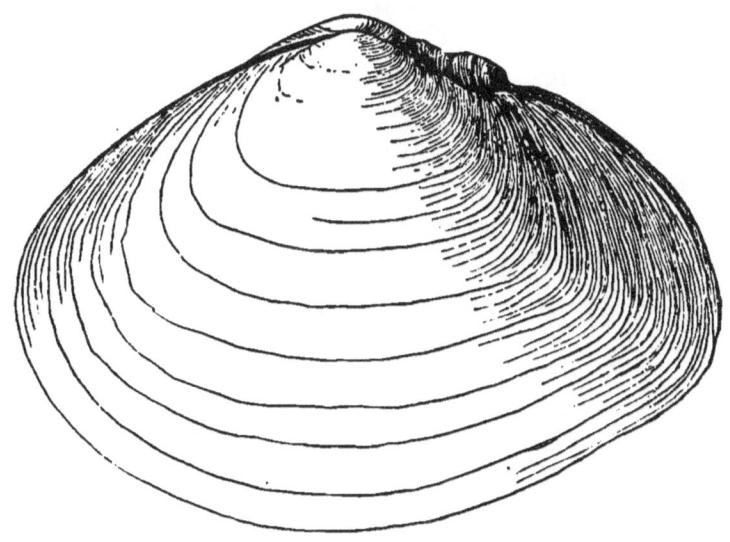

Fig. 163.

sek'-ta. The general form of the shell is oval, but the posterior end is suddenly contracted. The pallial sinus, as in all of the group, is large, indicating that the animal is a good digger, and the ligament is strong, broad and external. A thin epidermis is frequently found round the edges. The length of this shell is two or three inches, and it is found from Monterey southward.

The little southern Wedge-shell is shown in Fig.
164.   Its name is *Donax Californicus*, Conr., Do'-nax

Cal-i-for'-ni-cus. It is short and stumpy,
cut nearly square off at one end and
tapering to a rounded edge at the other.

Fig. 164.   It varies much in color, sometimes being
nearly white, while other specimens are striped with
bright tints.   Its surface is smooth, though marked
with narrow radiations.   The edge is finely crenulated.   Its length is an inch or less.

Donax flexuosus, Gld., flex-u-o'-sus, likewise a
southern species, resembles the foregoing, but the
rear part of the shell is not cut off so obtusely. Shell
white, usually covered with a light brown epidermis.
There are dark colored spots on the interior.

Cardium quadriginarium, Conr., is a rare southern
species, resembling Fig. 153, but having about forty
delicate ribs.   It sometimes grows to a great size.

CHAPTER XXIV.

INDIAN SHELL-MOUNDS — MACOMA — ANGULUS — THE TEL-
LENS — SANGUINOLARIA — MY ADVENTURE WITH THE
SAND-CLAM — HABITS AND BEAUTY OF THE MOLLUSK —
THE FLAT RAZOR — OTHER SOLENS — ENTODESMA — PER-
IPLOMA.

AT various points around San Francisco bay are great heaps of rubbish which mark the site of old Indian camping-grounds. They are always situated close to some spring, or are near some stream of water, the presence of which is now generally indicated by a growth of willows. They are of various shapes and sizes, and often cover as much ground as would suffice for a large garden.

A big conical one, situated in the western part of Oakland, is well known to picnickers, as it forms a part of "Shell Mound Park." There is a large and gently sloping mound near High street, in the City of Alameda. In this one I have dug for relics, without remarkable success, though odd stone implements have occasionally been found there.

These mounds are largely made up of old shells, ashes and charcoal dust. This shows that the Indians had their fires there, and that they threw away the rubbish which was left from their meals, and then returned to repeat the operation on the slowly rising pile. In my digging I came upon lumps of half-burned clay, which had probably served as a hearth; under these would be a layer of shells, ashes and bones, and then another hard beaten hearth. The great extent and depth of these mounds indicate either that there was a great rush of visitors to these primitive watering-places, or else that they were used as camping-grounds for many centuries. Perhaps both suppositions are correct.

It is interesting to examine the shells of these old heaps, and thus see what species formerly abounded on the adjacent mud-flats. I have found various kinds of shells, but by far the most abundant ones are those of the species named *Macoma nasuta*, Conr., Ma-co'-ma na-su'-ta, shown in Fig. 165. Although so abundant then, this species seems now to be dying out, and its place is being rapidly occupied by the

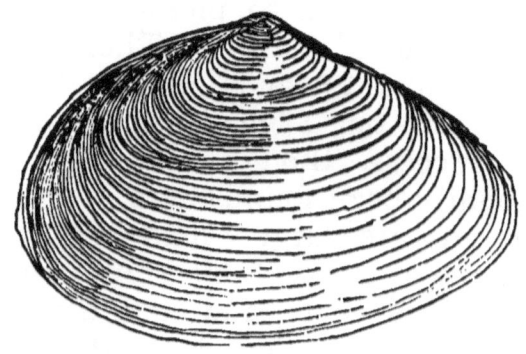

Fig. 165.

introduced Rhode Island clam, of which I will presently speak, but not a specimen of that shell is found in the mounds.

Macoma nasuta is a common species on the coast, extending from Kamtchatka to Mexico. It inhabits muddy flats, burying quite deeply, and reaching the water by two small, red siphons. The shell is smooth, flat and thin; rounded in front, but narrowed and bent to one side behind. The hinge-teeth are small, the ligament external, and in one valve the pallial sinus reaches to the forward muscle scar. Its color is white, and its common length is two inches.

Macoma inquinata, Cpr., in-qui-na'-ta, a northern species, resembles a small specimen of the last. In this, however, the pallial sinus does not touch the forward muscle scar in either valve. Shell white, an inch and a half in length.

Macoma inconspicua, Brod. and Sby., in-con-spik'-u-a; Fig. 166. This little mollusk has a thin, flat, pink or white shell, about half an inch in length. It is found from Monterey to Puget sound. Dead specimens are frequently washed up near the Cliff House, in San Francisco.

Fig. 166.

Macoma indentata, Cpr., in-den-ta'-ta, resembles a small specimen of *M. secta*, but the lowest edge of the shell, near the rear end, is indented and beaked. Thin, white, glossy, southern.

We now have a group of little shells to examine, which belong to the same great family as many of those we have been studying, namely the *Tellinidæ*, or Tellens. The first one is shown in Fig. 167, and its name is *Angulus modestus*, Cpr., mo-des'-tus; and in fact it is a modest little thing, with a shell thin, white and glossy, and marked with fine concentric lines. The ligament is external, the pallial sinus very deep, and there is an internal ridge near the forward muscle scar. It is a northern shell, about three-fourths of an inch long.

Fig. 167.

Angulus obtusus, Cpr., ob-tu'-sus, resembles the last species, but has more obtuse beaks. By this is meant that the ligament continues in a nearly straight line with the upper edge of the shell, while in *modestus*, as shown in Fig. 167, it slants sharply downward. The shell is white, about an inch in length.

Angulus Gouldii, Hanley, Gould'-i-i, is small, oval, inflated, a little angled at the beaks and slightly bent at the posterior end. About half an inch long; southern.

Angulus variegatus, Cpr., va-ri-e-ga-tus. Similar in shape to Fig. 167, but smaller. Pink and white, glossy, flat and narrow, hardly half an inch long.

Œdalia sub-diaphana, Cpr., E-da'-li-a sub-di-af'-a-na. This species has a thin, white, glistening shell, which appears quite swolen. The hinge-teeth are central, and the short ligament is situated almost between the prominent beaks. Length half an inch; southern.

Fig. 168 gives us a good idea of the shape of our next shell, *Cumingia Californica*, Conr., Cum-in'-gi-a

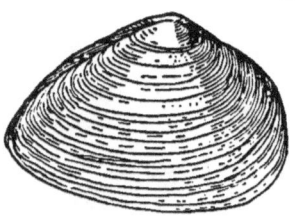
Fig. 168.

Cal-i-for'-ni-ca. It is somewhat triangular in outline, with the front end rounded, and the rear end narrower and slightly twisted. The lines of growth are very distinct, forming concentric ridges. The shape of the shell varies considerably in different specimens. Pallial sinus large, color white, length about an inch. It is occasionally found in Monterey bay, but is more common to the southward.

A very pretty little shell sometimes found at Monterey and sometimes far to the north, is named *Mœra salmonca*, Cpr., Me'-ra sal-mo'-ne-a. It is nearly rectangular in outline, the beaks being near one corner, and the external ligament at one end. The surface is very smooth and glossy, but showing distinct lines of growth. It is nearly white on the outside, but within it is beautifully salmon-tinted. Its length is half an inch or less.

Lutricola alta, Conr., Lu-trik'-o-la al'-ta. Shell round oval, wrinkled at one end, marked with fine and distinct lines of growth. Hinge-teeth central, ligament external, depressed, behind the umbones. Pallial sinus large, color white, but yellowish inside between the muscle scars. Southern; length two inches.

The Bodega Tellen, *Tellina Bodegensis*, Hinds, Tel-li'-na Bo-de-gen'-sis, shown in Fig. 169, has a very pretty shell, smooth, thick and heavy, and about two inches in length. The surface is polished, of a

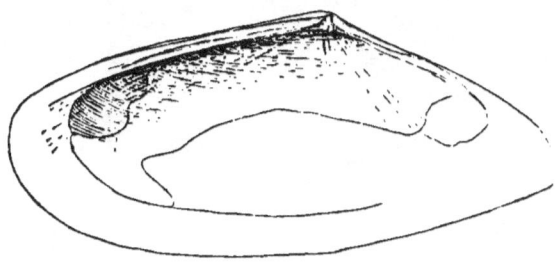

Fig. 169.

creamy-white color, and is marked with fine concentric lines. The posterior end of the shell is narrow and somewhat bent to one side. The ligament is external, the hinge teeth very small, and the pallial sinus very long and narrow. Old specimens show a marked tendency to thicken the shell from the inside. It is found at points along the whole coast, but chiefly to the northward.

Sanguinolaria Nuttalli, Conr., San-guin-o-la'-ri-a Nut-tall'-i. Shell thin, oval, flat on the right side, but bulged on the left. Ligament large and external, hinge-teeth small, sinus very large and acute. The color of this beautiful shell is white and lilac, somewhat rayed, but the coloring is partly concealed by a brown epidermis. It is a southern shell, two inches or more in length.

While returning one morning from a ramble over the rocks which had been left bare by the fall of the

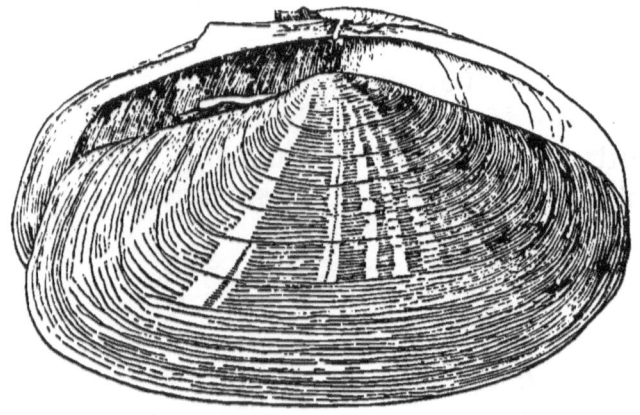

Fig 170.

tide, I was much surprised to see what seemed to be two white worms moving about in a little hollow between two mossy rocks, which was filled with sand and water. They were round and long, and about the size of a lead pencil. As soon as I disturbed them a little, they quickly disappeared beneath the surface of the wet sand. Suspecting what these singular creatures might belong to, I at once began to dig, and soon came upon a fine sand-clam, with a shell like that shown in Fig. 170. I was exceedingly glad to make the acquaintance of a real, live

Psammobia rubro-radiata, Nutt., for so I had learned to call him. I think his long name should be pronounced Sam-mo'-bi-a ru-bro-ra-di'-a-ta, and it means that he lives in the sand and has red rays on his shell.

Well, when I came to him down in his bed of sand, the two white tubes had vanished, and there was nothing visible except an oval shell, the valves of which were some three inches long. They showed distinct lines of growth, and were covered round the edges with a thin, brown epidermis. The color of the shell was white, with rays of red shooting down from the umbo, looking when I turned the shell over like the red rays of the setting sun. Besides a huge external ligament, there was nothing else to observe in my friend's outward appearance.

But I wanted to see more of him, so I took a large jar, filled it half full of beach sand, added as much sea-water as it would hold, and plunged my prize into the same. He rested quietly for a few minutes, and then began to open his shell and cautiously put out his two siphons. Soon afterward, from between the edges of his shells came his big, white, spade-shaped foot. He drove it down into the sand, curved it a little to one side, gave a vigorous pull, and, lo! his shell followed, though just why I could not clearly understand. Though the jar was large, he reached the bottom before his shell was wholly covered with sand, and had to content himself with a half-above-ground tenement.

Next morning his siphons were stretched out some six inches in length, and explained the appearance which led to his capture. I never thought before that there was any particular beauty to the siphons of a clam, but for this red-lined one my opinions quickly changed.

Imagine two tubes made of the finest pink and white silk, stretched over delicate hoops arranged at regular intervals; then think of them as endowed with life and waving with a graceful motion through the water, and you will have a faint idea of their exquisite texture and elegant appearance.

I kept my mollusk as long as possible in the jar of water, and then, not bearing to part with him, I quickly deprived him of life and took his shell home to my cabinet. It now lies open before me. Within it is of the purest white, resembling delicate porcelain. The pallial sinus is large, the hinge-teeth small, and behind them is a thickened portion of shell about half an inch long, which terminates quite abruptly, exposing part of the ligament.

According to Doctor Carpenter this species has been collected both in Puget sound and at San Diego. It completes our list of the *Tellinidæ*, which began with *Semele decisa*, and it is a worthy ending for our representatives of this beautiful order of the Plaited-gilled mollusks.

Once more I will quote from Captain Geo. Dixon's "Voyage Round the World," published in London, in 1789:

At the mouth of Cook's River, Lat. 59° 61', are many species of shell-fish, most of them, I presume, nondescript. * * * For a repast our men preferred a large species of the *Solen* genus, which they got in quantity, and were easily discovered by their spouting up the water as the men walked over the sands where they inhabited. As I suppose it to be a new kind, I have given a figure of it in the annexed plate. 'Tis a thin, brittle shell, smooth within and without; one valve is furnished with two front and two lateral teeth; the other has one front and one side-tooth, which slips in between the others in the opposite valve. From the teeth in each valve proceeds a strong rib, which extends to above half way across the shell, and gradually looses itself toward the edge, which is smooth and sharp. The color of the outside is white, circularly, but faintly, zoned with violet, and is covered with a smooth, yellowish-brown epidermis, which appears darkest where the zones are; the inside is white, slighly zoned, and tinted with violet and pink. The animal, as in all species of this genus, protrudes beyond the ends of the shell very much, and is exceeding good food.

The foregoing is declared by Doctor Carpenter to be "probably the first description on record of mollusks from the Pacific shores of N. America, by the original collector."

I will not add to it except to say that the species is now known as *Machæra patula*, Dixon, Ma-ke'-ra pat'-u-la, Flat Razor-shell. A picture of a small

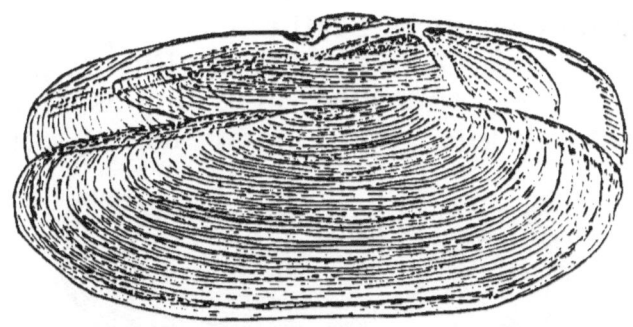

Fig. 171.

specimen is given in Fig. 171. Sometimes it grows nearly six inches in length. It is more common to the north, but it is also found on the coast of southern California.

Somewhat similar to this is the Short Razor-shell, *Solecurtus Californianus*, Conr., So-le-cur'-tus Cal-i-for-ni-a'-nus, shown in Fig. 172. The epidermis of this shell is not so glossy as that of the last, and the hinge is more nearly in the middle of the shell. The

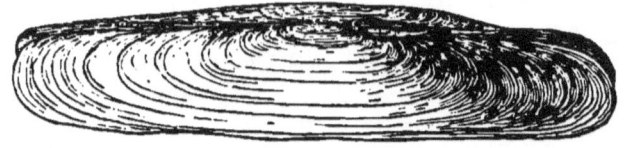

Fig. 172.

wild ducks love to find a colony of these edible mol-lusks, and have been known to lead the shell-gatherer to the right spot to look for them. Length two or three inches; southern.

Solen rosaceus, Cpr., So'-len ro-sa'-se-us, Rosy Razor-shell. The shell of this species resembles a small flattened tube. Ligament external, near the anterior end of the shell. Straight, rosy white, with glossy, brown epidermis. Length two inches; height less than half an inch; southern.

Solen sicarius, Gld., si-ca'-ri-us, Fig. 173, Short, slightly curved, truncated in front, as if chopped square off. White, with glossy, brown epidermis.

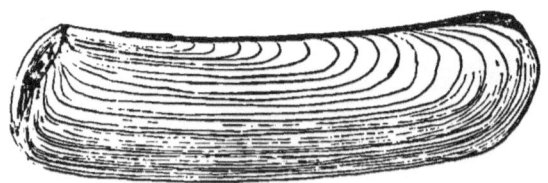

Fig. 173.

Length two inches; height more than half an inch; northern. The hinge and ligament are very near one end of this shell.

Lyonsia Californica, Conr., Ly-on'-si-a, Fig. 174, has a delicate little shell, which is occasionally found on the shores of the San Francisco bay, and which

Fig. 170.

lives along the whole line of coast. In shape it is oblong, bulged at one end; while at the other it is narrow, thin and crooked. The outer coat shows many concentric striæ, but this is easily rubbed off, revealing the inner layer of the shell, which is nacreous or pearly. Its length is an inch or an inch and a half.

Our next species is named *Entodesma saxicola*, Baird, En-to-dez'-ma sax-ik'-o-la. It is a singular mollusk, living in holes of various shapes and taking whatever form is most convenient. Its shell is oblong, bulged at the hinge end, gaping beneath, and prolonged at the rear end into a somewhat irregular and elastic tube composed chiefly of epidermis. The whole shell is thin and is covered with a yellow epidermis; internally a little ossicle or plate covers the hinge.

The variety *cylindrica* has a thicker shell, is very rough, and is somewhat wedge-shaped. Length about an inch; northern.

Entodesma inflata, Conr., in-fla-'-ta, resembles the last, but is smaller, thinner, and more irregular, and is composed largely of epidermis. Narrow in front, wider and thinner behind; southern.

Mytilimeria Nuttalli, Conr., Myt-il-i-me'-ri-a Nuttall'-i, is a singular mollusk which may sometimes be found imbedded in a soft substance, probably a kind of sponge. The shell is very thin, white, covered with a brown epidermis. There is an ossicle under the hinge. In shape it resembles an inflated bladder, with the spiral umbones at one end. Its height is about one inch.

Thracia curta, Conr., Thra'-shi-a cur'-ta.   In form
and markings its shell resembles Fig. 151, but it is
somewhat oblong and wrinkled at the rear end of the
valves. Ligament external, hinge-teeth small, pallial
sinus shallow, length from an inch to two inches.

Periploma argentaria, Conr., Per-i-plo'-ma ar-gen-
ta'-ria, Fig. 175.   This is a pretty species, easily recognized by its peculiar
spoon-like hinge-teeth. Oblong, beaks near the posterior
end, pallial sinus small, right
valve bulged, left one flattened. White, smooth, with
fine lines of growth, silvery

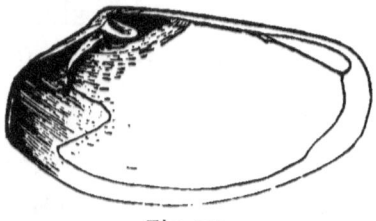

Fig. 175.

within.   Length an inch or two; southern.

Corbula luteola, Cpr., Cor'-bu-la lu-te'-o-la.   Shell
shaped somewhat like a small Donax, yellowish,
marked with lines of growth. Ligament internal, in
a small pit; pallial sinus small. Valves rather thick,
incurved at the edges, angled at one corner. The
length of this southern species is only three-eighths
of an inch.

CHAPTER XXV.

THE great Washington clam is a huge, burrowing
mollusk, living sometimes fully two feet below
the surface of the mud. For such a situation it is
provided with an enormous siphonal tube, through
which it holds communication with the upper world.
Living so deep in the mud, they are rather hard to
capture, but when they have been traced and spaded
out a very few of them are sufficient to make an ample
and excellent chowder.

The shell of this *Schizothærus Nuttalli*, Conr., Shi-
zo-the'-rus Nut-tall'-i, for that is its name, is oblong,
bulged, rather thin, and it gapes widely at the end
where the siphons pass. The hinge-teeth are small,
and the large internal ligament is lodged in a triangular pit. As you might suppose, the pallial sinus is
very broad and deep to make room for the huge
siphons. The white shell is sometimes covered with
a thin epidermis. This great mollusk delights in
muddy bays, where its shell sometimes grows to a
length of ten inches. It is found along our whole
western coast, from the Sound to Mexico.

Cryptomya Californica, Conr., Cryp-to'-mi-a. Shell
elliptical, slightly gaping, nearly smooth, sometimes

marked with faint lines. The sinus is small, and the right valve is provided with a large spoon-shaped hinge-tooth, on which is the ligament. Shell rather thin, white, with ashy epidermis. Length one inch or more.

Mya arenaria, Linn., My-a' ar-e-na'-ri-a. Fig. 176 represents the inside of the left valve of this well known and higly valued mollusk. The shell is oblong-ovate, thin and brittle, gaping at the ends, whitish, and covered near the edges with a gray epidermis. The left valve has a large spoon-shaped hinge-tooth, supporting the ligament and fitting into an appropriate flattened space on the right valve. The pallial sinus as shown in the cut is deep, for this mollusk is an active burrower, and the muscle scars are unequal. The common length of the shell is two or three inches.

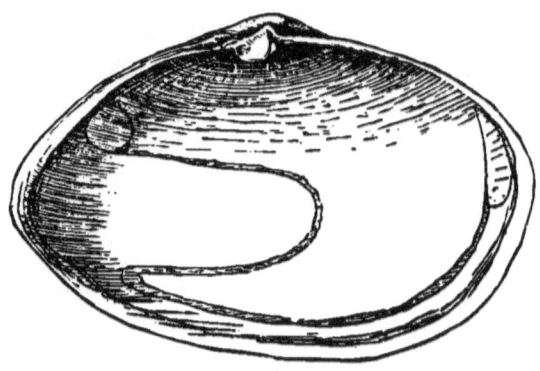

Fig. 176.

Though very common on the Atlantic coast, this clam was unknown in San Francisco bay before the year 1874. In November of that year a few specimens were discovered near Oakland and were named *Mya Hemphilli*, Newc., on the supposition that it was a new species. In a little time, however, its true nature was known, and it multiplied so exceedingly that soon specimens could be gathered by the hundred. Next to the Oyster, it is by far the most important food mollusk sold in the markets of San Francisco.

Its sudden appearance in these waters was doubtless due to the introduction of a few specimens in connection with the barrels of young oysters which were imported soon after the completion of the Pacific railroad. These young oysters were planted in the bay; they grew finely, but propagated feebly. The clams, on the other hand, though coming here by accident, found the situation quite to their liking, and the mud flats for miles around soon became thickly inhabited by their rapidly maturing descendants.

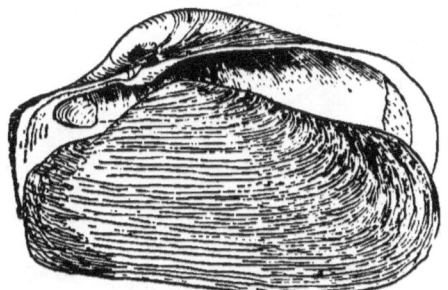

Fig. 177.

Although not quite so good for food as the more aristocratic oyster, the Mya furnishes the basis of a delicious chowder which can be afforded by all. Already this Rhode Island clam is crowding out the Macoma of the Indians, even as the eastern whites have already built their cities on the red man's hunting grounds. Even among mollusks—

"Westward the star of the empire takes its way."

Platyodon cancellatus, Conr., Pla-ty'-o-don can-sel-la'-tus, Fig. 177. Closely resembling the last is the species named above. The genus takes its name from its broad hinge-tooth, which is not equal, however, to that of the Mya. The valves are thicker than those of that species, greatly bulged, and gaping posteriorly. Concentric markings are very plain, but radial lines are faint. Color white; length two or three inches. I found them abundant on the shore of Bolinas bay; they are found also to the southward.

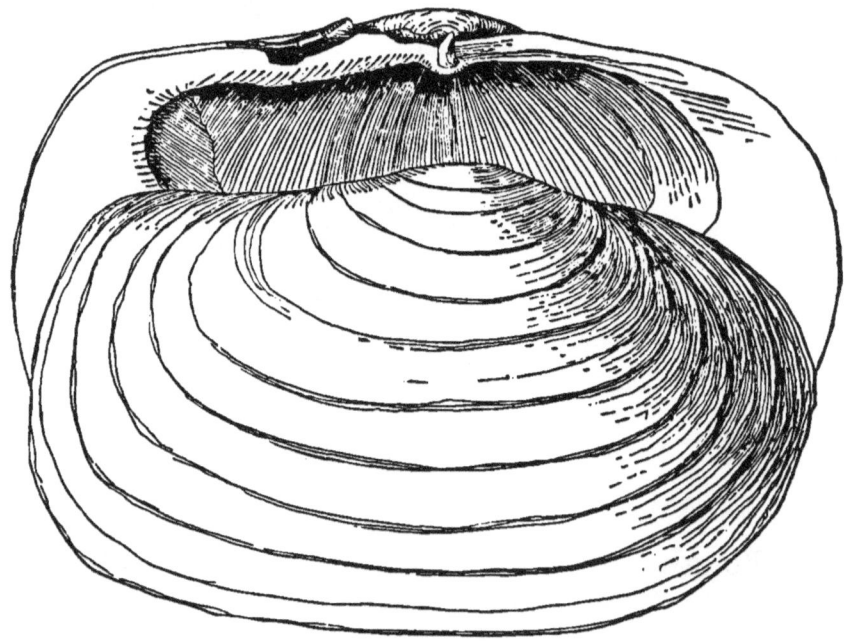

Fig. 178.

The shell of the little *Saxicava artica*, Linn., Sax-i-ca'-va arc'-ti-ca, is small, thin, wrinkled and irregular. The beaks are near the front of the shell, which is abruptly terminated. Ligament small, external, behind the beaks. Color ashy white; length from one-fourth to one-half an inch. Found on the roots of kelp, and in similar situations.

Glycimeris generosa, Gld., Gly-sim'-e-ris gen-e-ro'-sa, Fig. 178. This huge mollusk, which is found chiefly in northern waters, sometimes grows to a larger size than any other bivalve mollusk on our coast. The specimen from which this figure was drawn is over six inches in length, while others are said to be much larger. The valves are oblong and nearly rectangular, quite flat, and marked with distinct concentric ridges. They gape widely where the siphons enter. Ligament external, hinge-tooth on the left valve shaped like a sharp horn, muscle scars very distinct, pallial sinus not very deep. Shells thick and strong; dull white without, pearly and shining within.

The last family of the Lamellibranchs is that of the Boring-shells, of which there are two divisions. The first of these includes the *Pholadidæ* or Piddocks, which bore into rock, shell, or clay; the second division, which consists of the Teredos, *Teredidæ*, work chiefly in wood.

Of the former division the first species to mention is named *Netastomella Darwinii*, Sby., Ne-tas-to-mel'-la Dar-win'-i-i. This little borer is found in rocks. The front of the shell is open and circular; the latter part is prolonged into a narrow, flattened tube, shaped like a duck's bill. The shell is marked with striæ, and is divided into two parts by a sudden constriction. Color whitish; length about half an inch.

Pholas Pacifica, Stearns, Fo'-las Pa-cif'-i-ca. Shell thin and delicate, long and cylindrical; marked with wavy, concentric ridges and faint radiating lines. The sculpturing is not sharply divided into two sections as it is in the next species. Within each valve, beneath the hinge, is a slender, curved projection, very narrow and delicate. On the outside, just above the ligament, is a long, protecting plate, with straight sides. This auxillary valve, as it is called, is curved in front and straight behind. The shells of this species measure two and a half inches in length, are widely gaping at the ends, and are of a white color. This mollusk inhabits muddy flats near the shores of San Francisco bay.

Fig. 179 gives us a good idea of the shell of the Rough Piddock, *Zirphœa crispata*, Linn., Zir-fe'-a cris-pa'-ta. This fine borer is able to force a tunnel

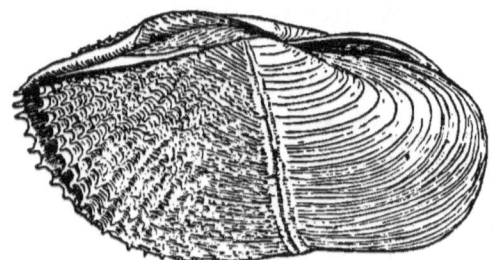

Fig. 179.

into the hardest blue clay by means of the sharp, rasp-like teeth, which are ranged in rows on the forward part of the shell. Within each valve is a delicate, spoon-shaped tooth or process, which joins the shell just beneath the umbo. There is no accessory plate over the hinge-area, but it is protected by a membrane, and in front of the umbones the valves are reflexed.

The shell is thin, white and very hard. The length is from two to four inches. This species is widely distributed, being found also on both sides of the Atlantic. I have dug fine specimens from hard blue clay near Bolinas. The internal organs of the animal as well as its shell are very curious and interesting. Among them is the hyaline stylet, a slender, transparent cylinder, looking like a piece of glass rod. Its use is not certainly known. Nearly all of the Piddocks are phosphorescent in the dark.

The great California Piddock, *Parapholas Californica*, Conr., Par-a-fo'-las Cal-i-for'-ni-ca, is represented in Fig. 180. The shell of this fine species is rounded in front, where it is marked with fine and delicate

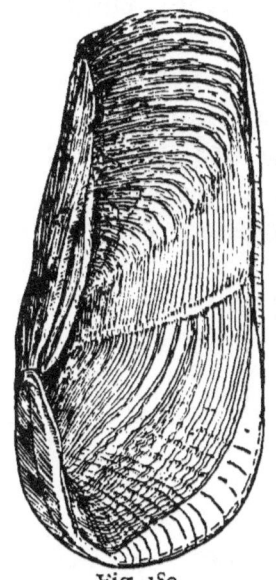

sculpturing. The rear end of the shell is tapering, and is mainly composed of large scales of epidermis. Near the line of union of the two valves, both above and below, there are accessory plates, long, straight and smooth. Curious spoons of white shell are seen within the valves, beneath the umbones. The shells are white, rather delicate, and are three or more inches in length. The rocky dust which the animal obtains in the process of excavation he uses in building up a strong, conical chimney, which protects the siphons.

Fig. 180.

Martesia intercalata, Cpr., Mar-te'-si-a in-ter-ca-la'-ta. This is a very small borer from the southern fauna, which is sometimes found in large shells like that of the Haliotis. Its presence sometimes disturbs the occupant of the shell, especially if its burrow has been carried nearly through the pearly lining.

Shells are frequently found with rounded knobs inside, which the occupant has built up to protect himself against this burglar, which in size and shape resembles a pea. Its valves gape widely in front, and the entrance to its burrow is quite small.

Fig. 181 represents a small specimen of the most common of our species of Piddocks. Its name is *Pholalidea penita*, Conr., Fo-la-did'-e-a pen'-i-ta. While it is often even smaller than the cut, it sometimes grows to a much greater size. I have one preserved in alchohol which, including the epidermal tips, is four inches long. Like the other Piddocks the forward part of its shell is rounded and rasp-like, while the latter part is narrow and smooth. A triangular plate covers the hinge-area, and the valves end in epidermal flaps or scales. It is commonly found in the softer rocks along our whole coast. There are several varieties, as *parva*, Tryon, which is very small. In young specimens the forward end of the shell is not wholly closed, but gapes widely like that of the Rough Piddock.

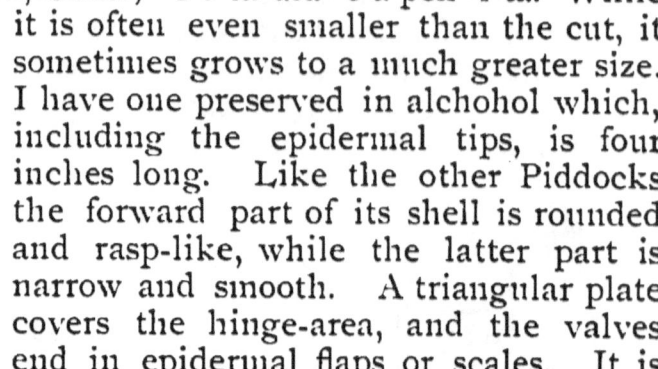

Fig. 181.

There is a very singular and very destructive mollusk, which lives especially in the harbor of San Francisco, and which is known as the Teredo, or ship-worm. Its true name is considered by Mr. Dall to be *Xylotria pennatifera*, Blainville, Zy-lo'-tri-a pen-na-tif'-e-ra. *X. setacea*, Tryon, is probably another name for the same species.

Its great end in life seems to be to bore as long a hole as possible; not for the reason that it desires the wood for food, but simply for the fun of boring. The young of this remarkable mollusk, like those of the other lamellibranchs, are free swimmers, quite unlike the adult parents. After a brief and sportive life in the water they find a post or a floating piece of wood, and begin to bore a hole.

At first this hole is very small, but as the creature grows the hole increases in diameter also. As he advances he lines the hole with shell, making a white tube, ever increasing in size. Communication with the outside water is kept up by the siphons, which reach to the original entrance. Through these siphons a current of circulation is kept in motion, bringing in food and breath, and carrying away all chips and refuse particles.

If our borer finds that his hole is approaching the tube of another of his species, he turns his course and bores on through undisturbed wood. Thus it happens that the timbers of which a wharf is built may appear perfectly sound, when, in fact, they are completely honey-combed. A little shock may break them open, disclosing the mass of tortuous tubes.

The valves of the shell of this mollusk are at the very front of the tube, and are nearly spherical in shape. They gape widely at both ends. The front of the shells is very beautifully sculptured, though the markings are so fine that a microscope is needed by which to examine them. There is an internal spoon-shaped process in each valve as in all the Borers. There are also two peculiar, oar-shaped, shelly appendages, which close the external opening of the burrow and perhaps perform other duties. The globular shell of the Teredo is about half an inch in diameter, and the pens or oars are some two inches in length.

Xylotria Stutchburryi, Jeff., Stuch-bur'-ry-i, has a very small shell, and is found in southern waters. The valves are white and triangular, and the pens are minute and club-shaped.

The Brachyopods are usually classed with the mollusks, though they have certain characteristics which ally them to the worms. In structure they are quite unlike the Lamellibranchs, but they resemble them in appearance, for they have bivalve shells. These shells, however, instead of being upon the right and left sides of the animal, cover the upper and under surfaces. The beak of the upper valve projects over the lower, and in this projection is a hole, through which passes the fleshy stalk that anchors the animal to its resting place.

Within the shell are two long, feathery arms, which may be extended and used for catching food. They serve also as gills; at least they partly perform that office. These curious arms were once considered analogous to feet, hence the name, Brachiopod, or Arm-footed.

Most of the Brachiopods had been dead for ages before the creation of man, and their fossil remains are very abundant in the earlier rocks. But there are a few living species, though specimens are rarely obtained, and most of them live in quiet deep water.

Terebratula unguiculus, Cpr., Ter-e-brat'-u-la unguic'-u-lus, has a wrinkled, gray shell, usually less than an inch in length. I have seen a northern specimen attached to the shell of a dead gasteropod.

Waldheimia pulvinata, Gld., Wald-hi'-mi-a pul-vina'-ta, from the north and *W. Californica*, from the state indicated by its name, have smooth, thin, subglobular shells, of an ashy color and a larger size.

Within the valves are singular shelly loops for sustaining the organs.

Waldheimia Grayi, Davidson, has quite thick, red valves, marked by eight or ten radiating ribs. The shells are rather flat, somewhat triangular, and are an inch and a half or less in length.

Our last engraving, Fig. 182, gives us a representation of *Lingula albida*, Hds., Lin'-gu-la al'-bi-da. The shell is shaped like a duck's bill, being thin, with nearly straight edges and a square end. It fastens itself to an anchorage by a long, fleshy stalk, which is shown in the cut as dry and curled. The shell is glossy, and is of a yellowish white color. It is a southern species, and is about an inch in length.

Fig. 182. Besides all these, there is another class of mollusks, which are the most highly organized of all. They are the Cephalopods or Head-walkers, so named because they have a series of large tentacles around the head, and these they use both for locomotion and for prehension. They include Squids, Cuttle-fishes, and Nautili, the last of which alone have true external shells. *Octopus punctatus*, Gabb, Oc'-to-pus punk-ta'-tus, is the eight-armed Cuttle or Devil-fish which is chiefly found in southern waters. It has power to change its color, but it is generally of a dark hue, marked with many small dots.

There are several species of Squid along the coast, the names of which seem at present to be rather uncertain. They have long, slender bodies of a light color, a dart-shaped tail, large eyes, and ten tentacles, two of which are much longer than the others.

With these, we close our descriptions of the mollusks, and turn to the remaining pages, which will help us in our study of what has gone before.

BIOGRAPHICAL INDEX.

ADAMS, ARTHUR, (A. Ad.). A distinguished English student and writer. One of the authors of the celebrated work on the "Genera of Recent Mollusca," published about thirty years ago.

ADAMS, PROF. CHARLES B. (C. B. Ad.). 1814-1853. Professor of Natural History in Amherst College, Mass. He was an extraordinary worker, and collected the very fine cabinet of shells still preserved at that college. He wrote chiefly on the shells of Panama, which region he carefully explored.

BAIRD, DR. W. An English naturalist of recent times.

BINNEY, AMOS. Born in Boston 1803; died in Rome, whither he had gone for his health, 1847. He was a successful merchant, and an ardent lover of nature. He wrote chiefly on the Land Shells of the U. S. He left money for the publication and distribution of his unfinished books on the same, which were completed by Dr. Gould.

BINNEY, W. G. (W. G. B.). Son of the above, and one of the leading conchologists of the present time. He has supplemented his father's work, and is the author of the volume on "American Land Shells," recently published at Washington, D. C.

BLAND, THOMAS. A naturalist of New York, who has given much attention to species of land mollusks.

BRODERIP, WM. J. (Brod.). An English naturalist, born in Bristol, 1817. He published several popular works on zoölogy, from 1847 to 1857.

CARPENTER, PHILIP P. (Cpr.). A very distinguished English conchologist, who spent considerable time in America. He studied the shells of the West Coast, and made careful reports to the British Association, one of which was reprinted by the Smithsonian Institution in 1872. He died soon after its publication.

CHEMNITZ, (Chem.). A German naturalist of the last century.

CONRAD, TIMOTHY A. Born in New Jersey, 1803. A distinguished writer upon recent and fossil shells.

COOPER, DR. J. G. A noted California conchologist and writer, who has made a particular study of the land mollusks. He resides at Haywards, Cal.

DALL, WM. H. One of the foremost of American naturalists; now at the head of the Department of Mollusca in the Smithsonian Institution.

DESHAYES, GERARD P. (Desh.). A French naturalist, whose publications date from 1835 onward.

DIXON, CAPT. GEO. An English sea-captain, who published in 1789 an account of his voyage round the world.

D'ORBIGNY, (D'ORB.), 1802-1857. A French naturalist and writer upon mollusks.

DONOVAN, EDWARD, (Don.). A very voluminous English writer upon insects, shells, etc. He lived in the early part of this century.

DRAPARNAUD, PROF. JAQUES, (Drap.), 1772-1806. His writings were chiefly upon the land and fresh-water mollusks of France.

DUCLOS, (Ducl.). A French naturalist who flourished about fifty years ago.

ESCHSCHOLTZ, (Esch.). The distinguished naturalist who accompanied the Russian explorer, Otto von Kotzebue, from 1815-1826. They visited this coast and collected valuable scientific material.

FORBES, PROF. EDWARD, (Fbs.). 1815-1854. An English scholar and writer. With Hanly, he published in 1853 the "History of British Mollusks."

GABB, W. M. A noted American naturalist; at one time paleontologist for the California State Geological Survey.

GMELEN, JOHANN F., (Gmel.), 1744-1774. A German professor at Tübingen. He edited an Edition of Linné's *Systema Naturæ*.

GOULD, DR. A. A., (GLD.), 1805-1866, was a native of New Hampshire, but spent most of his life in Boston, in the practice of his profession. Yet he found time to write much upon Natural History, particularly upon mollusks. His advice to a young naturalist who had more enthusiasm than riches is full of golden thoughts: "You must go ahead and earn your living, and use your leisure for study, as I have done, only don't wait for the leisure to be greater; do something, if but little every day; otherwise, when wealth or age give you greater leisure, your interest will have faded and your opportunity will be gone."

GRAY, JOHN E., 1800-1875. For nearly fifty years he was connected with the British Museum, and finally became its keeper. He wrote valuable catalogues of the same.

HALDEMAN, PROF. SAMUEL S., (Hald.). He was born in Penn., in 1812, and became a distinguished writer and teacher. His writings on mollusks refer chiefly to fresh-water species. He wrote also upon philology.

HANLEY, SYLVANUS, (Hanl.). An English scientist, associated with Prof. Forbes.

HEMPHILL, HENRY. A well-known student and collector of mollusks, particularly those of this coast and of Florida. His catalogues and collections have been of great assistance in the preparation of this book. He resides in San Diego, Cal.

HINDS, RICHARD B, (Hds.). The English naturalist who accompanied Sir Edward Belcher on his voyage round the world, in "H. M. S. Sulphur," from 1836 to 1842.

INGERSOLL, ERNEST. Naturalist of the U. S. Geological Survey of the Territories, under Prof. Hayden.

LEA, ISAAC, L.L. D., 1792-1886. Dr. Lea's ancestors came over from England with William Penn. Most of his life was spent in Philadelphia, where he was connected with a large publishing house. His writings are very voluminous, relating chiefly to the *Unionidæ* or River Mussels.

LEACH, DR. WM. F. Curator of the Natural History Department of the British Museum, during the early part of this century.

LINNÉ OR LINNÆUS, CARL VON, (Linn.), 1707-1778. The great Swedish naturalist, and author of the modern system of scientific nomenclature. His early life was full of difficulties, but when he became professor of Botany at the University of Upsal, his department soon became filled with eager students. He wrote many valuable works, and received great honors.

MARTYN, THOS., (Mart.). An early English naturalist who published in 1784 a beautiful work entitled "The Universal Conchologist."

MIDDENDORFF, DR. A. TH. V., (Midd.). An early scientific writer upon the shells of this coast. His reports were published in St. Petersburg from 1823 onwards.

MÖRCH, OTTO A. L. Part of his writings, on the *Vermetidæ*, were published in London, in 1861. But few of his species are found on this coast.

MORSE, PROF. EDWARD S. Born in Maine, 1838. A distinguished writer upon zoölogy, particularly noted for his skill in illustrating his works.

NEWCOMB, DR. WESLEY, (Newc.). An American naturalist, and collector of one of the finest cabinets of shells in the country. It is now at Cornell University, Ithaca, N. Y., where Dr. Newcomb, now an old man, still has charge of it. He formerly lived and explored in the Sandwich Islands and in California.

NUTTALL, PROF. THOS., (Nutt.), 1786-1859. His birth and death both occurred in England, but he spent most of his life in America, being professor of Natural History in Harvard College, from 1822-34.

PFEIFFER, LOUIS, (Pfr.). A celebrated German conchologist, author of numerous works, published from 1847 onward.

PHILIPPI, E. B., (Phil.). Another German naturalist of about the same date as the last.

PRIME, Temple. An American naturalist who has given especial attention to the smaller fresh-water bivalve mollusks. His check-list of the same was published by the Smithsonian Institution in 1860.

REEVE, LOVELL A., (Rve.), 1808-1865. A London author and publisher of extensive and beautiful conchological works.

ROWELL, J., REV. A clergyman of San Francisco, who has described several new species, and who has collected a very fine cabinet of shells.

SAY, THOMAS, 1787-1843. One of the earliest and most distinguished of American naturalists. He was a native of Philadelphia. His work had a most healthy influence on the cause of scientific investigation.

STEARNS, ROBT. E. C. A distinguished conchologist, formerly connected with the University of California, now with the Smithsonian Institution.

SOWERBY, GEO. B. JR., (Sby. or Sowb.). An English conchologist and artist, born in 1812. Both his father and his grandfather were eminent naturalists.

SWAINSON, William. Author of "Exotic Conchology," published in London, 1821-35, and a very voluminous writer upon Natural History.

TRYON, Geo. W., JR. An American naturalist, and a writer and publisher of extensive works upon conchology. He is connected with the Academy of Natural Sciences in Philadelphia.

VALENCIENNES, (Val.). A French naturalist of the first half of this century.

WOOD, WILLIAM. A London author and Natural History bookseller. He published many books on shells, from 1818 onwards.

KEY

FOR THE

ANALYSIS OF SHELLS.

MARINE UNIVALVES.

FRESH-WATER UNIVALVES.

MARINE BIVALVES.

Valves somewhat circular, joined by one large muscle . .   XXI
Valves dark, mussel-shaped.   XXII
Valves white, circular   XXII
Valves cordate, no pallial sinus   XXIII
Valves rough, attached to rocks.   XXIII
Valves mostly white, strong, sculptured; with pallial
    sinus   XXIII
Valves mostly thin, smooth; ligament internal   XXIII
Similar, but with ligament external, sinus deep . . XXIII, XXIV
Valves somewhat razor-shaped   XXIV
Hinge tooth spoon-shaped   XXV
Valves thin, inflated, irregular   XXIV
Valves with dissimilar ends, borers   XXV
Brachiopod shells   XXV

FRESH-WATER BIVALVES.

Small and nearly circular.   XXII
Larger and oblong   XXII

MARINE MULTIVALVES.

Shell composed of eight plates . . .   XV

LAND SHELLS.

Shell very thin, slender   XVIII
Shell minute, cylindrical   XVIII
Shell spiral, varying from flattened to globose. . . . XVIII—XX
Shell rudimentary, often concealed under the mantle of
    the slug-like animal   XX

GLOSSARY.

	PAGE.
APERTURE, the mouth of the shell	12
BIVALVE, a mollusk with two shells	157
BYSSUS, a bundle of fibers	166
CANAL, a tube or channel	12
CARNIVOROUS, flesh-eating	12
COLUMELLA, the shelly axis	12
CORALLINE, a stony sea-weed	100
CORDATE, heart-shaped	180
CORRUGATED, ridged	34
DEXTRAL, right-handed	48
EPIDERMIS, the outside skin	20
FUSIFORM, spindle-shaped	12
GENUS, a group of similar species	17
GLOBOSE, like a globe	132
LIGAMENT, the elastic substance at the hinge	159
LUNULE, a heart-shaped depression	178
MOLLUSK, a soft-bodied animal without joints	16
NULLIPORE, a kind of stony vegetation	99
OPERCULUM, door to the aperture	14
PERISTOME, rim of the aperture	37
RETICULATIONS, net-work	40
SINISTRAL, left-handed	48
SINUS, an inward curve	159
SIPHON, a breathing tube	41
SPECIES, a distinct type	27
SPHEROIDAL, somewhat like a sphere	46
STRIÆ, fine parallel lines	34
SUTURE, line between two whorls	13
TENTACLES, feelers	155
UMBILICUS, central opening	13
UMBO, beak of a bivalve shell	158
UNIVALVE, a one-shelled mollusk	12
VARIX, a periodical ridge	14
WHORL, a spiral turn	13

CHECK LIST

INDEX OF SPECIES.

www.ingramcontent.com/pod-product-compliance
Lightning Source LLC
Chambersburg PA
CBHW021437020726
47499CB00006BA/2033